Zaheda Ghani and her family arrived in Australia from Afghanistan as refugees in the 1980s. At nine years old, Zaheda, also known as Zoe, handwrote her first story using a HB pencil, in a scented diary with a lock and key. The heart of what she wrote back then developed over many years to become her debut novel, *Pomegranate & Fig*, which was shortlisted for the Richell Prize for Emerging Writers. Zaheda was also a recipient of the Western Sydney Emerging Writers' Fellowship. Zaheda served on the board of Australia for UNHCR, the private sector partner of the UN Refugee Agency, from 2017 to 2021. She is now an Ambassador for Australia for UNHCR and has an active interest in UNHCR's humanitarian work. Zaheda lives in Sydney with her husband.

pomegranate & fig

pomegranate & fig

ZAHEDA GHANI

hachette
AUSTRALIA

hachette
AUSTRALIA

Published in Australia and New Zealand in 2022
by Hachette Australia
(an imprint of Hachette Australia Pty Limited)
Gadigal Country, Level 17, 207 Kent Street, Sydney, NSW 2000
www.hachette.com.au

Hachette Australia acknowledges and pays our respects to the past, present and
future Traditional Owners and Custodians of Country throughout Australia
and recognises the continuation of cultural, spiritual and educational practices
of Aboriginal and Torres Strait Islander peoples. Our head office is located on
the lands of the Gadigal people of the Eora Nation.

NATIONAL
LIBRARY
OF AUSTRALIA

A catalogue record for this
book is available from the
National Library of Australia

ISBN: 978 0 7336 4760 4 (paperback)

Cover design by Christabella Designs
Cover images courtesy of Shutterstock
Author photograph courtesy Qais Wadan
Typeset in 12¼/17¾ pt Adobe Garamond Pro by Bookhouse, Sydney
Printed and bound in Australia by McPherson's Printing Group

MIX
Paper from
responsible sources
FSC
www.fsc.org
FSC® C001695

The paper this book is printed on is certified against the
Forest Stewardship Council® Standards. McPherson's Printing
Group holds FSC® chain of custody certification SA-COC-005379.
FSC® promotes environmentally responsible, socially beneficial
and economically viable management of the world's forests.

*This book is dedicated to the courageous
women and girls of Afghanistan*

part one

HERAT

HERAT

Henna

If anyone asks thee which is the pleasantest of cities, Thou mayest
answer him aright that it is Herāt. For the world is like the sea,
and the province of Khurāsān like a pearl-oyster therein, the city
of Herāt being as the pearl in the middle of the oyster.
— *Jalal ad-Din Balkhi 1207–1273 A.D.*

The youngest daughter of Khoja and Koko is so delicate that
the 120-day winds of Herat could blow her away. Her bones
are made from porcelain, rigid and fine. A diaphanous girl
in cotton dress and pantaloons, she is lifted high above Herat, to the
height of the ancient minarets of Queen Gauhar Shad and carried to
a far corner of the world. As she floats, her hair twists and wraps itself
around her white face, enfolding the arch of her long slim nose and
the glass lids of her large, closed eyes.

Family and friends tell her lovingly that she is too sickly, too thin.
She is not beautiful by the standards of the time which prefer curves

and flesh. Her two rose-cheeked curvaceous elder sisters, Nargis and Roya, are considered beauties by all. But they become jealous. Because their beauty doesn't seem to be enough. Because she receives so much more attention. They do the chores around the large house, they study through the night for exams. Henna studies alongside them. She stays awake all night to feed her brain, to replace her lack of beauty with an abundance of knowledge.

She must study even harder, given her mind seems never to settle long enough on one idea, doesn't retain the biology, the maths, the chemistry. It retains the poetry and prose, but even that for only a short while. Every good mark she gets is the result of twice as much study as her sisters do.

This morning, she is wrapped in layers of woollens, proud and blue with cold. Her thin waist threatens to break as she lifts her heavy schoolbag onto her shoulder. Like most days, her elder sister Nargis will carry it for her through the forty-five-minute walk to school.

This evening, the strain over her study of several days and nights dissolves into a fever that lasts a fortnight. She takes medicine to alleviate the fever, but it cannot settle her anxious mind. She wishes for her life to be uprooted and scattered by the rush of the 120-day winds. She doesn't know how real this wish will later become, this uprooting, brought not by nature's fury but by the ferocity of war.

Henna and her family live on a large fertile estate filled with orchards and flower gardens. They share the land with the families who bake the daily bread, who clean the house, who drive the cars. Her father, Khoja, is an artist. Family legend has it that her father lost his first wife, Shah Gol, to childbirth, that Shah Gol died alone without him beside her; that the last time they saw each other was when she gave him water to drink from her cupped hands beside the well. A story he does not himself tell, a tale spoken about him in whispers.

Spring finally visits and she brings with her the nargis flowers. Henna and her sisters make afternoon picnics of sheer chai, creamy milk tea, and samosa pastries filled with sweetened ground beef. The bulbul birds sing and Henna finds two caught in the hedges of Khoja's gardens, trapped dead in their romances.

Her elder brother, Hamid, doesn't believe in her frailty. He sees a girl who will be someone someday. A girl who will perhaps join an important advisory board or lead a delegation of women contributing to education planning. He sees her struggle to take charge of her life. He sees her yearning to learn about life through her voracious reading of books. His mission is to prove the worthlessness of mere tradition; he questions the myths that underpin their lives. He recruits her on his landscaping projects around their home. He doesn't heed Koko's warnings that Henna's bones will break, that the girl will end the day in fever and chills.

Now, a lady beetle lands on Henna's dress and she brushes it away. It's pretty but still, it is an insect with thin crawling legs which irk her. The sunlight through the naju tree carves pretty patterns on her hands and in her lap, on the rug around her, as she sits to daydream.

Later, a single drop of perspiration forms on her white forehead. She wipes it away with the back of her hand as she carries dirt in a wheelbarrow with handles thicker than her wrists. The sun shines on her. Today, she is made of the stuff of the mountains which mark the boundaries of her world, the weight of things she can lift, a contrast to the person she is on other days. She cuts a snake in two, using the courage given to her by Khoda jan, dear God, Allah. She uses the mouth of the spade as her weapon. She watches how the monster coils and twists in pain, surrendering to the permanence of death. Hamid approves. You must protect yourself in this world, he says.

Henna's life unfolds languidly against the backdrop of Herat's respected past and unsettled present. The year is 1973 when Prince Daud Khan leads the coup d'état to overthrow his cousin, King Zahir Shah, and becomes the first President of Afghanistan. Henna is seventeen. She is growing into a woman with narrow hips, cream skin, and serious eyes. Her proudest moment unfolds before her as she walks onto the stage to accept an honour award for her final year of outstanding secondary school. This award she holds close to her heart, the key that is opening the next two years of study at the teachers' college, after which she will become a teacher.

She is of the age when khastgar, suitors, begin to visit. The wellbred, educated, and wealthy call upon Henna's family to ask for her hand in marriage. They bring their sons dressed in suits and furnished with university degrees. Only a few families will have the means to look after a girl so spoilt and educated, from a family such as theirs.

Khoja manages things amicably so there is only a slight bruising of egos when they turn the suitors away, protecting his affectionately named hippy girl from the turmoils of adult life, from being pushed into marriage when she believes that she will never marry. But then, fate makes a date for Henna to meet Rahim.

Rahim

An incessant mosquito lingers, landing now and then on his brown hand. There is a constant hum of insects in the air, of wing clapping against translucent wing. The warmth is thick like honey, the air smells green and yellow. He strikes the back of his left hand with the palm of his right, catching the insect between two hands. He opens his right palm to find the body of the mosquito lying in a flower of blood. He wipes his hand on a leaf, goes back to his reading, his mind building pictures as the words meet his eyes, sitting under the shade of the pomegranate trees, the book in his lap.

Rahim wears slacks and a shirt with the sleeves rolled up and ready for action. He has long legs, which carry him as he strides Herat's footpaths and multicoloured bazaars, negotiating a clump of sheep being led by their shepherd, blocking the tight streets of the villages nearby, walking the length of local lantern-dotted festivals late in the night with his friends. He is a man of the law, so he sees what most people don't see, the ugliness of crime, chasing criminals down Herat's alleyways, rare alleyways which are unknown and forbidden to the clean women who exist in his life, his mother and aunts and cousins. He traverses this world hidden underneath the beating heart of Herat as if he is crossing a mud puddle, hitching up his bell-bottom trousers to cross. This is what he has learnt of life. That all people are created clean, like a fresh linen sheet, who, with misdeeds throughout life, create stains upon the sheet of their souls. He does everything he can to keep his sheet clean.

He loves his job as a prosecutor, doing his part to rid the world of crime, to make the underbelly of Herat clean, to make it safe, to rid it of the vampires who were once human but now survive by consuming others. He becomes possessed by some of the victims from the cases which come his way. Like the man who was thought to be murdered but whose body wasn't found. The thought of a body discarded, abandoned without a burial ceremony, stayed with Rahim, day and night. Rahim dreamt of this man, and from the dream acquired memories of a time together with him.

The man began to linger here and there amid the shadow and the light of Rahim's week. Finally, he appeared in Rahim's afternoon nap one last time with a message. Rahim found the body by following the directions in the dream. The man's wife, surprised that the old, long-hidden well could ever be found, confessed to the crime, thinking Rahim a friend of the djinn, spirits.

Another time, a Sufi master showed Rahim globes of light that nobody else could see, the lights floating just above the surface of the river late at night. Rahim saw them as a sign that he was being guided towards the beauty of a pious life which he strives to closely follow.

His hair is prematurely thinning and whitening because he reads and thinks too much, his mother says. He thinks of his mother a lot, perhaps too much, not because he is broken in some way but because he feels that she is. Underneath her stoicism and strength, Bebe is fragile like a bird.

He knows that many women open their eyes to the world in the same way that Bebe did, given in marriage at a young age, learning the traditions the hard way, by saying the wrong things, by being too honest about their thoughts. Bebe fell into traps set by women who came to visit the new bride, caught like a simple-minded sparrow in the net of nuances tied together by adult conversation.

Ah, you don't miss your family? That's odd, you must have been glad to get away from them. They asked her these questions, their eyebrows raised, their painted lips cast into shapes of cruelty, looking directly into her face, waiting for a response from the girl who openly liked married life.

She fumbled and was rescued by her watchful mother-in-law. She followed her mother-in-law's ways, was enraptured by the wealth of the new city which became her home, the city that flourished, in tune with her own life, or maybe it was the other way around. Rahim hopes that if he marries, his bride won't be subjected to the same social cruelty as his mother. That she may be prepared for those things said in adult company, that she will hold her own.

Bebe can't read and write but she has taught herself enough to run the household finances, to manage the servants, to order things for the house, and this makes Rahim proud of her. She plays the role of gracious hostess to the wives of high-ranking officials, merchants and lawyers who arrive as guests of her husband Haji Mama, the Governor of Herat. His wife will be different, she will be educated. That is if he ever finds the girl. Bebe discreetly shows him girls at social gatherings; he is irked by her directness.

This isn't a shop window, he tells her firmly, which makes her stop only to bring it up again next time.

Despite these frustrations, Rahim believes that heaven is found at the feet of mothers and so he knows that he exists inside her love, which exists inside the family, which exists inside Herat's wild floral springtime, which exists within a vast universe of Khoda's making. And while Rahim lives in a manner expected of a man of his lineage and station, he also occupies another world inside his mind. This is a scholarly world scaffolded by books and ideas which are sometimes controversial as they question tradition. But he is firm in his being, in his belief that Khoda made the heavens and the earth, gave man the ability to retain and pass on knowledge; that knowledge of the world and the sacred knowledge of religion are not separate avenues. Instead, the knowledge of the world leads to appreciation of the creator. So he reads about the sciences, about foreign belief systems and philosophies as if they are an anthropological study of the human condition, leading him to uncover the beauty of all creation.

Hamid

Hamid can feel the sting of hunger, there are small insects gnawing on the lining of his stomach, creating little volcanos of pain as they go. *Not long now*, he thinks, *it will be time for iftar*. Time to break the fast. Even after a long fast with no food or water, Hamid likes to not rush his food, to taste every morsel, to eat and drink only until he is two thirds full. One third for food, one third for water, one third for air, as the Prophet did. *We are not to fill ourselves, not on food, not on wealth, we are not to be extravagant,* he tells himself. He loves to fast, he loves how close the feeling of hunger brings him to himself, how clear his mind feels, how free his hours from the thought of his next meal. Koko reminds him daily to eat, eat, eat, as they all settle on the cushions after sunset around the large dastarkhon, eating cloth, spread on the floor covered with food, fruit, dates and water.

Hamid, your stomach is stuck to your back, Koko says. Eat more.

I do eat, he says, in those moments when his mother nags him. Yesterday, when she did so, he looked up at Henna sitting across from him with mirth in her eyes; his sister knows their mother's need to force-feed. Right now, he doesn't want to think of the feast that will be in front of him later, it's too tempting to start imagining the food.

Hamid is passing the washing fount in the Masjid-i Jami of Herat, the great mosque of Herat. He walks in the spaces between large columns. The columns and the walls are decorated with glazed tiles, which are being restored by his father Khoja's tile studio, a schedule of maintenance which has been under way as long as Hamid can remember. He feels like he is in a garden when he comes to this mosque, a garden of blues cut into curvaceous flora, stubborn materials moulded to perfection, the dance of blue and white ceramics. Geometric intricacies swoon in between the garden of flowers and frame the calligraphy made by the flourishes of generations of different hands, like his father's hand, in perfect strokes.

Men pour from the central courtyard, weaving in between the columns, mingling, chatting, a subtle grace defining their movements. They move beneath an arch that leads them to the steps and garden outside. They patiently wait for each man to gather his shoes from the wooden shelves near the outer door, to put them on, to bid goodbye, before they leave.

Hamid is a star in the constellation of bodies, moving slowly towards his sandals. He is scanning his skin for sensation with his mind's eye, with his mind's breath, from the top of his head to the tips of his toes as he walks, greets, talks.

Through muraqabah, meditation – which includes the five daily namaz, prayers, and zikr, remembrance, of Allah in seclusion – you can observe your spiritual heart, gain insights into the state of it. It's where you find peace, Khoja used to say when Hamid was young, when Khoja wanted to teach him how to live. Khoja had taught Hamid that his physical heart is a vessel for his spiritual heart, which is a gift Allah gave him as an amanat, a loan, which he must return to Allah in the same state of purity that he received it. Hamid tells these things to Henna, reminding her often, to her delight. He can see that she enjoys this way of thinking. She likes to see another dimension to this life. Nargis and Roya laugh and tease them, but the two of them can see and feel what others cannot.

He likes to be present in his body, especially during namaz as he recites the words of the Quran. Sometimes it doesn't work for him, and sometimes it does. When it does, he can feel his life force within, an energy that beats like a warm light within the palms of his hands, up his arms, down his back, around his waist, inside his stomach. He can feel his skin stretched tight across his muscular limbs, his organs, his bones, his veins flowing with blood.

He squeezes his hands into fists now, he can feel his arms flex inside his sleeves, his chest tightens under his embroidered white shirt. *I need to increase my training sessions*, he says to himself. He is going to compete in a local bodybuilding tournament in a few months' time. Zibayi andam, the beauty of physique, as people call it.

Men of all ages greet him, he looks into their eyes as they smile – black, brown, amber and green eyes, eyes with specks of sunlight in them, eyes that crease in the corners, wrinkling with friendship.

He thinks of those in the north and centre of Afghanistan, who suffered a lack of rainfall and shortage of food in recent times, hopefully now recovering after crippling drought. He prays for them and for his country.

He is grateful to be in a crowd of men hungry with purpose, hungry with the purpose of cleansing the body, the soul, the heart, grateful for the quiet that comes from giving up something as precious as food and water. *Khoda has given us free will*, he thinks, as he watches the faces around him, *we can use this will to fast, to abstain. Free will is the burden which the mountains refused to accept upon their shoulders, which only man is strong enough to bear.*

Everyone knows him by his name, Hamid, the son of Khoja. He has a wide circle of friends, he loves to be in the company of others most of the time, especially when things are going well inside his mind. Greetings touch him from different directions, from the dry lips of men who stop and take his two hands into their own, warmly.

Salaam, how are you, how is Khoja, we are going to come see you tomorrow . . . Roza o namaz qabool, may Allah accept your namaz and fasting.

Some are dressed in business attire, some are dressed like Hamid in perahan tunban, long shirts worn over roomy pantaloons. Some of the men have turbans perched upon their heads, the long end of the turban flipped over their shoulder, donning an air of nonchalance. For some these clothes are a namaz shell, which they wear when they come to the masjid, leaving their business suits behind for a couple of hours.

Hamid lets himself be carried in the crowd, like a river carries a flower petal that has fallen from its branch.

Hamid thinks of Nixon and Johnson, his two Tazi dogs; they need to be fed before he eats his iftar. He grinds his teeth as he moves, his square jawline a delight to his friends who tease him about his good looks. The shadow of his beard is already there despite the morning shave, his thick hair is shiny with health. He steps into the sunshine, squinting, his feet reunited with his sandals.

He wasn't always this healthy, this balanced. This state feels temporary at times, temporary and fickle and threatened. Threatened by what happens in the world around him, like news of the recent drought, like news of the unstable politics of his homeland. These things nearly break his calm, break his sense of self and send him back to that dungeon of guilt, back to the edge of the place he dragged himself from only a year ago.

Rahim

An argument is raging inside Rahim's head. It's a violent cacophony rising and falling. The angry voice is his own, the other, his father sounding apologetic. It's an old argument being repeated, which is theoretical given Haji Mama is never apologetic in tone or action in front of anybody, let alone his son.

Rahim turns the car into the alley, too fast for the space he has, narrowly missing the boy on the corner who sells anar, pomegranates. The boy stares at Rahim's car with his large green eyes, his thick, sand-coloured hair standing in spikes from his forehead. The boy's instincts are shaped by the wisdom of all the anar sellers who have gone before him, and he bends his chubby body over his red pyramid of fruit on the table to protect it from the car, like a mother duck protecting her eggs. With this movement he flattens the pile, causing the fruit to roll off the table in all directions, as his voluminous shirt fills like a large balloon with the gust of wind made by Rahim's car.

Reckless rich haromzada, bastard, the boy mutters.

Rahim comes to a sudden stop at the gates of his destination, the tyres screech, dust scatters into miniature clouds. He is suddenly awake as if from a dream, still angry at Haji, not sure which way he came. He turns the engine off and, in the process of putting on his coat to leave the car, he misplaces the keys and finds them – twice he does this – wasting precious minutes, lost in the repetitive thought loop that yet again here he is, a grown man, who has allowed himself to be sent on an escapade, organised and forced upon him by his father.

Rahim is greeted outside the teachers' college gates by Professor Abdel Hadi. He walks quickly to take both of the professor's hands into his own. *How disrespectful I am*, Rahim is thinking. He met the professor for the first time many years ago. That time his father had asked the professor to visit them at home, to sit and drink tea. Later, when the talk had become stale, Haji Mama asked for Professor Hadi's opinion of Rahim's choice of law for his university degree. Haji Mama wanted the professor to intervene, to dissuade Rahim from this direction in life. But Abdel Hadi had his own views. Even though he knew that disagreement with the Haji usually leads to an angry retort, he took Rahim's side.

I am sorry, Professor Hadi, I am late, Rahim says, standing taller in stature than Abdel Hadi, but feeling small, a nuisance, like a mosquito come to spoil a lazy afternoon, an interruption in the day of this learned man, an elder who has been waiting for him. The professor's cheeks glisten even though it isn't a particularly hot morning, his forehead is oily, his lips wet.

Rahim holds the professor's limp hands too long, he lets them go, feeling forgiven by the sunny smile beaming at him. Hands to chest, bowing slightly, Thank you again for seeing me, Rahim says.

Come, I will show you, says Abdel Hadi, his long lashes bold with promise, leading the way quickly to his office.

They walk past several large brown doors, which line the teachers' college corridor, and abruptly stop outside one of them. An old man in a blue uniform stands from his stool and opens the door.

Should I bring tea, sir? the doorman asks.

Yes, for Rahim jan, please, the professor says.

No, no, Rahim says. I will not take up too much of your time.

Nonsense, says the professor. I want you to spend as much time as you like. The doorman walks out to fetch tea.

The first thing Rahim notices about the office are shelves from floor to ceiling with volume upon volume of books creating a temple dedicated to the worship of knowledge. A window on the right interrupts the wall of books with its parted lace curtains, through which Rahim can see the path they have traversed.

The professor's wooden desk stands at the back of the room as they approach. Its scratched legs mingle with the legs of two faded black chairs placed on either side. The desk has three tidy piles of paper and a few pencils and pens in a rusty tin box. The professor takes a book from the shelf behind his desk. He hands it to Rahim, beaming encouragingly. Rahim feels the heat rise from his neck to the top of his head.

The college emblem on the cover of the book is embroidered in gold thread and feels rough under Rahim's thumb as he takes it from the professor.

Here is a seat, have a look at all the girls in there, all from respectable families who care about morals, education, and family, Abdel Hadi says. He walks off as soon as he has spoken these words, his steps quick, his belly bouncing, and then the door is closed behind him.

Rahim realises his mouth is gaping, he closes it quickly, recognising himself as the idle fool in Haji Mama's stories, stories about useless boys becoming useless men through a lack of structure, education, ambition, who spend their lives standing around the bazaar with mouths open, eyes vacantly staring, brains empty. Rahim pulls the chair across from the professor's desk, he sits down and puts the heavy yearbook on the table in front of him.

As he opens the front cover, a strong smell of freshly printed paper fills his nostrils. He likes this smell, the smell of books, the smell of ink; the pages are like the petals of a fragrant rose in full bloom being pulled apart slowly. Page by page he looks through black-and-white photos of girls, their faces submerged just beneath the surface of the paper, peering at him through it, their names floating neatly beneath.

He turns the pages slowly to take enough time, to make it seem that he has genuinely considered the option of finding a wife from a college yearbook, as arranged by Haji Mama. He is embarrassed to be doing this, a discreet act only possible because of the close friendship between Haji and the professor, one of deep trust, something he is confident would not be open to any other bachelor in Herat. He wants to leave as soon as possible, thanking the professor. But a photo on page ten makes him stop. Her long dark hair, her large-lidded eyes, her sharp nose rising from her face like a mountain peak, her angular jawline standing out against the high-necked blouse she is wearing. Her shoulders, like a bird's wings, pushed together to make herself small. Her forehead a mass of land upon which her future life will imprint lines. He closes the book and lets it stay closed, only to pick it up again and open it to Henna's face.

He is embarrassed, but he doesn't know why. He is shivering, but it isn't cold.

Thank you, he is saying to Professor Hadi later, as Hadi is patting down his combover.

Have some tea, Professor Hadi is saying. *When did the doorman bring the tea?* Rahim didn't notice, he thought he was alone in the room, alone with the books, that book, that photograph, those eyes. He tries to shape a sentence.

His mind, where Rahim has spent all his life, is now giving way to his body. He can feel that his limbs have a pulse, that his body occupies space, that movement is the dance of the body and the mind. He feels that he doesn't have much control over body or mind right now. The room is spinning slowly around his head, in a cruel cycle. He and Abdel Hadi are exchanging a long respectful goodbye.

Have a good day.

Yes, you have a good day too, thank you.

No, thank you for coming, please pass on my regards to . . .

Earlier this morning, the day didn't begin with such dizzying promise, nor even a hint of serendipitous adventure, of such foreign knowledge now flooding Rahim's body and mind. The yearbook sits closed on the table; the memory of Henna's photo is resting heavily upon his eyelids.

Rahim must focus firmly on his movements and speech. He needs to shake his mind free from the memory. An embarrassing memory of a slurp of words dripping from heavy lips as he struggles to suppress the hypnotic, kaleidoscopic film of possibilities projected upon his forehead by his mind. He must summon his long limbs to make the necessary movements that will take him out of the professor's presence to his car. And, somehow, back to his office.

What is funny? Bebe asks.

Nothing, Rahim says. The smile on his face dissolves like a snow-flake, jagged edges softening into droplets. Bebe is sitting next to him, in the back seat of the black Volkswagen. She has assumed the rigidity of a statue in her posture. She appears to be light because she is small, with long knotty fingers and a narrow oval face, but removing her from her seat will take the strength of Rahim plus ten men. They call her Bebe Hawa, where Hawa means Eve from the story of Adam and Eve, a name that evolved over the years on the tongues of those who form the society around her, a way to show her respect by using a sobriquet. When she was a girl her name was Mariam, but everyone who called her Mariam is now long dead.

When Rahim was young, Bebe told him stories as she cooked and supervised the servants. Every day the rice boiled in a pot big enough to hold Bebe, to soak and soften her aching bones, to soften her memories, making them pliable so that she was able to talk freely. She checked on the grains as they swam to the top of the water. She taught him how to cook rice, which he made for his friends while they were studying at Kabul University. He liked seeing the small horizontal lines appear along each grain of rice, the grains themselves becoming tasma, flexible, swirling and folding without breaking in the tide of angry bubbles. Bebe taught him to drain the rice at this point, any more time on the boil will turn these elegant grains to mush; how to measure the perfect amount of stew to be added; how to taste a grain for salt, taking another between her forefinger and thumb, pressing hard to test the softness.

One day when he was thirteen, sitting beside the pot a small distance away, she told him how she had lived most of her life with a sense that she was in the wrong mould. A sense that the spirit of a much older woman was contained within the vessel of her body, an ancient woman of tradition. He pictured his mother then, seeing her born not as a baby, but as an old woman, intolerant of youth and its associated beauty, its fickle love and sense of wonder. She told him that she played the character of Mariam for as long as necessary, up until her marriage. He wanted to ask many questions about Mariam and his mother's mould, but he was afraid to break the spell of her memories, lest she stop talking altogether.

And she did stop with her stories when he turned fourteen and the shade of facial hair began to appear on his face; she stopped her stories so that he could spend time with his father, orbit in the company of men. But the stories stayed inside Rahim, and although he wished she would bring them back, tell him more, it never happened.

Rahim believes that her body is manifesting the true self and name she once told him about, and her appearance is finally matching the old woman inside. Her grey hair, the most prominent symbol of her stately age, is parted at the centre of her head and braided into a long thin rope that rests down her back like a snake. The lines of history on her face are framed by a translucent white silk scarf, her chadar, which also covers the tops of her narrow shoulders. The edges of her chadar are hand embroidered with sond, silk thread, like her white cotton pantaloons, the embroidery stacked a hand high on each leg. Ten buttons are neatly sewn in a straight line down the front of her dress. They are like gems marking the milestones of her life that Rahim knows so well; her marriage, the birth of each child, the death of her parents and siblings far away in Gurian.

Now she is squinting through the side window of the car as if there is smoke blowing in her face. It's the same look he remembers from when she visited the cook in the kitchen to check on the rice, crouching low to see under the large pot. Her kohl-blackened eyes are sharp and nimble and fit for purpose.

Bebe doesn't like to leave her home and mingle in the streets with people, but Rahim is pleased she came out with him. Today is different, she is here to ensure that a job is done, to find him a wife. For him to choose and be done with fate's biggest question. After all, Rahim is thirty, already too old to marry.

He shifts in the car seat, and it yawns audibly as the upholstery stretches beneath his pinstriped suit. He bends his body towards the side window of the Volkswagen, facing away from his mother, so that his thoughts can be his own, so that he can dream with eyes open, so that the veil of thought can cover his dark lashes. His black leather shoes are slightly tight, he curls his toes inside. He is still aware of the presence of his body; since that day in Abdel Hadi's office, his body has made itself known. He looks at the watch on his wrist; it's 3.15 pm.

What does she look like in real life? What will she be like to live with? He has thought so much about that photograph of Henna since his visit to Professor Hadi's office. *Marriage.* The word brings with it a rush of tiny ripples which begin as a tightening in his chest and make their way into his belly. He noticed the same ripples appeared when he stood in court this week. He notices that he likes the ripples, they make him feel alive, they show love for his job, the artful extraction of a confession, the hunt for truth in between the intended and unintended lies.

How can two people live in the same moment or even a lifetime together and have two different truths? Sometimes he can see people as they do not see themselves; their decisions, their words, their reactions. Sometimes people surprise him and show him new parts of themselves. Other times he can sense the vibration of power in every word, bouncing back and forth, back and forth, a current between two or three, or a room full of voices.

Marriage will be full of complexity and of vice. People are not born sinful, over time they grow an awareness of it, follow it slowly and incrementally. The chicken thief progresses to a camel thief, as they say.

He once read that he must multiply a behaviour by the population to help test what is right and what is wrong. Take the example of telling lies; multiply this by the population and what kind of society would there be? Getting to know this girl, Henna, before engagement, if he multiplies this behaviour by the population, then all couples will meet before they are engaged. But what if they fall in love in the process of getting to know each other and then discover that they are incompatible? The horses of Plato's chariot cannot be reined in at that point. Marriage then becomes hell for life.

His parents have made arranged marriage work . . . but then . . . He thinks of his father's temper causing a rupture in a moment that could have been sublime. Childhood memories of his father come back to him like a series of small paintings that start with yellow happiness, before blotches of purple and red rage mar them.

He has some of his father's volcanic anger. He recalls how the rush of it spread like a bruise across his heart earlier this year. How he allowed himself to slap an accused wife beater in the face with the full force of his body, making the man stumble and fall back. It was the thought of the victim, a helpless woman, that made him do it.

Now, he is talking in a low voice, he smiles and says, Ahh, in response to a facetious comment Bebe makes about a neighbour. The driver, Fawad, is sitting quietly in the front seat, they talk as if they are alone. Mostly it's small talk. The conversation is there only to fill the gaps in the waiting, it will be interrupted soon by the girl they have come to see.

Bebe is describing Henna's family, their heritage, Henna's education and upbringing to Rahim in small bursts of enthusiasm, in between the small talk. She has learnt a lot about Henna, discreetly asking people about her, feeling blessed that Haji Mama already knows Henna's father well. This isn't the first time she has shared these insights about Henna with Rahim, but he can see that she is happy about this possibility, that she likes the sound of herself sharing the descriptions, telling the stories, hoping the words will sink in.

The union sounds perfect, but will the girl's family choose Rahim? He is older than most grooms, he has thinning and already greying hair and small round eyes. His skin is darker in their milieu, far from the sorkh o safid, rose-cheeked, white faces that are considered beautiful.

You are tall and healthy, at the height of your career as a public prosecutor. You are well read and you love the arts, the girl is from an artistic family, there will be a connection, she says, as if she has read his thoughts.

Now, Bebe points with her chin, look, there they are, she says, dragging him out of reverie into the Volkswagen, back into the seat beside her.

Rahim sees two women come out of the large cream gates of the teachers' college together. He watches Henna, recognising her forehead first, as she walks with her arm in her sister's arm. She is taller than he imagined and thinner than she seemed in the photograph. She is bidding goodbye to the school gatekeeper, a fragile old man with a bent back and faded green uniform.

She is a tightly packed bowl of aash noodles, Rahim thinks, *like all people*. A bowl of interwoven complexity of perception, pain, joy, anger . . . He can share his world with her, but he knows that she will never fully see things as he sees things. Yes, she may fill the space next to him one day and cut her shape into his life.

25

Henna and her sister get into Khoja's bright blue beetle parked on the roadside. The beetle is an unusual colour, it stands out like a jewel against the dusty road, a fitting accessory for the successful, eccentric artist Rahim has heard so much about.

Barem, Rahim says. He squints, making his eyes small as if he is trying to pierce a hole in the seat in front of him.

Let's go, Bebe tells the driver, a smile hidden beneath the mask of her straight face that he knows so well.

As they follow Khoja's car, Rahim sees a curve coming up in the road ahead. He can see horse-drawn carriages and cars, including Khoja's, turning one by one and disappearing around the curve. This road is so much like fate's road guiding him to his next destination in life. He can't see what it will be like once he turns the corner, once he is consumed by the curve in the road. His fingers are knitted tightly in his lap as he contemplates the future.

Hamid

Hamid is sitting on a bench, his body folded, his elbows on his knees. His fingers are interlaced in a loose knot, he is looking through them to the paved walkway below. The walkway is in a park, or a garden as people call it, in the middle of Herat city. It is a round patch of grass with concrete benches circling it. Each bench is painted a glossy blue colour, each shaped like a throne, with a tall back and oversized armrests. Concrete planters surround the benches, marking the boundary to the garden. Inside the shiny white painted planters, small flowers sunbathe, residing prettily, each leaf and petal fresh from the rain that fell this morning. A steady stream of cars, horse-drawn carriages, bicycles, motorbikes, and people make up the body of this serpent that glides and grunts along the roads surrounding the park.

Hamid is here to clear his head. He must take breaks in between the events that make up his days. Now, his mind is silent, finally, as he recounts the names of Allah. His consciousness is flowing in his veins, following the blood as it pulses around his body.

A lethargic donkey walks beside a turbaned old man nearby, the donkey's tail swaying from side to side, interrupting the party of lazy flies on his back, on his bony hind legs, on his thin fur. The donkey carries a sack filled with pomegranates. The sun's rays pour upon the donkey, the man, the world. The man calls out, Come get your anar, fresh delicious anar. From behind this man and this donkey, the figure of a young man emerges. The young man belongs to a past that lives in Hamid's mind, one that he is trying hard to forget.

Suddenly a sharp sound breaks Hamid's concentration. It causes a rupture in his recounting; he imagines a vein torn asunder. It's the feeling of a slap, as the palm of the young man's hand connects with the skin in the middle of Hamid's muscular back.

In a movement, filled with the grace of a dancer, Hamid pivots his body towards the slap with a tightly formed fist. As soon as he sees the face before him, however, he loosens his fingers, releases the fist, and the breath of mighty Rustam, legendary warrior, escapes from his chest. He feels his tongue tighten against the roof of his mouth. The figure is crouching, like a sinuous cat; it is shrinking back from him. This is the last face Hamid was expecting to see.

You could have broken my face with that fist! Zahid's mouth says.

Hamid finds himself in a tight embrace with Zahid.

It's good to see you, bacha kaka, cousin, Zahid says, running his hand through his hair as they pull apart.

When did you get here? Hamid asks, beginning the walk towards home, his legs feeling heavy, like ancient tree trunks with roots burrowed deep in the earth. Before Zahid can answer, Hamid says, Let's go home and have tea and catch up properly.

Zahid is smiling, still holding on to him.

Koko will be so happy to see you, Hamid says to Zahid as they walk.

Tea is served in the family room with the velvet red-and-gold embroidered bolsters and cushions on the floor. A dashlama sweet is slowly melting in Hamid's mouth, the aftertaste of failed dreams. Hamid thinks of Koko somewhere in the house fussing with something unimportant, her mind conjuring pictures of the conversation between Hamid and Zahid. She is telling Khoja the news of Zahid's arrival in her thin voice. She is repeating the things she always says that irritate Khoja, that Hamid's world has been turned upside down by this visitor. Within the innocence of her motherly love, Hamid knows that she hates Zahid for visiting and Khoja for being so calm about it all.

Hamid pours tea for Zahid.

Are you tired? Do you want to lie down? It must have been a long bus ride.

Yes, I am tired, Zahid says. But let's stay together and if I fall asleep mid-sentence you can laugh at me.

The last time Zahid visited was on his late brother Haidar's anniversary, two years ago. He stayed for two days. Now, he is explaining his life plans to Hamid; he is brimming with opinions about everything from politics to religion to art. The words come in the rapid-fire excitement of Zahid's speech, sometimes specks of spit spray ahead of the words themselves. He says he is on his way to Kabul. He has decided to join one of the new youth groups, against his parents' wishes. He is thinking he will sign on with the Khalq group, one of the main groups of the PDPA, the People's Democratic Party of Afghanistan.

He says the PDPA's ideals of learning from the Russians and taking socialism as a philosophy will help make Afghanistan better, more modern, with equality for all. Most importantly, people who are sick, like his brother Haidar was, can find a cure, and if not a cure, then care, proper healthcare, so that people don't gossip, so that their family doesn't become the ridicule of the whole village.

He wouldn't have had to go to Germany for care if he could have found it at home, Zahid says. He pauses to run his hand over his closely cropped hair, front to back and back to front again. I just came to say hello, Zahid says, you remind me of him. There is another pause.

Hamid blinks wordlessly. *How can I make you forget me?* Hamid thinks.

Lunch arrives and is laid out on the dastarkhon. Zahid digs into the challow, rice, with his fingers. He pulls soft pieces of lamb shank from beneath the mound and folds it with the rice into his fist, before stuffing it into his mouth. *Where does the food go?* Hamid looks at Zahid's skinny arms protruding from his shirt. His face has grown even more square with age, he has a scattering of red pimples on his chin, he is thin like one of Khoja's paintbrushes. Zahid's eyes are like his brother's; it's as if his pupils are covered with a layer of protective film to keep others out. Dark like the colour of night, not blinking often enough, there is something unsure within them.

Hamid doesn't touch much of the food, his spoon resting beside his plate, but Zahid, full now, sits back. The servant boy clears the dishes and begins to fold the dastarkhon away. Hamid watches the grains of rice roll inside the plastic surface of the dastarkhon, surrendering to the folds created by the boy's hands. Zahid washes his hands in the water that the boy brings to him, he lies back on the cushions, stretches out, breathes deeply, is quiet. Zahid is soon lost in slumber.

Now that Hamid thinks about it, he shouldn't be surprised that Zahid arrived today. Last night, Haidar appeared in a dream. Hamid agreed in the dream to pay a debt to Haidar. Every act in life has a ripple effect, like the ripples that dance on the water's surface as they expand eventually to touch the other side of the riverbank. Hamid feels a rush of warmth towards Zahid and a rush of hatred towards himself. *I need to be the brother I took from Zahid*, he says to himself.

Hamid was close to Haidar, they grew up inseparable and wandered the halls of their childhood together. So, it was not a question when Haidar's parents asked Hamid to accompany Haidar to Germany for treatment. Hamid planned the trip meticulously; he learnt the basics of the German language. He had a different brain then, a bright mind which sponged up the foreign words his German teacher taught him, immediately imprinting knowledge within him.

Hamid wanted to help heal Haidar, to create for Haidar the serenity he needed, the clarity to stop his mind from listening to the dark voices which only Haidar could hear. We all have voices in our heads, Hamid knew this, even now he can hear them – voices which conflict, repeat, drive him crazy with guilt. But Haidar's voices were louder, more aggressive, more pervasive, more violent, and they made him do things he didn't want to do.

And ten months later they flew to Germany. They settled in Hamburg, where Hamid found an apartment, spent Haidar's parents' money to set up a life. He made appointments to see doctors and specialists. At first the medication was working, things were settling down, but then Haidar drew a knife, attacked the girl Hamid had met in Germany, the girl he thought he was going to marry one day, held her by the neck when they were at the shops and threatened to kill her. The police came but it was Hamid who talked Haidar out of it, with the promise of a quiet place where they could be alone, a promise to give up his relationship with the girl, to talk, to reminisce, to calm Haidar's demons. Haidar dropped the knife and ran to Hamid, held him tight, whispered, Save me brother, she is trying to kill me.

A week later, a rush of paperwork, a strained conversation with the frightened girl to say goodbye, and they were deported back to Afghanistan. Back to Herat. Back to the ennui of life.

Haidar's mind began to derail completely. His person was undone, he became suspicious of their mutual friends, his family, even of Hamid. He decided he hated Hamid. Suicide is a sin, but Haidar committed this sin and it felt to Hamid that he shared in it.

With the death of Haidar, Hamid became the embodiment of loss. He retired to his room in the large house, to the Quran Khoja gave him, to repair the tear in his soul. Hamid didn't know what to do with the different shades of feeling arising within him. The thoughts which made his chest burst into a scream, a purple scream, the force of which shattered his peace forever.

A year passed until slowly he emerged from his room, with the help of namaz, and of dua, prayers, of fasting and abstaining, of chilla nashini, of reading the Quran through the night for forty days and nights; then one night he found himself lifted by an invisible power, lifted from the floor of his room, to find the top of his head touching the high ceiling.

He felt that he had made a breakthrough of some sort, but it didn't last, he wasn't able to control it, he had come crashing down to the floor, falling to the ground in a heap of pain. He wasn't strong enough to control it, or to reach the ecstasy of the place where Sufi masters find sacred knowledge.

The next day, he began to look for a job. He worked more hours than was expected. He created a routine. Wake early, pray, work, lift weights, pray, sleep early. He worked on the roads, repairing the wounds caused by daily traffic. For the first time in a long time it felt like the family, especially Henna and Koko, did not worry about him. For the first time in a long time, he felt like he was contributing to society in a small way that mattered.

Now, Hamid watches as Zahid sleeps. He thinks of the girl, her face faded, and shakes his head at the realisation that she was an infatuation, and nothing more; she was so easily forgotten. Zahid is leaving tomorrow morning. He will soon wake, they will drink tea, they will not talk of Haidar. Hamid stands slowly, he tiptoes and leaves for afternoon namaz. Today he will pray a few extra rakat, a few extra surah, a few extra requests for forgiveness.

Henna

The women arrive first, on an afternoon like any other, when Henna is safely enclosed behind her desk at the teachers' college. They come to start a conversation that is both taboo and a normal part of life. A small, intimate group led by Rahim's mother Bebe and a lady long known to the family, the wife of Professor Abdel Hadi, Shazia jan. Precious stones decorate their necks and fingers, the sond on their pantaloons and translucent veils catches the afternoon light. Their eyebrows are groomed into elegant curves. They float on a cloud of perfume to Henna's family home.

The women are led to the formal reception room by the maid, Nana. Shortly after being seated, they are joined by Henna's mother, Koko. The arrival of people Koko knows only by name is a sign of the purpose of their visit. They are here for Henna, Koko's only remaining unmarried daughter.

Like her daughter, Koko isn't made for small talk with strangers. She isn't a society wife, doesn't enjoy playing the hostess; carrying the conversation and managing the formality of new acquaintances is grating. Nargis and Roya were married in quick succession, perhaps too fast, so that Koko didn't get a chance to say goodbye or mourn their loss until one day she realised her home felt empty. Nargis and Roya live near each other at least, in Kabul, so they won't be lonely. They have lost touch with their parents and siblings, only writing a couple of times a year, and are immersed in the life of motherhood. Being closer in age to each other than to Henna and Hamid, Koko is pleased they found suitors from the same family to take them away. Now, Hamid is at risk of losing his beloved Henna to Bebe's proposal.

Koko glances at the bangle snug around her bony wrist as she adjusts her chadar on her head. The bangle reminds her of her own engagement, it came as a gift at her engagement ceremony, in the tray that Khoja's family gave her family. It was placed on top of a large bundle of money and other jewellery boxes on a bed of white sugared almonds. She remembers holding the thick gold band of interlocking chains for the first time.

She was sixteen when she was betrothed to Khoja, a contrast to Henna who finished her secondary school with honours two years ago, is now in her final year of teachers' college, already nineteen with no intention to marry. Koko and Khoja's families had a history of conflict, a war over lands and property that had started in the days long ago. The marriage was a form of peace agreement, a truce to put an end to the conflict which had at times been violent. She knew none of this history then.

Love your husband but never let him know how much you love him, Koko's mother had taught her. This had been sage advice; it had worked well for her. She had felt special then, being able to exercise this power over her husband, a thing all women wanted but rarely got. Years later, she received a slap in the face from fate. She overheard a conversation between Khoja and little Henna in the quiet of his studio. She heard Khoja say that he had loved his first wife but respected his second wife. Respect is also a kind of love, she reminds herself now, pushing down this thought into her chest so it doesn't spring back up as doubt.

Now, Koko returns from the faraway land of memories to the present moment in her lounge room, to the expectant gaze of Rahim's mother, Bebe, and her firm words about the future. There is no subject left to discuss. From the uncomfortable pause that happens with strangers, the proposal is emerging like a fresh green leaf from a dead dry stem.

Koko has heard this kind of talk before and she can see that Bebe knows how to prepare the room for this talk to become possible, to gain the permission she needs to address it. It takes courage to place her son in the equation of marriage with Koko's daughter without being disrespectful. She follows custom, she says the right things about Koko, their family name and status in society. She assures Koko that she and her family have thought about the boy, and about the girl's future.

Why don't they go to Kabul for this? In the modern city of Kabul, girls freely choose their husbands, Koko thinks but doesn't say.

Bebe leans into Koko and intimately relays that Rahim is in Farah working on a complex and dangerous case involving a violent gang. Koko can smell Bebe's sickly sweet perfume, Bebe's two dark beads looking into her own large almond eyes. Koko doesn't want to know about Rahim. *There are no ties that bind him to us*, she thinks.

She knows from experience that it can all change in an instant. That a ceremony will change everything, from Rahim being a stranger to Rahim becoming her son; even though nothing about them has changed as people, they will have made a pact expressed through ceremony. *Then my heart strings will become attached to him*, she thinks, *and I will want to know when he will return from Farah, is he safe, does he need his shirt mended, are they getting along together as a couple?*

Koko feels like her heart cannot bear a new connection, a new attachment to yet another person who she must worry about, care about, love. For love is so hard to give, takes so much pain, so much sacrifice and torment. She feels like all her available heart strings are tied to her children and her husband.

The people she loves are floating out there in the world, their decisions out of her control, their future out of her reach and influence. When her children hurt, she hurts, as if the umbilical cord was never broken at birth, it's still there, attached to each child, lingering and tugging and transmitting their pain to her body. *I will wait to see the day when I love Rahim as my son*, she thinks, suspecting that such a day will never arrive.

The visit ends with Bebe saying they will come again, and Koko saying, Henna is too young, she has a long road ahead, and wants to be a chemistry teacher. This is your home, come any time but leave the talk of proposals out of it.

The doorman closes the door behind them only to reopen to them again in a week when they arrive with a larger group, including Rahim. Khoja will join the guests this time, given there are men in the company.

In the weeks that bring autumn to a close, Rahim's family return many times. They seem more determined at every visit, having investigated Henna's family, her behaviour in public, her educational record. They bring mutual friends of Khoja with them. They walk with purpose to the reception room, they know the way now, they are familiar with the orange song of the leaves crunching beneath their feet in the courtyard, the thick of the green hedges, the faces of the life-sized horse statues which Khoja has carved to stand guard at the doorway of his house.

Hamid

Hamid opens the front gate of the house. He has been thinking about how he will approach Henna all day. The skin on the palms of his hands is burning from pushing the wheelbarrow and then the weights. He steps over a small puddle, pulling his pantaloons up around his waist so as not to get dirt on the edges. He plans to walk straight to Henna, wherever she is in the house, and wants to appear calm, clean and respectable.

In his hands, his pantaloons feel heavy even though they are made only of white cotton. This is because his biceps feel tight and strained, as if he is still carrying the makeshift dumbbells he has been working with the last hour at a gathering of men like him, all of them working on their bodies in a small room with a roller door to close at night, and a handful of equipment. They watch their bodies as they lift in front of a large mirror that covers the wall and is kept cleaner than any mirror he has ever seen. He has noticed a parallel between the way his training companions admire and work to sculpt and refine every muscle on their bodies and the way Khoja sculpts his statues.

Now, he has a job to do. Heavier than the weights he lifted this afternoon, in the pocket of his black vest, is the photo of a man, a photograph inside a white envelope that he stole from the drawer where Koko hid it, following a visit from Bebe. A photograph he is going to pass on to his sister. If said out loud this thought, this scheme, this plan, this aberrant behaviour would forever brand him as dishonourable and lacking the decency expected of a brother in Herat society.

A man who passes his sister the photograph of another man is, more than anything, an abomination. But this plan, this risk, this acquiring of the photograph of Rahim, under strict privacy, is to save his sister from being betrothed to a man she will not see face to face until their engagement day.

Hamid knows there are reasons for the modest rules of their family and society, but allowing Henna to walk this path without knowing who her companion for the rest of her life will be – this life, with its unpredictable and precarious turns – is not decency at all. Besides, his relationship with Henna is different from all the brothers and sisters of Herat. He has already joked with Henna, talked about Rahim with her, been a confidant to her when Koko would not be. In a situation like this, Hamid believes he must take matters into his own hands. If they are found out, if she is blamed for this act, then he will lay his life down for her and will accept the label of shame.

He believes this isn't how Khoda intended women to marry – for women to be blindly wed against their wishes. Even if society shuns him, he knows that Khoda will not. He is going to save her from the mistake of regretting her future before it has even begun.

He stops with his hand outstretched to the door handle. What if Henna becomes angry that he did this? This is a likely outcome, given Henna appears to be angry at everything these days.

He thinks for a moment. Standing still. Hearing his own heart beating. A thought arrives. He will save them both the embarrassment of a conversation about this photograph. He will seal it inside its envelope, write her name on the front and his own on the back, and leave it under her pillow. Now, he smiles. He thinks, *Yes*, and he heads to Khoja's studio, tiptoeing to borrow a pencil.

Henna

Henna is yet to set eyes on Rahim, despite the many visits to their home over the last year. She has finished her final year of teachers' college in that time and is now starting to teach her beloved sciences, specialising in chemistry. She wishes she could ignore Rahim and this engagement proposal and focus on her new career which is blossoming like a fresh rose bud. It is turning into a stable future she always dreamt of. She loves to stand in front of the students and impart the secrets of Khoda's creation to them in the form of the periodic table of elements and their various duties in forming the world around them.

She hasn't seen that Rahim goes to a lot of trouble for his visits. Her brother Hamid has been the main source of information on Rahim as a person, and how he has black hair and wears suits to the meetings. At first this conversation about Rahim, between brother and sister, felt strange. Usually, a girl's brother is the last person to joke with her about a suitor, but Hamid began to involve himself, shyly at first, and Henna is relieved that someone is on her side. Hamid has been telling stories about Rahim, full of mirth and teasing; he told of the last visit, how Rahim sipped hot black tea, squeezed next to his parents on the leather sofa, sweat dripping down the side of his face. He wiped his sideburns with the white handkerchief he took from his pocket and Hamid saw that it came away black.

Henna cannot help herself wanting to hear about Rahim. Sometimes she loses her temper at Hamid, but today she is calm and resigned.

She has Rahim's photograph in her hand now. Her eyes are tracing his features, his thin curly hair and long sideburns. His round face, his small black eyes, his distant gaze looking out from the photograph, as if he is looking at something behind her, his parted full lips about to speak. Hamid describes him as a sangeen, grown-up, with gravitas.

She gives the photograph to Hamid with a half smile. She knows that Hamid is trying to help her. He shouldn't have been so forward as to give her this photo. He puts it into his pocket quietly.

Henna walks to where the pomegranate and figs grow, a walk she has taken a lot recently. She walks through grapevines, row by organised row, when, at just this time of day, an orange tinge colours her skin, like the orange sky, orange trees and orange earth.

Henna's family is steeped still in the oldest traditions. As a child she was taught the traditions her mother introduced, preached and pressed upon the family from her own time. Koko used to describe Henna to her visiting lady friends as a curious and serious child, more mature than her three elder siblings. Koko would say that she worried less about Henna being reckless in her life. Overhearing this as a ten-year-old made Henna feel proud, made Henna more serious, more thoughtful, wanting to weigh things up even more carefully to please her mother. She liked being thought of as more mature than all her other siblings. Nargis and Roya teased her and called her Coco Shereen, sweet old lady. Hamid stuck up for her, but she didn't mind her sisters' teasing because she had Hamid to explore the gardens with, to catch grasshoppers with, their beautiful green bodies a delight to behold.

Over time, Henna has created a new moral code, shaped in part by her mother's traditions, and in part by her own innate desire to retain a sense of self, to live the rest of her life as a single woman with a purpose.

Henna thinks the man who is meant to marry her, as destined by Khoda, will be alone if she chooses to remain single. This is the punishment she wants to inflict as a protest against society. She will not marry, not bear children. She will work as a science teacher; she will travel to Paris like the hippies who visit their property from foreign lands to purchase her father's paintings.

The Germans and the French arrive in the springtime, looking like peasants dressed in faded cotton clothes and gratefully gorging on fruit, food and hospitality from their home. These tourist gadah, beggars, loiter around Khoja's studio; they talk to him with funny Dari accents, they take photographs and accept his polished gemstones as gifts. Henna doesn't know that her laugh fills one photograph, which was taken by a man from France while she was talking to Hamid.

How is it that these people won't accept no? Other suitors were so much easier to dismiss, their visits never impacted Henna in this way. She didn't give them a second thought, but this time it's different, they are persistent beyond measure. A pain grows inside her belly, a sickly feeling like she needs to vomit but there is nothing to throw up.

She knows their society well; she knows that saying no will impact her father the most. A man much loved by his friends of long ago, friends who have been beside him most of his life, all entwined in this mess by Rahim's family. They have been called upon to give their word of honour that Rahim is a good man. Those friends are now going to be offended, all of Herat society will know of the rejection. Their friendship will be strained if she does not proceed with the betrothal.

This is the first time her father has asked something of her but the idea of a man in her life is unthinkable, the fear of it is like a vice tightened around her whole body.

Her future life rolls past at high speed like scenes from a dream; with this man, engaged; with this man, married; the wedding night, the children – her life as she knows it, lost forever.

She can see that this is her death, the end of her, the end of who she is and who she wants to be. She will need to become someone else, a married woman. A woman whose life will be lived under a burden of expectation from all sides, her family, his family, society. She will be loaded up like a mule with life's heavy baggage, many children, housework, old age.

The proposal lives inside of every moment, it weighs down on every part of her person, lingering in the background of all she says and does. The conversations about the proposal that follow with Khoja, with Koko, are brief, but each one rekindles the intensity of her pain.

Months go by and a strange thing begins to happen. With the passing of each moon, with the alignment of the planets in the vast universe that Allah created, she becomes less fearful.

Her insignificance is the same as a small insect's fears and feelings on a giant planet; what weight can her wishes carry compared with the enormous power that turns the wheel of the world in its predetermined direction? Fear begins to lose its sharp edge and eventually turns dull, a thud of a drum in the distance. She is a resilient creature and, just as all humans can, she becomes slowly accustomed to that which torments her. That which was once so foreign, over time, becomes familiar. What was it like to be herself before these events?

She decides to face this drum playing inside her chest. Slowly, day by day, she begins to take each aspect of it apart. *Me . . .* she thinks, *I am . . .* she thinks, *to be married . . .* The first time she says this to herself, she cries, but over time the tears reduce and give way to a stillness.

Many days pass, the khastgar visits continue, and one day she can speak to herself about it, using more words than before. *Me, I am, to be married, to leave my home, my family.* She is looking over the edge of a deep, dark well with nothing nearby to steady her swaying head and body. *This is vertigo of my spirit*, she thinks.

Now she dreams, a dream with mountains in the distance. There are dark grey clouds, she can almost touch them, they are close to her face. A fierce and angry fire has passed through this place in which she is now standing, leaving only shades of ash behind. A fire that has burnt the sky and the land and everything in between. She recognises this place as the gardens around her home, Khoja's gardens burnt to ash. Screams are coming from behind a grey door that stands in front of her. A door suspended before her with no walls or hinges. She pushes it open. There is shouting and blood everywhere. An invisible hand with a bloody sword slices through the air, cutting through limbs which appear from nowhere and belong to nobody. Henna can see flesh and bones, cut red and fresh, like the meat the butcher cuts, cleanly sliced into pieces.

She walks through the door into this horror, but the sword does not react to her and busily continues to cut limbs around her. She notices there is a sound nearby and it is coming from a hole in the ground. It's a sucking, whooshing sound and it gets louder as she walks towards it. Everything is being sucked into this dark deep hole. She finds that she has also fallen in, headfirst. She cannot see an end to where she is going, the sound of falling fills her ears, becomes louder. She awaits the moment of impact, to be shattered, her narrow pelvis breaking to free her bones, her ribcage opening to expose the space where every fear resides. She awakens.

Her eyes open and she hears her own heavy breathing. She sits up on her mattress in the calm of the room. She thinks of Hamid next door, on his mattress, covered like a butterfly in a cocoon as he slumbers. The lambent wood in the fireplace is burning yellow, red and orange. Small specks of light float away from the flames and fall back in, unable to escape. Dawn is about to break; Koko will wake them soon for the morning namaz. Today, when they ask her about Rahim, she will not protest the engagement, having come face to face, in her dream, with the darkest possibilities within her.

Henna is reading a book, lying on her belly. Her thoughts are distracting her, the words are hitting her forehead and dropping to the floor instead of penetrating her brain. Hamid is writing something in a notebook, his tongue sticking out, as it always does when he is concentrating. Koko is lying on a toshak, a large thick mattress on the carpet-covered floor under the window. It's teatime on a Friday, their day off, and that time of calm in the afternoon that Henna loves after her midday namaz, after a long, delicious lunch and a nap, when she, Khoja, Hamid and Koko drink tea with dashlama and talk before praying Asr. Now, Henna sees movement in the curtains that separate the sitting room from the hallway and Nana walks in. Henna has noticed that Nana likes to hide behind these curtains when her parents argue; she likes to listen to the family conversing to see if they will say bad things about her.

Nana has been with the family since she was a young woman. Koko hired her when she knocked on the door one day, with her two young children, to ask for a job. The man who turned her life upside down became a loyal friend of charse, hashish, and he smoked everything they had. Nana's back is now hunched. Henna isn't sure exactly how old Nana is, and even Nana doesn't know this, having lost track of time. She has spent the best of her years sweeping, polishing and pushing tea trays around for Henna's family. Even so, Henna cannot remember a time when Nana liked Koko.

Shast shakast, when you turn sixty, you are broken, Nana tells Henna as she rubs her aching back, saying how almost daily she is finding a jolt of pain in her joints that wasn't there before. Henna thinks of Nana as a cracked plate, fragile and liable to break.

Henna watches Nana tuck her thick black headscarf behind her ears, her amber eyes filled with glitter as she surveys the room and everyone in it. Henna remembers spitting out a small mound of butter that Nana had pushed with her coarse fingertip into her mouth when she was a child.

Now, Henna sees that Nana is looking pleased with herself.

What is it? Henna asks. Nana opens her mouth, her top lip stretching across her gums, producing an empty gap where three front teeth used to be, a gap she refuses to replace with the dentures Khoja purchased for her at Henna's request.

They have come, the khastgar are here, Nana says, looking down at Koko who uncovers her face from behind her folded arm to reveal a furrowed brow. Henna looks back down to the page in front of her, then up at Nana and then at Koko. Their eyes meet.

Koko sits up, pauses, then stands.

Iblis, the devil, won't let us rest, she mutters.

Henna can feel her heart, a small bird fluttering.

What do you expect? Nana says to Koko. You have kept your daughter like an antique and your son too, when is he going to marry? They should both be gone to their homes by now, making children, running households. But nobody will listen to this old woman, Nana says.

Hamid looks up for the first time and shakes his head with a knowing wink at Henna as if to say, There she goes, the mad woman talking about us again. Henna smiles back at him and rolls her eyes, then makes a soundless shhh motion with her lips, shaking her head as if to say, Don't get them started.

Henna looks back to her book, not wanting to mediate between the women today. Koko straightens her dress, giving it a pat down with both hands, and adjusts her cotton pantaloons. She covers her head with a translucent cream veil, which was hanging on the wall, smoothing down a stray hair from her plait. Henna pretends to read as Koko turns to follow Nana into the studio to get Khoja.

Rahim

There is a new face among the people who are sitting with Rahim's family today in Khoja and Koko's formal reception room. The new face and noticeably large belly belong to Professor Hadi.

Rahim has learnt this week that Abdel Hadi has a son who works with Khoja as an apprentice, helping to carve sculptures for Herat's public spaces. In the past, did Abdel Hadi harbour hope that his own son would one day be worthy of Henna's hand? He must now see that this chance has passed.

Rahim hopes that Abdel Hadi's presence today is a good sign. Professor Hadi's position as a friend of Khoja, even though he is also friends with Haji Mama, means that he can represent the girl's side of the equation and everything he says can be taken as speaking on behalf of Henna's family. Rahim hopes Abdel Hadi will say yes to this match, which Khoja cannot bring himself to do. Rahim also knows that

Khoja cannot really afford to say no, that if he does his reputation and his friendships will sour. That Haji Mama will be insulted personally.

Rahim has been in social settings with Abdel Hadi before, and he is usually more talkative than he is being today; usually he talks about his political views, which stretch the sensibilities of Rahim, Haji Mama and their circle of friends, espousing the People's Democratic Party of Afghanistan's Khalq agenda, saying the Parcham side is too slow in the process of wanting to move away from the traditionalism that holds their country back. He is also critical of President Daud Khan, saying he is suppressing the freedom of alternative parties such as the PDPA as they were outlawed last year.

Rahim believes the Khalq, Parcham and a handful of smaller groups are all different shades of the same socialist belief system, which wants to invite the Soviet Union and its influence into Afghanistan, over and above the friendship they have historically enjoyed, including the Soviets' training of the Afghan army, aid and economic dealings.

Lucky for Abdel Hadi, he has deep friendships with important people and his status as an educated man yields respect, so most people turn a blind eye to what is politically dangerous talk.

So far, Abdel Hadi hasn't said much, the talk has centred around everything but politics. Abdel Hadi seems to be waiting, to see more of the conversation unfold, only chiming in with the general dialogue, sometimes causing laughter to ripple with his self-effacing comments. Rahim watches Abdel Hadi in his reclined position on the dark-blue leather sofa, his belly a large mound sitting in his lap.

Rahim is also unusually quiet, but he is the groom-to-be so it is his role to sit among his elders and listen. He watches his father, well built, tall, with a fully shaved, shining head and dark brown skin. His hands and fingernails are clean and broad. Rahim likes to look at a man's fingernails, the shape of them; the broader the nails, the more honest the man.

Haji Mama talks in a decisive, philosophical way, with respectful pauses, and listens attentively when someone else speaks. Rahim's mother used to tell him that some people have a high star. Their presence makes others seem small, they dominate the room. Rahim thinks that his father, Haji Mama, is such a man. Next to him he watches Khoja, the genteel artist with a heart made of love, a delicate man known to reside more inside his imagination rather than the dunya, this world. A man who can say so much with the stroke of a brush or convey agony and strength and desire by the stringing of words into a poem, a man Rahim believes is of the ilk that Rousseau describes in his *Confessions*.

Abdel Hadi crosses his legs, his fat fingers resting on his large belly, his tie woven between his fingers. His large bulging eyes see everything but hide his private thoughts. He begins to twist his thick silver ring around his index finger. Rahim shifts on the sofa, enjoying the feeling that he does not need to be in control of this gathering. Abdel Hadi leans forward as if he is about to make a move, to say something important. The bald patch on top of Abdel Hadi's head glistens.

Khoja, he says, forgive me for I am here as your friend and I know you trust me as such. I must speak on your behalf and say the things which are right to say at this juncture, that your modesty prevents you from saying. It is my duty to be true to your friendship.

Rahim feels like his body is a mashcoola, a water bottle, full of heat. The thing is about to happen. The room comes to a hush, and Abdel Hadi continues as everyone looks at him.

Khoja, you are the pride of Herat as an artist, a writer and a sculptor, Abdel Hadi continues. And you know me and my intentions. Henna is like a daughter to me, she has grown up before my eyes, she is an educated, intelligent girl.

Haji Mama is also the pride of Herat, and our beloved governor. Rahim is an educated, accomplished young man. Khoja, your families have known each other for generations and have much in common as respected names who have defined the right way of life for the rest of us. I hope you both don't see me as being disrespectful, but this life is but two days long. I say we accept this union with Rahim and let the young people start their life together. They will make many children, so that you will be truly wealthy, they will live in the comfort of the blessings that Khoda has bestowed on your families.

Rahim breathes out, his eyes lowered to the ground, his face burning. Khoja could say no today, could tear his pride and his family's name apart. Abdel Hadi has finally done what good friends do in this situation, he has spoken on behalf of Khoja and therefore Henna. Haji Mama speaks next on behalf of Rahim.

It would be an honour if you were to allow this, Khoja, he says. We have come with this intention and will continue to bother you until the soles of our shoes have worn out, even if it takes another year.

He stands and all who are present also stand. He takes Khoja's two hands into his own and presses them gently before taking Khoja into his arms and giving his small body a strong friendly squeeze.

Rahim sees that Khoja has tears in his eyes but he is not resisting the finality of Abdel Hadi's comments. He sees Khoja look over at Koko, she gives him a small shrug. It is Khoda's will, she seems to say, who are we to stand against Him? Rahim knows that the union has been blessed, that Henna will be his.

Bebe and Koko exchange kisses on the cheek, Abdel Hadi embraces Rahim and then both Khoja and Haji Mama. Rahim's parents and new in-laws embrace him, others shake his hand; Abdel Hadi's wife who must have known and come prepared, takes a handful of sugared almonds from her handbag and throws them over his head. The almonds scatter on the floor and get stepped on, leaving white sugary marks on the beautiful red rug.

Nana brings the black tea, but today she also brings sugar cubes, dates and the large buttery cookies that Rahim loves. The sugar will sweeten the acceptance, he smiles to himself, feeling large, as though his happiness is filling the room.

Rahim is visiting his new in-laws on his own for the first time since the acceptance ceremony a week ago, following on from the agony of uncertainty and repeat visits to Henna's home. Finally, the day has come when she is his fiancée.

He hopes to see Henna today, in person, standing in front of him, but she doesn't come to the door and doesn't bump into him in the hallway and isn't waiting in the reception room with the dark blue couches, the ornate antique furniture in carved timbers and the red handwoven carpets. Despite her absence, which he feels strongly, like the absence of the moon in an inky sky, the room seems to be filled with a new resplendent beauty. Rahim kisses Koko and Khoja's hands when they come to greet him. Nana brings tea, talk ensues, and he finds the ambiance in the room has shifted from the tense politeness of previous gatherings to a convivial and friendly mood.

Hamid joins them moments later, walking into the room with sure gentle steps, bare feet on carpet, wearing his perahan tunban the colour of blue sky, his gaze warm upon Rahim. If Hamid is like other brothers of brides, Rahim will need to create a relationship with him first, to help Hamid see that Rahim will take care of his sister, will be there for the whole family, will become a confidant to Hamid. This is the expectation placed upon Rahim, and Rahim will happily comply.

Rahim has heard many things about Hamid, but mostly that he is the slightly mad son of Khoja. Just how mad, Rahim will need to find out as he watches Hamid's words and movements over time. Hamid sits cross-legged on the sofa opposite Rahim, an unusually familiar posture given they haven't exchanged many confidences yet. He has cupped his steaming glass of tea in his two hands through which Rahim can see undulating green tea leaves in limpid green liquid. Hamid is leaning forward towards Rahim as he is quietly listening and watching Rahim's reactions to what Khoja and Koko are saying. Koko is beaming from Hamid to Rahim, urging them silently towards friendship. Both men avoid her gaze, Rahim feeling like he is a young boy being encouraged by his mother to play with the new boy at school. Khoja is sitting next to Rahim oblivious and friendly as expected, his body turned towards Rahim fully, Rahim the centre of his attention at this moment, looking as though he is ready to reach out and hold Rahim's two hands in his own.

Rahim has brought flowers for his new bride, which caught Khoja's eye, and Koko felt compelled to leave without water, given it's impolite to be forward about accepting gifts. She left them at the centre of the coffee table, their heads tilted towards the door, slowly withering, watching the proceedings and waiting for Henna to walk in. Rahim is wondering where Henna might be, will she come at the end of his visit to say goodbye or in the middle of his visit to say hello? He tries to carry on meaningful conversation as his mind dances in her direction. He doesn't know that she is close by, that she is sitting in the garden contemplating the future.

A few days later, following Rahim's disappointing visit – disappointing because it was empty of Henna – the betrothal is made official through the sweet-giving ceremony at Henna's house.

On that day, Henna does come to meet him, her face covered with a veil. She enters the room where Rahim waits, her place on the throne next to him is empty. The room is full of beaming faces watching them both, the smiles of friends and parents and family like lanterns dotting the room.

She walks into the room slowly, with her two sisters at either side of her, one of them holding her by the elbow, gently. Henna's eyes are cast down. She is dressed in a deep green velvet dress with wide sleeves and lace trims. She appears to be drowning in the dress, and as Rahim watches her walking towards him, he wonders if she chose it, its shape bubbling around her small figure. Everyone claps as she stands next to him and they smile into the faces watching them.

Without looking into her eyes, though he desperately wants to, he will place a ring on her finger, after they have sat beside each other as stiff as knives. This is the ring his mother has given him for this purpose. He doesn't try to exchange words or glances longer than necessary, pretending to be caught up in the ceremony of things. Instead Rahim chats to Khoja, Hamid, and others that fill the room. As the hours pass, it is time for the gift giving to begin. His family members place gifts on the table for Henna. Bebe hangs earrings from Henna's ears and a matching gold necklace around her neck, then two bangles around her wrists. The boxes pile in front of Henna as the women in Rahim's family put offerings of jewellery and clothing in front of the bride.

She is beautiful, Rahim thinks many times as he sips his tea. His hands shake as he puts his cup down on its saucer, which he holds with his other hand. He believes that he will happily wait for the moment she decides to look at him, be it for the rest of his life.

The ceremony is painfully short, a few hours that Rahim will come to cherish, memories of when she entered the room, when she sat beside him on the decorated couch, when he touched her hand to put on the ring.

Rahim's family take with them an elaborate tray of sugary treats decorated with ribbons and flowers. They take this tray home as the symbol of Henna's acceptance and celebrate with a feast and dancing long into the night. Rahim would gladly exchange all this merrymaking for one more moment with Henna. All night he thinks of the sombre and quiet mood they left behind at Henna's house. They brought the joy of the engagement home with them and left a shell of an incident behind. *How strange is our culture*, he thinks to himself, as his cousins dance and eat around him, *that we are celebrating, but their home is silent and sad at the thought of losing their daughter to my family. Why must marriage mean such a loss for Henna and a gain for me?*

Henna

The branch of the apple tree, heavy with the weight of small green apples, bobs up and down beside Henna's head to the beat of a secret melody played by the wind. Mother and daughter stand in the shade beneath.

Henna has been dreading the conversation which her mother must now have with her. Now that Henna is an engaged girl there are rules to follow. Khoja has requested a long engagement from Haji Mama, Rahim's father, as one of his conditions for letting Henna go. Henna knows the agreement between the two men has made Koko unhappy. Khoja is delaying the inevitable, exposing his daughter to a world of possible miseries, Koko keeps saying, shaking her head as if Henna is to blame.

You will adjust better if you have a short engagement, get married quickly. Less risk that way, just like I did and all the women in my family before me have done, Koko says.

Henna thinks about this. She agrees that nowadays the hammam, public bathing house, is full of women with stories about girls getting pregnant while engaged. She understands the things Koko is not saying, for it's shameful to mention them outright.

Henna wasn't raised like those other girls – lacking morals – and her mother's lack of trust in her is disappointing. Yet there is no winning when Koko is in her fearful state, when Koko takes everything Henna says as a knife to the heart.

Henna must now listen to Koko about how to behave with Rahim; to be respectful, keep her physical distance.

You can both visit public places; he must bring you back each day before dark. You must never go to their house alone or enter his quarters, even in the company of others.

Enough, Henna says, I understand, don't say any more.

Koko pauses, having gotten the words out. Henna's hair is glistening amber and brown in the sun's rays. Koko walks into the house, leaving Henna standing alone under her favourite tree, looking at the ground, her eyes overflowing with tears she did not want to show.

This man isn't like a winter to be endured for a few months and then he is gone, this will be your companion for life, Henna can hear Koko say in the distance.

Hamid

amid feels guilt gathering at the edges of his heart and in the taste of the words that come from his mouth as he looks at Rahim's smiling face, as he tells Rahim about his work, as he carries along the easy conversation. They have spent a good two hours together, with Hamid trying his best to be distant, but becoming entangled, absorbed and immersed in Rahim's stories every time, thinking, *Is there no end to the depth of this man? This man who is a deep sea of insight about himself and others.*

I gave his photo to my sister before she saw him in person, Hamid says to himself, watching Rahim carefully sip steaming tea when there is a lull in the conversation. What would Rahim think if he knew this? Hamid imagines the tea spilled into Rahim's sharp-suited lap. He imagines Rahim's polished demeanour startled and his arms flapping. The imagined gestures seem completely out of place for this real Rahim sitting before him. Hamid smiles to himself.

A fond memory? Rahim asks, looking at Hamid, his head cocked to one side.

Yes, Hamid says, one of our childhood together. With Henna. Picking grapes and getting stung by a bee, Hamid says as he looks over Rahim's shoulder through the window with no glass, which opens directly onto the street and its bustle. Hamid is relieved he came up with a memory on the spot for Rahim.

They are sitting in a restaurant in Herat's bazaar. The table, which was full of kebab skewers of tender meat, a platter of rice, sabzi, finely chopped salad and bread is now bare, with just the two cups of tea and sugar cubes in a small, clear plastic bowl.

Hamid's stomach is stretching inside his pantaloons from the big meal. He ate too much, his nerves overcoming his habitual restraint. Rahim is older, wiser, more educated, his sister's fiancé. Hamid ate too much because he was distracted by all this.

So, Rahim says. What are your plans for life?

Hamid smiles. Big question, he replies. I am a leaf being carried by the stream of life towards an ocean, and so, only Khoda knows.

You talk like a mystic, Rahim says, as he smiles gently in response.

Far from the Sufi mystic myself, I do love the poetry of Khoja Abdullah Ansari, Hamid says, thinking of the time when he tried to access the sacred knowledge and failed.

Yes, Rahim says, I love to read him and also the works of Rabia Balkhi and Jalal ad-Din Balkhi too. It's a universe of literature right there.

Balkh did breed great poets, Hamid says smiling into Rahim's smile.

Hamid asked for this meeting with Rahim today to penetrate Rahim's refined exterior, to dig for flaws that could inflict suffering on his sister, but he became nervous when Rahim said yes. Not that Rahim could have declined the invitation without causing a family fuss at this point, since he is engaged to Henna. But Hamid feels now that Rahim isn't here because of duty, he is here because of who Hamid is – Henna's brother, shadow and friend.

Now, Hamid wonders if he has left any questions unasked, has he done his best to find a flaw which would be a risk?

Henna

Her strappy platform heels are slippery on the insole and one of the straps, which cuts across the back of her foot, is rubbing against her small toe, making it painful to walk. She is wearing brown bell-bottom slacks and a white pussy-bow silk blouse with her hair out over her shoulders.

Rahim is walking slightly ahead of her, a little too fast for the leisurely romantic stroll this is meant to be. He is tall, so when she loses him in the crowd, she can see his fluffy hair bobbing ahead. His blue bell-bottom slacks are wide, and his shirt neatly tucked behind his belt. He began to speed up a little while ago, suddenly seeming to be in a hurry, abandoning the conversation about Nietzsche.

She isn't catching up with him now, she is drowning in the river of the crowd filling the street; men, women, children, bright street lanterns, bustle and scent from flowers and cardamom and fried fish and syrupy jalabi layered on boards and in baskets by street vendors.

A young boy offers her a bolanie pastry. It's potato, he says, holding it up in his grimy hands.

Later, she says, as she continues to walk.

The plan was to go to the cinema on their first outing, but they wanted to walk through the festival first. Why is Rahim like a horse broken free from the carriage now? She replays their conversation in her mind, word by word, to see what it was that she said to upset him. Her anxiety turns to anger. What is he doing, leaving me alone like this? Hamid would never have behaved this way.

She has countless memories of being with Hamid in a public place when they argued and though he walked off in a huff, he never would abandon her for long. He would be angry but still hold her hand to cross the street or help her carry the shopping or hold her ice cream when she had to tie her shoelace.

She finds Rahim standing up ahead in a clearing, a bicycle swerving around him, nearly hitting him. Rahim, oblivious, his eyes narrowed, looking down at his feet in his big shoes, kicking an invisible ball, hands in pockets.

Henna doesn't speed up to reach him, she takes her time, almost hobbling from the pain in her toe which now has a blister. She is feeling guilty for leaving him waiting.

Let's go, he says, when she approaches. His eyes are empty and unfamiliar, a stranger on an outing with her.

What was she thinking to accept an outing so soon, just after the engagement announcement?

What's happened? she asks.

Nothing, there is too much attention here, he says.

This is when she realises, he is jealous, she has been attracting attention.

She immediately begins to walk beside him. She tells herself they are a couple, and if it looks this way to anyone who can see them, then perhaps there will be less attention.

They walk briskly to the car and, in silence, he drives to her home where he drops her off with a distant smile. This was Henna's first outing as an engaged woman, her first outing to see a film, walk in the bazaar, do the things she's heard couples do. She is relieved to be walking to the house so soon after she left it; the less she sees him the better.

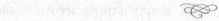

A year after their engagement, the time has finally come for Henna's wedding night. Despite her resolve, despite her belief that she has accepted marriage, it has taken a year for Henna to get used to the idea of being engaged and for the wedding to be booked.

Through the year that passed, her parents have been patient and Hamid attentive to how she has been adjusting. Beneath their support she has suspected that they worried about her and may have feared that any day her fiancé would leave her given how disinterested she has appeared to them. They were under the impression that all their outings had been the same as her description of the outing to the festival.

But they haven't been so. He has come to the house to see her; they have visited restaurants for lunch and she has studied him the way she studied grasshoppers when she was ten.

She has been learning much about him but has been too shy to speak of it to her family, even Hamid. She now knows that Rahim is kind from the way he has shown patience to her. He has talked about the future in gentle terms and taken his time to win her trust by giving her space. He helped her prepare for her teaching college exams and they have talked about the books they read. On one occasion, Rahim described her as a knowledgeable conversationalist. He told her he likes that his fiancée holds her ground when it comes to the pace of the relationship. She was relieved that he didn't find her a burden and flattered that this intelligent man thought her knowledgeable. Although she has grown fond of their friendship, she still finds the idea of separation from her family, especially Hamid, unbearable. She still finds the idea of living with Rahim difficult.

Now, the time has come for these changes to take place in her life. Now, she looks at herself in a mirror, a mirror with a heavy golden frame, a mirror twice her height and multiple times her width that fills the wall of the dressing room of the reception hall. Her reflection wears a long ivory-satin gown that flares at the hem. A layer of silver lace shimmers on the satin and drapes over her body, forming a train at her back.

On her head is a tiara, tall and white, and it sparkles, distorting her figure and distorting her gaze. Her straight hair has been transformed into an elaborate bun on top of her head, with ringlets flowing down the sides of her face like streams down a mountain. The beautician has applied a multitude of eye shadow colours on her eyelids and brushed bright rouge on each cheekbone. Even though her mother allowed her to wear make-up during her yearlong engagement, Henna chose not to, she felt it to be immodest and gratuitous.

Henna is now seeing her multicoloured, womanly face for the first time in her life. The beautician stands next to Henna, also inside this cage of reflections, beaming, her own eyelids painted green and gold.

Can you please remove some of this? Henna says.

The beautician frowns, But you are the bride, what will people say?

Henna remains quiet, standing very still, looking into the mirror. *I don't want to be the bride*, she briefly allows herself to think.

Henna's eyelids sting from cotton ball and brush stroke, as if the beautician is peeling off the skin from Henna's eyes as punishment for ruining a masterpiece. Henna doesn't complain about the pain, her eyes water and watch as the woman walks off. Henna wants the woman with the coarse dry fingertips and green eyelids to come back so she is not alone.

In the room next door, she knows that Khoja, Hamid, Haji Mama, Rahim and the mullah are settling the dowry, signing the nikkah papers. She has chosen Hamid as her witness, to speak on her behalf, to say that she accepts this union when they ask him three times as is required. In this moment, certain words are spoken, words as old as time, and those words are attaching her to Rahim, she is becoming connected to Rahim in a way that is both spiritual and different to all that she has ever known.

Rahim is the first suitor Hamid approved of; Hamid says that Rahim's age gap with Henna means he will be a good husband. He is mature, he is accomplished, he will take care of her, he will have an open mind.

Henna picks at the corner of her bright-red nails. She can hear the band playing mast music – mast, meaning lost in the madness of love; mast, meaning lost in the flow of the moment; mast, meaning losing control to the ecstasy of heavenly love. She doesn't feel mast, she thinks of the dream she had, that dream where she is swallowed by the earth, but she shakes her head.

Her sisters Nargis and Roya, Koko and her mother-in-law, Bebe, will now be standing side by side with her cousins, in a glittery row, at the entrance of the great hall, to welcome each guest as they enter. These women form a caravan of glossy happiness, kissing cheeks, bowing heads, shaking hands and inviting multicoloured guests to take their seats. Inside the great hall, the light – a shard of it, a fragment of it – bounces on the crystal drop of a chandelier, the glass face of a watch on the wrist of Professor Abdel Hadi, the sparkle of a red jewel on a necklace around a long white neck, the golden door frame, someone's shiny black shoes, an old woman's dentures as she smiles – to settle, finally, in the centre of Bebe's dark delighted pupils.

The light, like Henna's mind, pauses temporarily in each place, before moving to another place, like a mad restless bird, a bird set to flee a beautiful golden cage. But Henna is not going to flee, there is nowhere to go, so she remains standing before the grand mirrors. Usually the bride's room is filled with her friends and family, but Henna has requested to be alone, so that she can say goodbye to herself in peace.

The door opens, startling Henna. It's Hamid.

Come, he says, taking her hand, it's time to go.

She looks at him, his voice is gruff, this is his brave voice. Later, when the party is over, it will be midnight, she will say goodbye to Hamid. It will be time for Khoja to tie the green sash of fertility around her waist; inside the layers of the folded sash there will be a gold charm which Hamid bought, some grains of rice, a cardamom pod, and that is how she will part her family.

One day, when Khoja has become a memory, she will think of this night and its ending ceremony. Of her father's hands tying a sash of green tradition to her waist, the smell of his cologne, the beautiful fingernails of his beautiful hands slightly in a tremor, but firm, his eyes fixed in concentration looking to the task at hand, his eyes, disguising his tears, blinking them away, Bebe at his elbow, whispering, instructing him, his head close to Henna's face so that she wants to kiss the bald place in the centre of his hair, but does not, fearing she will cling to him to let her stay, and then a flood will come and all that has not been said will be said, and they will drown in the flood she created and Rahim's wedding will become a tale told to frighten young women, a tale which old women will tell their grandchildren as they sit in the doorways of their homes, in a village far away.

You look handsome in this suit, Henna says to Hamid. One day soon you will be the groom.

You can be my witness then, Hamid says, and they both smile.

Henna sees Rahim waiting for her outside the doors of the reception hall. Rahim is wearing a dark navy suit and a burgundy tie with a white shirt. His greys are hidden with black hair polish. Nargis and Roya are wearing matching long green velvet skirts with silver short-sleeved blouses. Their thick hair is gathered high on their heads in large curls. Khoja wears a black tuxedo and bow tie. Henna knows that he is the only man in a tuxedo at her wedding, or any occasion in all of Herat. Koko and Bebe have chosen the unusual option to dress the same. They are wearing calf-length dark blue dresses made by the same tailor. Both women have opted for the ease of matching pattern and cloth from the same catalogue, over the fuss of having to browse numerous styles and look at numerous fabrics. They wear their white silk veils loose around their heads. White silk pantaloons cover their legs and the embroidery along the hemlines skims their elegant shoes.

Henna walks to the doorway with Hamid and stands next to Rahim, her bridal veil falling just below her chin. She lets her mother's hands adjust her dress and her sisters fuss about her hair as the men stand patiently, talking in low tones. Her feet ache. She can feel Rahim standing next to her, she can feel there is a magnetic force between them now which wasn't there before, during their yearlong engage-ment, as they stand next to each other, an invisible string attaching them thumb to thumb, fingertip to fingertip. She doesn't dare look at him, her eyes cast down. Finally, the grand and heavy doors of the great hall open to velvet chairs and white tablecloths, to 400 pairs of eyes, watching, waiting, standing still, here to celebrate their union. *Ahesta Boro* is sung by the live band as Henna enters a room with her husband for the first time; *Go slowly, my lovely moon*, the singer sings.

Henna walks slowly towards two decorated thrones on a stage; she walks side by side with Rahim, as she will for the rest of her life, side by side, step by step, as the wedding song plays. The family is walking behind them, Hamid is holding a Quran above the couple's heads. The guests watch like owls, the birds she fears the most, turning their heads, their heads move with her movement, their pupils fixed on her as she walks down the never-ending red carpet of her new world. Her spine tingles, her breath sleeps within her chest.

In front of the couple is a table with two glasses of sherbat, a sweet juice, and a seven-tiered wedding cake covered with white and silver fondant. A tall cone made entirely of sugar and covered in silver foil is on a silver tray surrounded by sugared almonds. A mound of malida, a sickly-sweet wedding breadcrumb, is next to the cake.

During the mirror ceremony, the couple are covered with a colourful silk shawl as they look at each other in the mirror. Rahim looks at her, he smiles, but Henna is far away, watching a distant corner of the mirror, at her own face. His smile shrinks. They quietly read a sura from the Quran together. Rahim takes a thick bundle of money and places it inside the Quran, this will be their khairat, alms, to the poor.

The photos of their wedding turn out black-and-white. The film is spoilt so that the colours of that night will only exist in the hearts of those who saw it first-hand.

Hamid

Hamid is looking down at his shoes; they are shiny, they hold his toes too tightly together, they make him look smart and his black suit with the white flower on the lapel is bringing out the best of his muscular body. He knows these things about this evening, about himself: he will dance the Attan at Henna's wedding to Rahim tonight; he will pray for their wellbeing.

It has been a long engagement, many visits, he has had a chance to investigate Rahim's character, to converse with him, but he will stay beside Henna as her protector; Khoda forbid Rahim doesn't turn out the man he seems to be. Henna is in the room off the main corridor of this large wedding establishment. When he visited her in the room where she awaited the start of the reception, he saw she was a beautiful ball of nerves.

He picks up his glass, drinks some of the sweet sherbat; he is seated at a table for ten with the bride and groom's families, their seats empty.

The white spotless tablecloth, the glittering silver, white napkins, too delicate to wipe your mouth with, the glasses that twinkle. Bebe, Rahim's mother, has irked him a little tonight; she has pointed to a pretty girl in a green dress and asked if Hamid has thought of marriage.

No, he said to her, his response short and disrespectful. *How intrusive of her*, he thought.

Now he looks at the orange-coloured sherbat, twirling it his glass. He is alone at the table, the families have gone to do various preparations for the henna ceremony, later they will apply it to the palms of Henna and Rahim's hands. He remembers teasing Henna on most Eids when they were growing up, about how the natural dye is her namesake.

He thinks of the Eids they spent together, her excitement at the prospect of a new dress, the days when they were taken from store to store, holding Khoja's hands, one each, looking for her dress and his outfit for Eid.

On the nights before Eid when they were young, their aunties applied henna to Nargis, Roya and Henna's hands in the shape of a duck. In the morning, she greeted him, holding her palms up to his face, so close he could smell the dye, showing him the deep burgundy ducks imprinted on her palms. Tonight, her hands will have henna on them for a different reason and Rahim will share the same colour as her. Hamid will miss their Eids together, and then the thought strikes him, the thought he has been trying to suppress. He is losing Henna, like he lost Haidar.

Now Hamid reclines in his seat, putting down his glass, removing his elbows from the table, resting his hands on his abdomen, buttoning his jacket, stretching his legs, scanning the crowd. The thoughts of Eids gone by and the loss of youth have made his heart beat faster. He takes a few breaths and looks down again at his shoes to distract himself. He will not weep like a boy when they sing *Ahesta Boro* tonight, he will be brave.

Rahim

They are in their month of honey, as they call it. He has chosen the Intercontinental Hotel for their honeymoon hoping Henna will like it. She hasn't stayed here before, in this mass of rooms stacked on top of each other like a layered cake among the cacophony and movement that makes up Kabul, the window of their opulent room showcasing the peaks of the Hindu Kush mountains. They are dressed for dinner, she in an elegant black gown with large chiffon sleeves, he in a tie and dark suit. They landed this morning and now they will have their first dinner alone as a married couple; the thought of the days ahead with Henna make Rahim feel like he did when he was a child purchasing a kite or brand new books for his new year of school.

He closes the door of the room behind him, leading her to the elevator, appreciating her height next to him as her legs carry her in silver platform shoes. She is wearing make-up; he loves the glittering eyeshadow on her eyelids. She smiles shyly as she looks at him when they both reach for the elevator button together, she withdraws her hand quickly, her painted fingernails glistening in the light of the corridor.

The elevator doors open to a couple; she is blond wearing a minidress, he is also blond wearing a grey tie and suit. Hello, hello, the couple exchanges polite greetings with Henna and Rahim as the doors close behind them.

Rahim feels like his skin is new, like his face is made of completely new skin, that his body, too, is covered with a new layer of skin. I am a married man, he says to himself, catching his reflection in the window of the jewellery store in the lobby of the hotel as they walk to the poolside restaurant. *I must buy her a bangle from here, an intricate thing she can wear around her wrist, made with blue lapis*, he decides.

Now, he looks into her eyes, which are amber because they are reflecting the candle on the table in the dimly lit restaurant. A fragrant buffet is laid out and the band plays a romantic melody. The blond couple they saw in the lift are sitting near the band, they stand up and begin to dance in each other's arms, then another couple rises to join them.

What shall we do next with our lives? Rahim says, looking across the blue of the pool, the dancing couples, up to the twilight sky above and turning his gaze to Henna.

Henna pauses, putting her water glass down. Let's make it what we want to make it, she says.

He nods and says, I agree. The Ahmad Zahir concert will begin at nine, he says. Shall we start there? He can hear quiet chatter in myriad languages. He can recognise English, French, Russian in the tables around him. While he understands most of the English from school, he wishes he understood all these languages. He imagines everyone is in love and on their honeymoon like the two of them. Dusk has just settled her wings around them, giving every sound a resonance that only she can bring about.

The waiter brings their food. Henna eats very little. She blushes when he holds her hand across the table. The wedding yesterday, together today, a life ahead of them, his chest feels like it will burst with happiness. There is quiet between them but they don't need to speak.

Later, after the sweet rosewater-scented firnee has melted on their tongues, they watch the concert from a corner table. The warm-up act before Ahmad Zahir enters and plays upbeat tunes, and Rahim can see a sea of dancing bodies and hair and dresses twirling. People are dancing but Henna and Rahim are content in watching. He rests his arm across the top of the back of her chair.

Now, Ahmad Zahir's shoulders are shaking, his hair flicking, his sweat pouring as he holds the microphone in his hand. The melody, his voice piercing Rahim's flesh, making the small hairs on his neck stand and sway. He has heard the song many times but never really listened to it like this, never felt it like he does now, inside his chest and stomach and along his new skin – this song is absorbed by every cell and is rewriting everything he has known about life to date. A new world is now open to him, new words and sentences formed by this music, flowing in his blood. He is reminded of a poem, a poem about a night like this, may this night never end. He leans into Henna's ear and whispers the poem to her, she finishes the last sentence of the poem for him, and he knows that she is as intoxicated by this night, by their togetherness as he is, all without a sip of masroob touching their lips.

Henna

They are in Farah for Rahim's work. Henna wakes up startled in the middle of the night, sitting upright, like most nights since the wedding a year ago. She is breathing heavily as if trying to suck the oxygen from the sky of the bedroom. There is a swell of heavy air pushing against her ribs, she has forgotten where she is, who she is with, why she is here. Teeth clenched, she wants to run for the door, run back to the bed on the floor next to Koko.

Rahim's snoring is loud, foreboding. Henna is scanning the room. There is cool moonlight streaming through the open window. It illuminates the high ceiling, the tall windows with the white wooden frames, the red cotton curtains moving like the tongue of a monster. Someone could enter through those windows and kill them in their sleep.

What have I done? she asks herself. She married this man, knowing she was not made to be a wife. She looks at him, lying there, his body in the shape of a rifle. She trapped this man into marriage by agreeing to the proposal and now she must become the wife. He hasn't said so, but he will expect children; her hand moves to her belly. Sitting here, in her long cotton nightie, her hair stuck to her cheekbones with sweat, she takes her thin arms and folds her knees close. *What if I am pregnant? How will I birth a child from this body?* The horror she saw when she was a child and walked in on the baker's wife pushing against the knees of the midwife.

Rahim is stirring in his sleep. His body is turning inside his sky-blue pantaloons and white singlet. He is good to her. So gentle. He sighs in his sleep and reaches to find her. She can see his hand search her empty spot and his eyes open when he can't find her next to him. He is up on his elbows, looking at her on the edge of the bed furthest from him.

What's going on? he asks.

Nothing, go back to sleep, she says.

He gets up, turns on the light and leaves the room. He returns with an onion chopped in half, still in its burgundy skin, its layers exposed, its scent heavy.

Here, he tells her.

She takes the onion in her two hands and takes a long deep breath to inhale the heat into her lungs, their nightly ritual as prescribed by Bebe to help her sleep. Her eyes water. She hands it back to him.

No, take another breath.

She does. He takes the onion and places it next to her on the bedside table. He helps her to lie back on her pillow, she curls up onto her side, facing away from him, facing towards the window, beyond which is her freedom. Freedom from what, to go where? Her legs are folded against her stomach, inside her nightie. The outline of her toes is visible through the stretched cotton, her toes bony, curled inwards like her mind. She feels him gently cover her with the sheets, and he goes to the bathroom, turning off the light.

Rahim

Rahim is sitting, waiting, in the stuffy lounge room of a stranger, where the windows are closed and there isn't enough air. The servant boy instructed him to do so, the servant boy who should be at school, who opened the door of the apartment in Macroyan to Rahim. Rahim has only heard this man's voice on the phone, this man he flew to Kabul to meet, but he has an idea of his appearance based on the booming voice he heard, as someone confident and well-educated. Rahim has a mental picture of a tall handsome man his own age, probably holding office somewhere among the elite of Kabul society. Rahim expects that this man is from the People's Democratic Party of Afghanistan, either Khalq or Parcham faction.

The invitation was to come for a talk, the call came through to Rahim's office. In this political climate it isn't prudent to decline an invitation such as this. It is prudent to vaguely agree to what they ask, gently remove himself from being counted as a party member but not appear strongly opposed to this man and his politics.

A man now enters the room, wearing a white outfit of perahan tunban and a black vest. He appears to be much younger than the man Rahim was picturing a moment ago. Rahim stands, they shake hands and sit down on wide, green corduroy sofas.

Masroob?

No, thank you, Rahim replies, wondering if this is a test of his religious inclination. The man walks to the next room and returns with him a drink of whisky and a glass of water for Rahim, his gold wedding band pressing against the crystal of the glass. He is tall and broad shouldered, and he says his name is Najim. He has a goatee and a full head of hair.

Were you at the Razi wedding last month? Rahim asks, recognising his face.

Yes, says Najim, that was me, as he takes a sip.

You danced a good dance, Rahim says.

Well, I was there for the damad, the groom, what else do the damad side do but celebrate?

Nice people, Rahim says.

Yes, very, Najim agrees as he settles opposite Rahim.

Congratulations are in order for you too, Rahim jan, Najim says. I hear you have married Khoja's daughter.

Yes, Rahim says, his eyes lowering to hide the hatred he feels for Najim at this moment, for mentioning Henna. Rahim tells himself that it is normal for word of marriages and deaths to travel along the lips of people between provinces, but somehow this thought gives him no comfort, this stranger knowing so much. But doesn't he feel this anger any time people mention knowledge of his betrothal to Henna? Is it because this stranger has spoken of her, or is it because he feels that she is a secret only he can know about, as if the knowledge of her existence now must only belong to him? He doesn't know, and Najim's voice breaks his thoughts.

So, Najim says, Rahim jan I am pleased to see you have come.

Rahim can see that Najim is a little nervous, or suspicious or something else, something uneasy, uncomfortable.

As you know our country is a wonder of history, culture and art. Our religion is Islam and I would wish nothing different for our beloved Afghanistan. Najim pauses, his black eyes settle on Rahim. He is a handsome man, or could be, Rahim thinks, if his teeth didn't poke out like so, protruding slightly too far.

Rahim jan, we are a group of men who are part of a growing group of men in Kabul, who are all working towards a modernisation of our homeland. Creating a country where education is accessible to children in all corners of the country, where land rights are just, where the traditions run alongside a new modernity.

Rahim has heard this talk before, he has been nursing his own private disappointment over the last four years with the way Daud Khan has ruled. He has heard Daud is arresting his opponents rather than debating with them in public and he has not been able to close the gap between rich and poor as he promised. University funding has suffered even though he talks about education for all. Rahim believes Daud is good for the country despite these setbacks, Daud just needs more time.

I am open to new ideas, Najim jan, he says. Knowing that while he is open to new ideas, this particular group's ideas do not fit his own values.

We need educated comrades like you, Rahim jan, and Professor Abdel Hadi, too, the good man who referred you to us, Najim says, sitting back. Waiting for the flattery to sink in.

Over the years Rahim has heard this sentence from many a political movement of being an educated man but it means nothing to him, though he can imagine the impact of such flattery on men like Abdel Hadi.

Last year a group of men made a mistake by trying to change things on their own, Daud imprisoned all fifty of them, Najim continues. We are going to arrange a series of peaceful demonstrations in Kabul and want you to help us create a newsletter to educate and inform the population. You can work from Herat through our university connections, help us tell real stories about the struggle of the people and we will distribute your work all over the country.

I will do what I can, I am busy with work and family, but I will see what I can do. Najim jan, you know that my family is young and my means are small.

As the words come out, he thinks of Henna again. She is suspicious of the movements which have arisen in recent times for the betterment of the nation. She knows enough of the politics to be right with her suspicions.

You will hear from us about the next meeting, Najim says, as Rahim puts his hand into his pockets and rises from his tight spot between the couch and the coffee table.

Hamid

Hamid knows that the sky is withholding rain from Afghanistan in the north. She is doing this with permission from Khoda. There is a reason for this. Everything happens for a reason, everything that happens is caused by an action somewhere else in the world.

These laws, they are a complex spider's web which is spread across the lives of all humanity, animals and every living thing in nature. These laws exist but we cannot see the invisible strings which bind us to them. Our actions and thoughts pull the strings of this web in different ways and once pulled the reverberations in this web are far-reaching across the world. Only Khoda knows what we will choose to do and what it's impact will be.

Hamid likes to contemplate this ripple effect each time something good or bad happens to him. Each time he makes a choice between two paths. He imagines the where and who and what that caused this thing to happen. As a human being he does not profess to know the actual causes and their effects, his consciousness is not a big enough vessel to hold all the moving parts; that is a job for Khoda jan.

Khoda does not control humanity, but He knows which path each person will choose. He set up the laws, provided the guidance and created their infinite variables based on our actions. Hamid cannot blame Khoda for bringing drought, hunger, war, death. He can only imagine that there was a reason for this, somewhere a cause was triggered by one or millions of actions to bring him to what he faces today.

Hamid is contemplating this on his jai namaz, prayer rug. He has just finished his morning namaz. He has also finished his conversation with Khoda, he has asked for forgiveness and guidance for himself, his parents and all of humanity.

He wishes he was a doctor who could save lives. But he doesn't act. It has been a while since he has taken decisive action. He has stayed where he is, closely tied to his routine.

He has not been determined since he left behind his dreams of going to Kabul University, abruptly. He thinks of his time studying, wanting to be an engineer, then wanting to study at university. These thoughts have visited him again, triggered by the morning when things are quiet and the voices in his mind have more space to speak, to be heard. Could he have been someone great, perhaps?

Am I regretting the decision to leave school and take Haidar to Germany? He had asked this of Henna, looking to read the answer in her face as they sat next to each other in the gady, the horse-drawn carriage, on the way to the shops one day. She had remained silent for a long time, thinking.

I don't know, she had finally said. Was there anyone else who could have gone? Wasn't it the last chance he had to get better?

He had turned away from her then, her eyes professing the truth of her love for him, that she hadn't wanted him to go with Haidar. He asks himself now, pausing all his movements, breathing consciously to wait for an answer from the child self who lives within the valley of his breast bones.

No answer comes but a memory visits him. He had overheard Khoja long ago talking to a group of his friends who had come for tea, about the first wave of euphoria that followed the abolition of the monarchy in 1973. Hamid and his friends had been following the stories, wanting to be part of the build-up of energy all around, a promise for young people that change was in the air.

In his memory, he is sitting with his friends under a tree. They were meant to be playing football but the heat had beaten them. He remembers the passionate words that escaped his lips on that day, about the future of Afghanistan being upon them, about Daud Khan and the potential for modernity, the end to the monopoly of a few rich and lucky men over the majority of hardworking, poor farmers.

Now, he feels ashamed of his boasting and bravado. He feels ashamed that once upon a time he thought he had the potential to be a right-hand to Daud, to work his way up into politics. Once there, he would work every single day to topple the aristocracy that ruled his country, even though it meant his own family would become part of the fallen.

He sits with his feet folded beneath him on the jai namaz, in his room. He misses Henna, she is in Farah with Rahim. He wonders what her life is like and is glad she will be back soon. His finger traces the pattern of an archway on the rug all the way to the top, causing him to stretch towards the qibla and, following the arch with his finger, to sit back down.

Henna

Henna jan, can you hear me, are you there?

Henna can hear Sofia, her singsong voice travelling over their shared fence and into the house where Henna is. She puts her book down to go and see. It's always Sofia calling to say, Let's visit the new threading woman, Sofia calling to say, Come to dinner we are having some people over, it will be boring without you.

I am coming, Sofia jan, Henna calls from her hallway, as she walks towards the front door, a smile across her face and a floral headscarf tied around her head. Outside, Henna can see Sofia's pink painted smile and big black eyes rising over the shared wall, and Sofia is inviting Henna to come tonight, Henna jan, I bought fresh gandana, I will make bolanie.

Should I ask the cook to make something too? Some challow? Henna asks.

No, Henna jan, just come, the bolanie will be enough, Sofia says.

Okay then, I will wait for Rahim, we will come around six.

Sofia is satisfied, her smile widening, she gives a small nod and runs back inside her house. Henna watches Sofia disappear into her front door, turns back towards her own door, but before closing it, Henna looks up at the blue, blue, blue of the endless Farah sky, not a cloud to be seen. Henna is waiting at the door, like she does many times during the day, looking at the small green garden, with the absent flowers. She takes a moment to listen to the mild breeze who has come to visit, the breeze is a young woman and the train of her silk gown is catching the treetops and making them sway as she passes. It's a silent, hot day, a dry heat, and then there is this soothing afternoon breeze which makes it all bearable.

It's been almost a year, living in Farah for Rahim's work. She is looking forward to going back to her own work when they return to Herat. She loved the thrill of presenting her lessons, always adding something extra to the class to make it interesting for the students.

Since they arrived in Farah, her mind has been more scattered, her body thinner, weaker as she spends long days by herself or talking with Sofia in the garden next door.

Henna has one of those headaches today which last all day, a throbbing behind the eyes, she knows that today she will waste the day and lose herself in between lying down and walking around. That tonight she will likely wake again with anxiety and fear about her life, fears which don't seem to have the same gravity when she thinks of them during the day.

She has a half-written letter waiting on the floor by the window, a letter she is writing to her parents about her new temporary life in Farah.

I am happy, Rahim is well, we are missing you . . . she can't finish what she means to say. She wants to colour her reality a bit, to not tell all the truths. A part of her wants to describe her situation in full to her parents, but they will worry, there will be fear and more tawiz sent to protect her from the evil eye. She wants to tell Koko about the vomiting, the heightened sense of smell, meaning she can't eat anything cooked in the house, she wants to talk about Sofia, to reassure her parents that she is not lonely. The words don't come.

She walks to the window, a breeze is blowing, sheer white curtains brush against her body. The two women have become friends, Sofia and Henna, faster than Henna thought they would, maybe she will put that in the letter.

We are both from Herat, both here for a time because of our husbands' work, both teachers, both homesick for Herat, yet fond of rural Farah and its gentle-natured people, she will say in her letter. Sofia has an eight-year-old son and her husband is a doctor, she will add.

In truth, to Henna, Sofia is a lifeline to the outside, the outside of what and where, Henna doesn't know, she just knows that she is lonely without Hamid, she was lonely as she sat beside the guests who filled her lounge last night, lonely in the company of Sofia even sometimes, lonely in the company of Rahim.

Every few nights there is a crowd for dinner, Rahim's colleagues, new friends, old friends, there are dinners at homes around Farah, but she runs out of words at these gatherings, she cannot fill the silhouette of Rahim's wife, the silhouette that people, especially the women around her, seem to expect her to fill. An old woman, the mother of Rahim's colleague said to Henna at a dinner party, This is the age when you tie your waist to work.

What work? Henna thinks. *There are no children whose noses and bottoms need wiping, no dishes or floors to scrub, no bread to bake, no meals to cook.* Rahim has everything set up so she doesn't have to lift a finger.

She calls Rahim at work, to ask when the cook is expected to arrive with the groceries today, knowing that he knows this is an excuse for a call. She is embarrassed, embarrassed to call and to distract him from his day, but the call ends, and the day stretches before Henna, getting longer, the longer Henna waits.

The winter was especially hard, the freezing weather was too cold for her to walk outside so she spent days reading books, trying to remember things to tell Rahim when he returned from work only to forget them; too lazy to write things down.

An unfamiliar and firm knock on the door startles Henna now, and she gets up from her bed, pulling the scarf away from her head to tidy her hair, she straightens her bell-bottom pants and blouse. Only a stranger would knock like this; yes, it's Sofia's servant woman with the lisp at the door.

Khanom, madam, she says in her crackling voice. Come, please, Mistress Sofia is making a frightening noise, she is not well.

What kind of noise? Henna asks but the woman has already turned and is walking quickly away. She follows the woman out into the small street and into Sofia's house next door. She goes directly into the bedroom to find her friend on the bed, a streak of blood coming from the side of her mouth.

I have the taste of blood in my mouth, Sofia says as Henna sits beside her on the bed. The servant woman stands nearby, watching with her hands folded against her thin chest.

I have cut up the gandana, but I got dizzy and I haven't done anything with them, Sofia continues, in a low voice.

Khaira, Henna says, let's not worry about bolanie.

Sofia turns her head away from Henna, closing her eyes. The servant woman moves closer and gives Henna a damp, folded chequered cloth.

Henna wipes the blood from Sofia's nose and mouth. What happened? Did you have a fall?

No, Sofia says, turning her head back to Henna. I think it's my stomach, Henna jan. Sofia puts her hands on her belly, Henna covers Sofia's hand with her own, noticing the swelling all over Sofia's body. *The ulcer must be acting up*, she thinks.

Call Najeb jan, Henna tells the servant woman.

I have already called him, she replies. He is on the way. Henna leaves Sofia with a kiss on the forehead and goes to the hallway to call Rahim.

I am coming now, he says, and Henna hangs up the phone to go and comfort Sofia until Rahim and Najeb come home and take Sofia to the local clinic. They hope a doctor will be present but fear the right equipment may not.

Now, hours later into the night, Rahim returns home to Henna. Henna doesn't know what time it is, she had been watching the big clock, sitting in the large brown armchair in the study, but the hands of the clock don't work, they are frozen in time. She has put a blanket on Sofia's treasured son, fast asleep in the spare room, unaware of the new world he will wake to in the morning, unaware of the way they laid Sofia gently, a broken ruby jewel, in the back seat of the car.

Rahim walks into the lounge looking for her, his shirt sleeves are rolled up, his face newly washed, his sideburns still wet. She understands from the look of him that Sofia will not be returning from the clinic, that he must have been covered in blood moments ago, that he took the time to clean up at Sofia's before coming home so as not to frighten her.

Henna takes Rahim's hand and walks to the bedroom with him. Her mind is unusually quiet, her body seems light and airy, her headache has disappeared. She lies down on the bed and pulls him down beside her, in the way she sometimes does in her dreams, she folds her body into the warmth of his, taking his arm and wrapping it around her waist. He responds by holding her tight, sharing the warmth and loneliness of their life for the first time. For the first time she has decided to go to him, and he has decided to let her into his grief. She folds her knees tightly against the bump of the child in her belly, the bump they both celebrated when the midwife told them, her back against the man she is learning to love. Not long until Rahim's transfer back to Herat; she will count the days even more closely now.

Rahim

ahim adjusts his trousers, looking at the ground as he walks, the sun casting a short shadow of him among a crowd of shadows. The shadow walking to his right belongs to Abdel Hadi. Rahim looks at Abdel Hadi, in his brown vest, white shirt, grey pants and a grey woollen flat cap. *A bit warm for this warm spring day,* Rahim thinks, although he likes the way the man is dressed. Abdel Hadi smiles at him, hopeful that Rahim has been won over to the side of progress, that Rahim flew to Kabul just for this, unaware that this is a game Rahim will play for as long as it takes to maintain equilibrium between old friendships and political views he cannot agree to.

Rahim doesn't know what the right answer is, he understands Daud's insistence on Afghanistan's independence from its neighbours and he also fears the passionate perspectives of People's Democratic Party of Afghanistan.

He wants the country to prosper, not by selling itself to the Roos, the Russians, or any other country, but as an independent, sovereign state. In all his thoughts and conversations with Henna on the topic, they both agree that Daud's time has been the most liberating and that he is a watan parast, patriot, but suppressing the PDPA groups seems to create more unrest.

Today Rahim is in in Kabul, invited by Abdel Hadi, so that he can see for himself the change that is descending upon the country, a change Abdel Hadi said Rahim must understand and be a part of. Too polite to decline, too politically aware of the consequences of declining, Rahim is now here. The sun's rays are relentless, the heat like a blanket wrapping his body; he should have left his jacket in the car, but now he wears it like a heavy secret, his body moving with the people around him, but his soul has floated back to Henna, to the comfort of Henna's arms and the security of the life he knows and loves.

Abdel Hadi is sweaty in all weather, and today is no different. He is breathing in quick spurts, his short legs moving fast next to Rahim's long strides. Abdel Hadi says he isn't eating enough, that he feels like he has lost weight.

Rahim glances at his protruding belly and smiles. Yes, I can see that, he says.

Abdel Hadi says he has a new daily routine, with the extra hours he is putting at his office, writing and collating articles, editing and refining the words, sharpening the meanings to the point of a needle. Then he is running around finishing print runs at midnight and distributing the shabnamah, newsletters, in discreet boxes to be sent to People's Democratic Party supporters.

Rahim understands that Abdel Hadi was invited to a few meetings, like Rahim was, where his ego was polished into a gleaming gemstone.

Abdel Hadi is still talking about a sense of something better around the corner, the promise of advancement for the country, gesticulating passionately, his short hands fluttering like butterflies and his belly bouncing, his eyes dreamy.

Some of our brothers and comrades have been caught and imprisoned, President Daud Khan doesn't take much time to shut people down, put people away, he says.

Today is proof that the party is gaining momentum, knitting old bonds back together, he says, clasping his short fingers together and showing them to Rahim.

Today we march alongside ten thousand or so men and women in Kabul. The occasion is the funeral of an educated journalist and thinker, who was brutally assassinated two days ago. This march and funeral is a good opportunity for the party to show the government it's time for change.

Rahim feels overcome with the feeling that he is an imposter; it's Henna's voice that makes him question himself, *if you aren't a supporter, why pretend?*

Because we will not be safe otherwise, because those who have declined invitations from the party are kept on file, for Khoda knows what. He regrets that he embarked on this trip after an argument with Henna, he regrets that if this turns into a violent protest, he may be imprisoned.

Abdel Hadi is talking now about his own wife; last week she threatened to leave if he is imprisoned. She threatened to take the children with her. He says women rarely leave their husbands, but she is not like other women, there isn't a soft heart under her skin. She doesn't let him talk about his new shabnamah at home, but soon she will be proud of where it has taken the nation, soon her eyes will open to the future like his eyes have opened and she will proudly talk of this time to all who will listen.

Rahim pushes his thoughts of Henna aside, also of the conversation with Khoja and Haji Mama the other night about needing to keep an eye on Abdel Hadi. Now as he is continuing to listen to Abdel Hadi respectfully, he knows that Abdel Hadi seems deeply involved. What were once ideas in Abdel Hadi's speech are now turning into action.

A group of people walking along the edges of the march shout anti-American slogans as they pass the American embassy. They wave red flags in the air, they are seeking reform.

Later, Rahim will see that Abdel Hadi trembles from passion for this cause and the power of the crowd. This power will elevate Abdel Hadi from respected professor to new heights, to a power within the party itself.

Rahim will tremble also but from fear for what is to come. A small voice in Rahim's heart has grown louder over time, and it tells him that his world has become a dangerous place, that the recent events around him are like small earthquakes which are building up, creating a large crack in the solid earth upon which he and his forefathers have stood.

He is resting his book on his belly, looking up at the sky, his head upon his folded arms. They have made a picnic in the sunshine today. Henna is sitting beside him, eating figs from a small bowl. In her middle is a mound, a mound that represents hope, love, dreams to Rahim. She is doing everything to hide her belly, she wears a large dress now with a shock of frills around the shoulders and neck. *A choice far from her usual elegant dress code*, Rahim thinks.

Henna is looking down at him, a look he cannot read. He gets up on one elbow, still watching her face. He has teased her about a busload of children; he is only half joking as he does want a busload but only if she does. He has spoken about a large house, more servants waiting on her, looking after her numerous offspring. Perhaps he has been too forward with her, it seems she hasn't found any of it funny. She tucks her hair behind her ear, puts down the bowl of figs and fixes her big brown eyes on him.

So rude, she says, so forward, let me get this one out of my body before you disrespect me. Look at our lives, she continues, the country . . . our world is so unstable, she says. Rahim knows that she is referring to the protests and Rahim's visit to Kabul. He knows what she means to say.

He wishes it was easier to dream together. Henna is right, the protests and unrest make him rethink his life. He will wait. Perhaps she doesn't want any more children at all. Perhaps he will never become a father to more than one child. But one child safe and sound is all he wants.

Rahim has hired a cook, cleaners, gardener, a clothes washer to maintain the household since they returned from Farah. Henna doesn't talk about the night Sofia died, but Rahim can sense that it's in her thoughts. He lies back down, goes back to his book, trying not to think of anything, to clear his mind of politics and work.

Henna

Henna is glad to be back in Herat, far away from Sofia's death, although it haunts her still. She embraces the rhythms of her large family, of their parents visiting, their stories, their questions about how she is feeling. She is happy to be near Hamid.

Bebe says the baby will be a girl because of the shape of Henna's stomach; Koko says it will be a boy because of the shape of Henna's stomach. Henna knows if it's a girl, she will be called Sofia.

Henna doesn't feel what she thinks she should be feeling. She thinks she should be feeling elation, gratitude, love for the growth inside her. All she can think about instead is how the child will come out of her body, physically tearing her apart. Henna remembers the whispering aunties in her childhood talking about how a neighbourhood woman had been torn from back to front because the baby wouldn't come. She remembers the stories of a cruel midwife, who made a woman suffer more if she didn't like them.

She thinks about the woman she will become as a mother, how the baby will push her mind to its limits, how her mind was never meant to cope with any of this. She must be tough, this baby, holding on to life, unlike the ones who came before and whose grip on life was loose and so they passed through Henna in a stream of pain and blood. She had heard of women losing their pregnancies like this. What Khoda ordained happened, and Sofia was meant to be.

What world will her imagined daughter, Sofia, enter? She will be like Rahim. She will be so strong-willed that she will eat Henna and take her life on arrival. And so, Henna prepares for her own death. In every exchange about the mundane there is a sad goodbye hidden, even though her face remains smiling and her eyes calm and tender.

The pains begin one night, when Henna couldn't sleep anyway.

Her baby lies next to her in the bedroom. It's mid-afternoon. They are alone for a moment of solitude away from doting Hamid, grandfathers and grandmothers. She looks at his tiny features, the curve of his left cheek as his head rests to one side.

She has so much to think about, her thoughts need to be assembled into themes and patterns, so that she can understand herself and her new life.

Henna runs a finger over the fine fair hair growing across his soft skull. She likes to look into the large, brown eyes when they are not closed, sleeping. She likes to smell the scent of his milky skin, the body so delicate, radiating a soft warmth. She is overwhelmed by how vulnerable, dependent, needy he is at just three days old. She is filled with a love she does not understand, never could describe, and a strong drive to protect him with her own life.

She remembers peering into a nest with Hamid at a crow and its ugly chick.

When it comes to offspring, there is a fine line between beauty and ugliness, Hamid had told her. Now she wishes that one day Hamid can feel this for his own child. She thinks it is a wonder how Tariq's crinkled little fingers and creased narrow bottom are beautiful to her.

How will I keep you safe? she asks. The Saur Revolution has brought in a new government, the PDPA is in power, Taraki's voice is on the radio often, promising a better world. Red flags hang across Herat's beloved public buildings, there is a new national anthem she doesn't want to learn.

She has heard of protests against the new government being suppressed with violence; how can a regime which came to power by killing Daud and his family lead to anything peaceful and just?

You will never know the Afghanistan of before, like the kids who played in the streets freely. They have made way for uniformed men who patrol and spy in the name of peace and safety. She is grateful that both Hamid and Rahim have undergone their army conscription in the days gone by, because nowadays young men are being picked up daily by the army.

Henna falls asleep with these thoughts, the infant beside her. An afternoon breeze trembles against the window. Moments later she starts awake, a nightmare that she has suffocated her child, the weight of her too much on the fragile caterpillar beneath her.

Stupid woman, she tells herself as she opens her eyes to find the baby still fast asleep beside her. Her body feels like it has been sectioned by scissors and then sewn back together. She fights against the pain, sits up. She can feel her hair sticking to the side of her face. *Where is Rahim now?* she wonders. Only he seems to be a comfort, but he had to go back to work today. She wonders too where Hamid is. She thinks of him meandering through the alleyways of Herat, holding his eyes to the blue of the sky, squinting from the sunshine's glow, dreaming of tomorrows to come.

The baby begins a half-hearted cry, she picks him up and rocks him in her arms, a jolt of pain down her spine with every movement. Now the child is quiet again, she puts him back in the cot next to the bed and lies down to slip into one of those dreams where everything is as it was, into one of those days with Hamid in the garden, when she is pushing seedlings into the moist, scented mouth of the earth.

Hamid

Hamid runs his hand across his forehead. His palms are wet with water from the bucket that the servant boy prepared for him to take his ablutions before heading to the mosque. He is walking where he shouldn't be walking. He is walking past homes made of small boxes, amid the makeshift town of Taraki's army.

A lot has changed recently. Hamid has become an uncle to Tariq and the politics of his beloved country have changed to something new and unknown.

It is after the Saur Revolution, which began about ten days after Rahim returned from the protest in Kabul. President Daud Khan has been overthrown by Taraki and the People's Democratic Party of Afghanistan. Hamid's Herat is now a city of red flags and slogans. A new national anthem fills the radio before the news. Daud Khan and his family have been massacred at the Arg, the presidential palace, by the military officers who had trained in USSR and defected to Taraki's side.

The propaganda is everywhere, Abdel Hadi was rejoicing when he came to tea the other day at Hamid's parents' house. He called it the people's revolution, but Hamid, Henna, Rahim, Khoja and even Koko and her sharp tongue were too afraid to disagree.

Abdel Hadi boasted about the powerful secret police and their work ensuring that insurgence and misalignment against the new government would be recognised and dealt with promptly.

We wanted this revolution as a people and now it is has come, Abdel Hadi had said, filling his chest with air so that it stuck out; a caricature, Hamid had thought as Abdel Hadi reminded him of the way the pigeons inflate their chests during their mating dance.

People have died and continue do so in skirmishes all over the country, and now the army is in Herat, trying to keep the peace. The soldiers rise at dawn with the voices of the muezzin and turn to face duty, instead of Mecca; the worship of routine, which rules a soldier's life, the worship of weapons. Hamid imagines himself in this situation – he could never abandon the world inside his mind in exchange for full absorption into the world of physical things. Taking orders while a commander barks at him.

Hamid has heard about the brainwashed youth of Afghanistan who went to Russia and came back strangers. In front of him on the street, a soldier walks by in his stiff uniform. He glances at Hamid as he walks, triggering fear in him, seeming to pass Hamid in slow motion. The man's eyes are set close together, slightly buried in the flesh of his face, a little too foggy to be fully awake, a little too glassy to be alive, lingering a little too long when he looks straight into Hamid's eyes.

Hamid's spine tingles with shame, he can feel his own white teeth too long like a horse's, standing to attention behind his smile. Too much attention from an older man, a man of power, a man driven by something greater than both of them, greater than the whole army. Hamid thinks of staying safe in the night when he retreats to his quarters at the back of the main house, locking the door.

Hamid can see a man fall, his knees bend beneath him like the bellows on a harmonium that plays a sad song. He knows this man. This falling man sells sheer yakh, ice cream, which he serves in a metal bowl. Hamid remembers the ice cream melting before he could get it home when he was a child. The scent of the rosewater is in his nostrils, he is keen to press a spoon into the mound and then feel the sensation of snow on his tongue.

This man, the sheer-yakh man, is bending now and is falling face down, kneeling in the last namaz of his life. Hamid watches this, can see only from between the gaps in the wooden door of the front garden. He knows there was much noise a moment ago, he knows there are shots being fired by the army onto the protestors.

But it's all quiet now, frozen, except for the sheer-yakh man, falling in slow motion. On his chest is a large red opening, his insides and skin and clothes melted together. He slips to the ground, without a sound.

Hamid had heard from Koko, who'd heard it from the women at the baths, that the protest started with a speech by an old man in a nearby village. He was angry, this turbaned farmer, with his black vest and clean white clothes. He was intending to visit a friend, but when he went, his friend wasn't there. The friend had disappeared in the night. Someone had come to knock, muffled words were exchanged about land he owned, words his wife said she didn't understand, then the sound of a car driving away. No sign of him since, he never returned to her.

The farmer grew angrier, his white beard the length of a prophet's, his asa, walking cane, bent to the shape of a question mark, the sun-baked skin of his forehead creased from working in the fields, his eyes quivering in their sockets, the edges red with small veins, electricity rushing through his body, his voice hoarsely crying for a jihad against the Taraki government. His rage swelled to the size of a flood, spilling into every crevice of every alley in Herat, gathering a crowd as he yelled.

The travelling crowd yelled Allah o Akbar and more men joined in along the way to make one powerful voice, marching through the streets, hands waving green flags and pitchforks. All the shops closed and normal life paused. Protestors had kept the government out of Herat, they had taken over the governor's office. Soldiers, supporters and officials had withdrawn inside the Masjid-i Jami; they were waiting for the army to rescue them.

This is just one example of people taking a stand, Hamid thinks, one of many around the country which blew up as unrest against the socialist reforms implemented by the new government. These reforms were meant to lighten the load but worsened the situation of this farmer and his friends.

Hamid has imagined this hero farmer who spoke up, the farmer who was prepared to die. The farmer is probably dead today, following the army's bombing raids and gunfire in their effort to get things under control.

Hamid has been behind the garden's wooden door since sunrise, afraid to break his mother's wish, until now. He is a restless bird hitting against the walls of his cage. His mother doesn't understand that a man such as him must fight, he must sacrifice his youth now or he will forever regret his cowardice.

His mother forbade him from joining the march last night as Khoja watched their argument unfold, throwing in his own argument for wanting to go and march with the flood of men too.

Now Hamid remembers this argument word for word.

We are cowards, he said to her last night, if we don't fight. He could not yell at Koko even though he wanted to. The march is right outside our house, let me go, he had said.

Koko refused. If you go, I go, she said.

The determination in her eyes spoke this truth, that she would follow. Better to follow and die with Hamid and Khoja than to stay, her eyes said to theirs. They didn't see her cry, she didn't shout in anger, hers was the quiet, steely stoic power of a jadoogar, sorceress.

Now, Hamid flicks the latch of the gate. He feels as though hay is stuffed into his mouth and throat, his limbs and mind and feet and hands are out of his control. He can save this life somehow, to make up for the one he lost. Haidar's eyes appear to him, looking into his own. He owes Haidar this much.

Hamid regains his focus and realises that it's still quiet. The latch gives to Hamid's push, the door opens. He crouches and half runs to the sheer-yakh man. There is death all around, slaughtered bodies on the ground. He tries to keep his eyes on the sheer-yakh man so as not to see too much. He thinks of Haidar's body, hanging from the tree by the river, so limp, an empty vessel. He steps on a detached hand, soft and squishy, dirt beneath the nails. The embroidered sleeve of the man it belonged to is still attached to the hand by the thread of its embroidered sond. An embroidery stitched by a wife waiting at home.

Hamid is crouched low next to the sheer-yakh man; the man is lying in a shape that Hamid's mind cannot comprehend. Then Hamid realises there is another man entangled with the sheer-yakh man's body. He bends down to hold the ice-cream maker's head, to kiss his eyelids, to take him home. But a sound gives him pause and then a burn, a wetness at his stomach, the loss of control of his own two knees.

Hamid thinks of the home searches looking for insurgents, a type of home invasion by the government that has started. He wonders if the sheer-yakh man was searched this week. The heat in his stomach has turned to a sharp pain, he feels thirsty and the world goes black.

Henna

enna awakes to knocking on the door, a fierce knock that isn't like Bebe's confident push, her usual brusque entrance into their private space, heading straight for the curtains and promptly parting them in one fierce movement. Saying, Salaam, subh bakhair, good morning, time to wake up. She does this most mornings. Henna doesn't understand this behaviour of Bebe's, unsure if this is an intended intrusion like she has heard mothers-in-law practise to establish their authority, or if it is because Bebe is trying to include them in her family's daily rhythms.

But today is not like other days, it is a fierce knocking, and Henna feels like her head is cracking with the sound, like the sound is coming from inside her head. She rolls over and falls out of bed, landing painfully on her wrist. Rahim picks her up, sits her on the bed, kisses her forehead and waits while she threads her dressing gown over her nightdress.

Rahim is calm, how can he be so calm? She watches him walk to the door, she knows the last time a knock like this came she lost Sofia, and she has heard stories of knocks like this on doors of friends she knew. These days the most innocent sounds can herald unimaginable horrors. She stands and quickly follows Rahim to the door.

They find the messenger boy from Khoja's house at the doorstep.

Rahim jan, he says, breathless, you both must come, something bad has happened. Hamid jan has been shot.

The boy's eyes are wide, his voice a croak, he abruptly stops speaking, looking from Henna to Rahim and back again. Henna's throat tightens and she feels everything become dark.

She wakes to find herself on the floor of their bedroom, her head in Bebe's lap. Her face is wet with the water they have splashed on her. Bebe is rubbing her temples firmly.

Where is Rahim, what's happened? Henna says as she sits up.

Then the memories of moments ago come back to her. The house is empty.

Where is the baby?

The baby is safe with the wet nurse, Bebe replies.

I need to go see Hamid, Henna says, standing, scrambling to her feet.

Yes, we will go, dress yourself first, Bebe says, the car is waiting.

She has red eyes, Henna can see that she has been crying. She is dressed in black, a sign for Henna of what to expect on the other side of the car ride they are about to take.

Bebe helps Henna as she dresses feverishly, absentmindedly. Her top is loose above her skirt instead of neatly tucked in, as is her usual way, the belt missing, a white scarf around her shoulders, her tears streaming.

Henna gets into the car and Bebe sits next to her. Bebe is holding her hand tight as they drive to Khoja's house without a word.

Henna's hands are wrapped around the veranda railing, her nails are digging into cold metal as she watches what's unfolding in front of her. She is mute, and she is deaf – aside from the sound of her teeth grinding together, every other sound is silenced by the scene before her, like the sound of gunfire in the distance, its rhythmic thud, thud, thud, pause, thud, thud, thud. It seems to no longer matter, it has been muted by the grinding of her teeth. This is a body being carried in a bedsheet, this is her brother. Four men are hurrying him along the garden path of Koko's house, each holding a corner as they approach where she stands, with quick steps and furrowed brows. She lets go of the railing and she screams his name, she stands in the same spot, her feet have grown roots into the earth.

And then she begins to laugh. The absurdity of how these men carry this thing, the urgency in their movements to get him here fast, when it's too late to save him. The mockery of pretending their actions matter, when the hospital has turned him back home, in a bedsheet for a shroud.

These thoughts make her laugh out loud, a burst of sound which falls flat onto the concrete floor, which nobody else can hear. There is no breath left in her to laugh, but somehow she laughs again. She doesn't double over as she laughs, like she does when Hamid tells a joke; this is a standing stiff kind of laughter, it's a draining, weak-in-the-knees kind of laughter. Her eyes are not laughing, just her mouth, her voice, her breath.

Henna knows this is her brother, not because she has been told but because she can feel her own flesh inside the shroud. Because she has already seen this scene a thousand times through her life, when she lay in a fever ready to die, in all those moments between waking and nightmare, when the room would spin, when the objects around her would simultaneously expand and contract in time with a faraway tune, in between those moments, she has seen this scene unfolding, she has been here before, rooted in this same spot.

Now, she is loud, her voice hoarse, angry, she begins to say, I told you so. I told you so.

They ignore her, these strangers, as they put the body down on the balcony.

Her laughter turns into a wail. She lurches at the men who are bent over Hamid. She catches the hair of one of them and she pulls hard. He falls back and she realises it is Rahim.

And these are the markings of death, these blotches of colour on the bedsheet, this stillness of limbs, the shape of an elbow or a knee pushing through the bedsheet, stretching the fabric like the skin on her belly when she carried her son. Now Hamid is in a womb made of cotton, stained and covered in dust.

She dives onto Hamid's body but someone grabs her elbow. A loud crack in her shoulder and agony runs down her weak body. She turns to see Rahim, now holding her tight in his arms, stopping her from collapsing to the ground to be buried beside Hamid.

She begins to hear other voices, many wailing sounds and realises there are people all around her. Koko is floating, blurry like a ghost, collapsing as she is being held by a woman whose name Henna cannot recall. She sees Khoja near Koko, part of the same blur, his face contorted, his hands holding his hair in bunches.

Other men – she doesn't remember their names – are bending over Hamid. Strangers take him away, away from the house, she isn't allowed to follow, because Rahim's arms are strong around her body, holding her against himself; like a rag doll her body wants to fold in upon itself.

Hamid

amid can feel himself moving. His body is in a dark enclosure that is in motion. His mind is struggling upon a thought which refuses to form itself. This is death. Finally, he is free. Free to go to Haidar and to talk. To talk a long while, to sit all night and talk about all that has happened, about all that has passed. To find out why Haidar did what he did.

They will watch the sun together as it comes up orange over the top of the wall. As it brings orange to Haidar's face, his clothes, his stubble, his hair and his eyes, as he reclines on his side. His voice will echo at this time of the morning, he will explain how he suffered at his own hands. He will be the old Haidar. I don't blame you, he will say, for my death.

Hamid remembers the night it happened. It was Hamid who left that night in anger, knowing Haidar could not deal with losing him. Hamid allowed himself to punch a wall, to imagine it was Haidar's face, he allowed Haidar to see him that way, to make his oldest friend think that he is leaving for good.

For what? For an argument so futile, over Hamid's dream to go to Kabul University. The rupture, so visible. Haidar had been in a dark mood all day, he had accused Hamid of using him, questioning his motives to leave Haidar behind alone, asking if he had joined Haidar's enemies in Kabul. But on that day, at that time, Hamid was tired; it had been a long day, a long struggle to calm Haidar down. At last Hamid lost his temper. He was horrified at himself, at this new anger he didn't know by name. Haidar had begged him to stay, to calm down, to forgive. Hamid had run, then, he had run fast out of the room, from the courtyard into the dark alleyway, running faster, feeling lighter the further he got. He had left Haidar alone with his own thoughts, to surrender to his madness, while Hamid ran and spent the night in the field, under the stars, where he cried for all the years he had not cried, and became angry for all the anger he had withheld, and screamed for all the screams which had been trapped inside of him until he had lost his will to even breathe. Sleep had covered him with her warm blanket of darkness.

He feels a sharp pain now, his body is hitting against something hard. He is swaying violently. The swaying stops abruptly, he feels like he's going to vomit, nothing comes out, only the sting of his stomach. There is stillness. There is the sound of voices much louder than before, they are fierce, angry, hysterical.

He can hear Koko, Khoja, Henna, Rahim, all talking and shouting at once.

I am here, inside this black cave, I am okay, he wants to say. His mouth doesn't form the words but he knows that they are here around him, he can feel them and hear them but cannot see them. *Am I home?* He doesn't know.

He wants to ask but the sound doesn't come from his mouth. Hay is still filling his mouth and his throat, harsh, scratchy, dry, knotted and compressed, layer upon layer of hay and the dust of hay, the particles trapped between his teeth. The shadow of the memory of the sheer-yakh man momentarily visits him, he fails to grasp its significance and it fades as quickly as it arrived.

Now, the darkness is spreading, he thinks of what he will say to Haidar when they meet. When they meet and they shake hands and they fly kites like in those summer days of their youth, in the fields and on the flat roofs of Herat's springtime. He lets the cold take over, he shivers violently and falls into the smooth black sea he has been avoiding. Inside this sea it's like a warm blanket on a winter's night, and he melts and he drowns, thinking and fearing nothing as the words lā 'ilāha 'illallāh Muhammad rasūlū-llāh unfold upon his lips.

It is five in the morning, the glimmer of first light graces the clouds in the sky, making their outlines golden. Two men are driving this van to Tehran, its exterior white and dented. Behind them, on the floor, inside a thin sleeping bag made out of a plastic tent, with the logo of an aid agency on it, is Hamid, in a death sleep.

He is wearing nothing on his torso and black pantaloons on his bottom half. His torso is tightly bandaged, his lips blue and swollen. Small cuts cover his arms and body. His wound is still fresh from two days ago. He has been in and out of consciousness.

Now, he wakes to the greeting of pain, which seems to have been with him forever. He tries to lift his head but realises this makes the cabin spin.

From the window he can see the sky blurring past, he doesn't yet know this is the Iranian border stretching across the horizon; it looks like a row of celestial lights floating in the distance. The van drives at top speed, he can feel its pull towards someplace new, or is that a push?

He can see the outline of two men who are sitting in the front seat. His body rolls from side to side with the movement of the van. He puts his head back down, only to realise that also hurts, a sharp red light shoots pain behind his eyes. He feels separate from his body, a mind outside its vessel. A mind that wanders and moves freely to the past and imagines a future without boundaries. He is thirsty, he can feel his lips are large, dry; he can only see from one eye. Tiredness takes him over and he surrenders, sleep coming to take him away upon the sea of dreams.

Hamid opens his good eye to see a silver shape coming towards him. It tips some water onto his lips. A teaspoon of water, just enough to make his lips wet. He moves his tongue slowly to feel the moisture; it feels good. He wonders if this hand with the water belongs to Rahim. He thinks of the time they met for lunch, when Rahim had become engaged to Henna. Hamid remembers feeling the sun, a thin sliver of it coming through the window, warming his forearm as it rested on the windowsill of the restaurant, warming his whole body as he sat opposite Rahim, questioning Rahim's motives and ambitions as indirectly as he could, with as much tact as he could muster.

Hamid was nervous then, as he ate the meal, as he sipped the strong cardamom-scented tea – he was so unsure of who Rahim was at the beginning of that meal but had left with an understanding of the depth of the man, which had come to be proved true.

Rahim, perhaps, is the elder brother I never had, he thinks as he drifts back to sleep.

Henna

It's just before dawn when Henna opens her eyes to a faint light. She is in a large room, the ceiling high, she recognises the ceiling. She begins to lift herself up, slowly, painfully, to sit up on her toshak, cushion, on the floor. She must have come to Koko's house. She finds the baby is next to her, fast asleep on a tiny mattress, swaddled tightly, his eyes closed. A sob breaks free from her chest as she remembers why she is here, a rude shock of pain in her shoulder ignites the memory of yesterday.

She picks the baby up and holds him in her arms. It will be time to feed him soon. She wishes Tariq's wet nurse were here, she wishes this small body could be passed onto the woman whose milk has nourished him recently on so many occasions. Henna is a broken mother to him, her broken body rocks him slowly as her mind pieces together the stories which make up the day gone by.

She remembers the men, the neighbours and shopkeepers who brought Hamid to the house, who took him away as the fighting began nearby, the lights, the sounds and smells of war were close, she could smell death lingering in the trees nearby. *Where did they take Hamid? Who were those men? Where is Rahim?*

She looks around and doesn't know who is who. *Rahim isn't here*, she thinks, *he must be with the men who took Hamid.* She thinks of Roya and Nargis, her sisters in Kabul. Their hearts will break, already they are drifting far apart, their letters being censored, their words to each other awkward and restrained since the revolution.

They took Hamid, he was alive, Koko's voice speaks from behind Henna.

She turns to find Koko sitting up, a tasbeh in her hand, the beads hanging from her fingers; she has been repeating the ninety-nine names of Allah all night.

Where? Henna says, her voice breaking, as Khoja sits up and Rahim too, and they blink at one another. She realises none of them were really sleeping.

Iran, Koko says, tears streaming down her face. He will live, if he made it across the border in time, my son will live.

Henna turns her gaze to the baby in her arms. One of her teardrops falls onto his cheek and he stirs, squirming inside his swaddle. Hamid is somewhere out there, somewhere far away from her. She didn't get to say goodbye.

part two

WAR

Rahim

The arrival of Soviet troops into Afghanistan is marked by the sound of a deep-rooted hum. This hum is followed by other sounds such as the new national anthem on the radio abruptly replacing the normal news broadcast and the announcement that the USSR have landed in Afghanistan. Rahim initially thinks only he can hear the hum, a continuous sound emanating from the earth beneath his feet, an earthly hum, deeply rooted, heavy and firm, forming a canopy of sound around his head, or is it rising from his own chest into his head, this sound? Regardless, it has been making its way deep within him – burrowing, burrowing.

The hum began so faintly that he tried to dismiss it; but later the voice of the new leader, Babrak Karmal, rose on the airwaves to declare the Democratic Republic of Afghanistan as the people's regime. Glued to the radio, with Henna, he squeezed close to listen to every word pouring from it.

Now he realises the hum was not from within but from without, from far outside of himself. Rahim feels it grow louder in his ears as his dry mouth and beating heart worry about what is to come. *This is the hum of the ingel, the angel of death, announcing his death, calling him to the grave.*

Now, Rahim bangs the top of the radio hard with his fist, it turns off then on again, but he has had enough of the repeating messages and the presidential address, played on a loop; there is no new information. Henna is sitting on the edge of the sofa, her hands in her lap, her face pale, her lips parted. She gets up and goes to the next room.

Rahim's face tightens into a knot. He wants his father's rage, which sleeps within him, to give him the power to destroy this home, to take his dreams one by one like porcelain plates and smash each dream against the hard floors, to shatter them to pieces and then to end his own life. He must destroy everything most dear to him. He wants nothing to fall into their hands. His anger gives way to the realisation that he is a coward utterly incapable of any of this destruction. He thinks of Henna, alone in her despair – alone in the next room – and he feels ashamed of his rage.

Later, around midnight, the hum has turned into a roar as Rahim stands and watches the sky overhead, seeing a bridge of light, as wide as their house, has formed across the night sky. A bridge which seems to come from over there, the valley of Takht-e Safar, and reach over their home, and end somewhere behind the house where the army base is.

Helicopters are hovering and flying in and out of the bridge of light like guardians of some precious bright caravan. Henna stands next to him, he watches her as she watches the parade above, the lights shining across the arch of her tall nose, her loose hair around her shoulders, her small body standing apart from his, her mouth open, tears running down her face.

He sees himself and Henna as two separate individuals for the first time since their marriage, standing apart even though they are bound together. *We are standing apart in the same way as we will stand on judgement day,* he thinks, *when no one will remember the bonds they held, and each woman, man and child will do his own bidding,* as the aeroplanes continue to pour out of the abyss, of the darkness, bringing lights with them.

Tears flow down Rahim's face and he makes no attempt to hide them, no attempt to put on a brave face and broaden his chest as they meet the monster that has taken over their sky and their lives.

Rahim will talk about this year as the year of darkness for as long as he lives. He will wear the scars from the events of this year upon his skin like markings on a map, and every hardship he sees and every happiness he feels will etch more scars and cause him more pain. Although he is not a superstitious man, he is a spiritual soul who begins to believe that his life could have been something else if this year had unfolded differently, if his time on Earth had not contained the year 1979.

Rahim has come to work today, as if nothing has changed. He is at the office as if this were a day like any other. He is sitting in his chair, staring at a pen upon his desk but not really seeing the pen. His throat is dry, his skin feels sticky even though he washed this morning and performed his ablutions and namaz. His coat feels heavy on his back.

He reflects how his world has changed irrevocably, as he leans into his desk, in the quiet of his office, this early morning, cupping his hands together, his elbows aching on the hard wood as he rests his forehead on his cupped hands. The news of the coup filled his ears when Taraki overthrew Daud Khan. In quick succession other events followed, with Amin taking power after Taraki's assassination, and the introduction of Babrak as a puppet of the Soviet Union, leading to a friendship treaty with the USSR. There was a clause in the fine print of the treaty that gave the USSR power to intervene in Afghanistan directly. And now they are here. Daud had wanted to keep Afghanistan an independent nation, but looking at it all now in reflection, Rahim believes the USSR was always going to overstep; their friendship, he suspects, included a hidden agenda, which Rahim believes cultivated and supported the formation of disruptive political parties, such as the PDPA, and their agendas.

He knows that today he will be moderating every smile, every word he utters, every emotion he shows. He will rely on the silence between his breaths to help him stay focused at work.

There is not a soul here with whom he can share the burden of his feelings and thoughts about this invasion, events that sit heavily on his chest. He cannot call any of his friends to talk about what happened, nor those men who admired his father in the past.

There is the sound of somebody walking into the office next door. His colleague must have arrived. His colleague with the thick moustache presiding over his smile, the man who throws his head back when he laughs, his fat neck thick and sturdy like the trunk of a tree.

This man was anti-party, but then he signed on and they let him keep his job. The party members will now be able to show their happiness; everyone else will be pretending, faking like Rahim, trapped like actors in a film, carrying out make-believe lives and displaying false emotions, but cracks can form easily in their masks.

This is a time of Khafaqaan, hysteria, Rahim tells himself as he walks out onto the main floor of the building. He rubs his hands together, the skin on the back of them is rough, a fine dust rises from his skin. He grimaces, *I am a human animal shedding skin. Actually, we are all much smaller than animals, we are flies trapped in a jar, in the middle of a fire we cannot acknowledge.*

Idti! Idti! Idti! Rahim hears it before the rest of the family do, the sound of the Russian word repeating, Go! Go! Go! He follows the noise outside, into the front garden, where he hears boots landing with a thump onto flower beds, crushing the leaves, the buds and petals and beetles and worms beneath. Bodies in uniform pour over the walls like spiders. Rahim stands still and puts his arms up, palms facing out. He waits for them to find their footing, there are about ten men. He knows that a twitch will cause them to fire, so he patiently waits for them to settle and organise themselves. As each one lands, they form a semi-circle around him. Rahim can't warn the family. They are all indoors. It's a cold Friday – Khoja is in his studio, Henna is napping with Tariq, Koko is knitting.

Rahim can feel the weight of eyes on him. The barrels of their guns are pointing towards him, he keeps his hands up next to his shoulders, his eyes blinking, his breath slow. He thinks of the pistol he has under the pillow in his room, he thinks of the mujahideen hiding in the grape vines, men who arrived injured only yesterday, who know to shelter here, who are fed and watered to recover enough to fight again.

Come and take me, he says to them in his mind, as four stand in front of him and the rest spread out around the house. These men will fill Khoja's house, they will shortly find Khoja's studio, the gardens, the living areas, the toilets, the beds, the wardrobes. Their clothes will be touched and their living space – the family space – will be invaded; tornado-like, storm-like, robbed.

He watches their faces silently, nobody is speaking, they are all sweating like pigs. They are the Roos, Russians, and with them are one or two Afghans. Within moments he sees Koko, Khoja, Henna walking out with Tariq holding her hand.

Stop, stand there, one of the pigs says, his gun pointed at Henna. Tariq hides behind Henna's legs and she turns to try to comfort him but the soldier asks for everyone to have their hands up. At this, Tariq begins to cry.

Rahim doesn't look at the others, he doesn't want to encourage Koko to try to comfort Tariq or Henna to react.

He wants Henna out of sight and Tariq to be quiet. He wonders if he will be next to be disappeared. They call those men disappeared because, somehow, they are lost in the dark of the night. A whole person is swallowed by an invisible hand and is never seen or heard from again. One by one, men have been plucked out of their homes, those suspected of anti-government activity, those suspected of siding with Ismail Khan's mujahideen. Women also, but that is a horror he dare not contemplate. Every day the ministry of the interior in Kabul publishes names of the people who have died in Pole Charkhi Prison. He prays for his family to be spared this fate.

A uniform steps forward.

You are helping mujahideen criminals, he says to Rahim. We have heard they are on the grounds of this property.

There is nobody here, you are free to search, it's just me and my family. Let the women and the child go, Rahim says. Let us comfort the boy.

No! shouts the uniform. He has pale green eyes, olive skin, leathery, and he is an Afghan. He is young and filled with the power of his uniform. Rahim knows what it's like to crave unquestioned authority as a young man, wanting to make a mark on the world, wanting to break the chains of power that hold you. The uniform, the gun, the men around this fool, following his every order, people on the street with fear in their eyes as he approaches them, it has all formed a potent concoction of power and testosterone for him; he is king.

Men can be so stupid, Rahim thinks. The other soldier's pig eyes scan Henna. She had no time to put her scarf on her head, Rahim is angry at her for this.

The soldier moves towards Henna, her eyes are cast down, she is shaking. Tariq is now wailing and the pigs seem unmoved.

Rahim can see from the corner of his eyes that Khoja's hands are shaking.

Hey, Khoja says to the green-eyed Afghan man. Rahim gets ready to throw himself at the man and his gun. That gun, poised, ready to unload into Henna.

Are you not Khadir? Khoja asks.

I am Khadir, the man says, walking over to Khoja to look him straight in the face for the first time.

What are you doing here, Khadir? How is your painting going?

Rahim wants Khoja to shut up. The man has a gun, Rahim wants to yell at Khoja, why are you asking about paintbrushes?

Khadir pauses, smiles, is visibly embarrassed, his shoulders smaller than before, he casts his eyes down to look at his toes. Khoja smiles nervously. Rahim knows this man's shame. He has seen it often, when a soldier has not been fully converted to a man who hates his own people, when a soldier momentarily remembers who he used to be before he put on this uniform.

Khoja, it's you, he says. I am sorry, I didn't realise. We will go. He signals to his men and within minutes the spiders have scattered.

Henna

It is the year 1981, Henna is teaching secondary school in Herat, Tariq is two. She is in the staff room at work. The room has begun to look different to her, even though the bare concrete floor, the tea things and the tables and plastic chairs are all the same.

There are new people teaching now, alongside her, but also the longer serving teachers are quieter, slower, things are slower, everything is slower. One of these original teachers is the cordial and capable Zora. She and Henna have common friends and have exchanged a few words over time. Henna knows that Zora is rumoured to be leaving work in a couple of weeks. When she asked Zora about it, Zora told her she wants to stay home and look after her family. That she is tired of working and wants to be a housewife. Henna suspected there was more to this, knowing Zora to be as driven as herself, but didn't want to pry further.

Anita, a new student in her class, has Henna preoccupied. She pushes the folder away. *You can't do anything about this, let it go.* But she cannot. She wants to tell Rahim, but she doesn't want to burden him further. He doesn't have the capacity for more, yet he isn't doing anything about their situation. She folds her fingers around her hand, then she changes hands and repeats this motion. Her wedding band and rings she received for her engagement are loose around her slim finger. She twists a ring so the ruby is facing out. It always ends up facing the palm of her hand, the ring is too big, she should get it fixed.

Henna saw Karima the other day, a new teacher who is built like a man, tall, broad. Karima has a tendency to look men straight in the eye, the way Henna knows men are not meant to be looked at, unless they are your husband. In the bathroom, fixing her hair, she remembers seeing Karima's stockings, thick, sheer, synthetic, and then the tip of a black gun showing at her thigh. Now, she thinks, *Karima wanted me to see this.* There are three other women teaching, just like her.

The school board officials are proposing changes, a memorandum said. Positive changes to support the freedom of women and girls and their access to education. This sounded good at the start. But now, when she wants to fail Anita because Anita is a bad student, she cannot. Nobody has told Henna this explicitly, but she can sense it. It's hidden in the smile Karima gives her when they cross paths in the narrow corridors; it's in the principal, Doctor Shams's new wealth, his new approach to student welfare; it's in the fact that Anita's father visits often and Anita's entrance-exam scores would never have been given a second look years ago.

Henna gets up from the table and walks to Doctor Shams's office.

Doctor sahib, she says, as the doorman opens the door for her to enter.

Bale, yes, he says, putting down a book. He is seated behind his desk; she can tell from the look in his eyes that he was captivated by what he was reading. A slight look of annoyance passes over his face like a shadow upon the surface of water.

His new suit is blue pinstripe and is made of fine wool, the kind he never wore before.

Doctor sahib, I wanted to raise the issue of Anita's results with you. You know she is failing the chemistry class, I wanted to have a conversation with her parents, we usually don't continue them to the next grade, she may need to repeat.

Henna stops. Waiting. He continues to look at her waiting, waiting. She expects him to interject with, Yes, yes, I know, let's . . . but all he says is, Yes, go on, so?

I have said as much in my report and recommendation paper on Anita, but I can see you have drawn a red line through my report and have asked me to progress her anyway. This may set a low standard for other students.

Doctor Shams takes off his glasses, looks out the window. His eyes narrow, he turns to look Henna straight in the face but he isn't saying anything. His face is closed to her now, it used to be an open book. She stands in the silence, thinking of the dinner parties he and his wife attended at her house. How they talked till dawn about Herat's great poets – him, his wife, Rahim and Henna. Anger grows within her. How can he disrespect her so, by not standing when she entered the room, by acting as if she doesn't exist?

What happened to his unctuous admiration for Khoja in days gone by? She feels the heels of her shoes are too high, the shoes she wears most days. As she waits for his eyes to come off her, she looks at the books that cover the walls, full of wisdom from great minds. She thinks of the springtime when she and Hamid were young, when this man was young like them, and when he visited with his parents to sit and drink tea near the pomegranate trees with her parents. *Hamid would have . . .* she stops herself. The memory of him, the gap in her life in the shape of Hamid has remained vacant . . . the way to cope is not to focus on this gap, but to accept the days as they are, despite this empty void. Khoda jan doesn't give us all that we want, but He lays out a path for us to get closer to Him, she tells herself.

I think you know what is expected of you, Henna jan, Doctor Shams says calmly, breaking into her self-talk. Henna blinks. And then he returns to his book, his movements slow and precise. Henna turns and leaves without a word, wanting to outrun her tears, but she walks away slowly, full of what she hopes is outward composure.

Rahim

I signed with them, he says.

Rahim is still in his work clothes, his armpits are wet, have been all day since that meeting where he thought he was going to escape from committing to the Hizb again, but he couldn't. He takes his tie off, loosening the shirt buttons at his neck. It feels like an elephant is sitting on his chest. He hangs the tie in the cupboard. Breathes out. He notices his hands shaking as the tie slips into the hook.

He looks at Henna's face and can see that she understands about the signature, about how he had no choice but to sign or they would take him away, he can see that he doesn't have to make excuses for his weakness, that she will not think him a traitor for signing, that she knows the psychological game of cat-and-mouse as well as he does.

She told him a few weeks ago how they came to her school as well, how they lined the room with teachers, just like they did in his office today.

They ushered the workers into a meeting room, putting a gun on the table in plain view but never referring to it during the briefing. They were given two options. First option was to sign on with the Hizb, the party. Second option was to sign on as an interested party who isn't yet ready to sign with the Hizb but pledging he would do nothing to stand in the way of the government.

When this happened at Henna's school, he knows that she got away without signing anything. She had told them she is a simple woman who doesn't have the capacity to understand politics, that the party and its needs wouldn't be met with her contributions in any capacity, she played dumb.

Given this is a democratic people's government, people have the right to choose to stay out of politics because they have limitations in their capacity to understand, no?

Yes, Doctor Shams had said. As long as we don't hear about traitors, because we deal with those people using this, he had said, pushing the gun towards Henna.

Henna was undeterred, and, after her, most of the teachers had used that same excuse to get out of signing up to the Hizb.

Rahim was ashamed he didn't and couldn't say something similar. Since his meeting with the party representative in Kabul long ago, he has been delaying his contributions to their new magazine, he has not attended any of the meetings; the clock has been ticking and today he couldn't push back the invitation to sign as an interested party.

Abdel Hadi was there, he says to Henna, so was another man I haven't seen before. They asked me to sit and talk about my beliefs, my hopes, my dreams, my family. Everyone was asked to do this, to share their story. I told them I would be interested to learn more about the Hizb, so they took my signature.

Okay, she says, closing her cardigan around her, the light from the alakain, lamp, glowing bright on the tip of her nose. One day at a time, she says.

Rahim begins to pace, his hands behind his back. He walks to the window, wishing it was smaller, checks the crack between the curtains, opens a curtain slightly from a corner, peers at the darkness outside. He imagines someone watching them now, the three of them in the house which suddenly feels too big. There will be gunfire later, no doubt, between the mujahideen, the insurgents, and the army; the routine of every night. She puts her hand on his shoulder, she wakes him from the nightmare.

We can hide in the storage room again, she says, reading his thoughts.

Henna

Henna arrives home early and heads straight to the bedroom. She throws herself on her bed and begins to cry. She lets the tears come, allowing them to flood her. She needs to pick up Tariq from Koko's house before curfew, before the sirens, before the streets are given over to bullets and bombs. She will do this before dinner, but first she will cry, then she will wipe her tears, and then she will talk seriously to Rahim.

Tonight, she will tell Rahim about Anita, about the risk they have taken staying in this country which is no longer their home. The streets don't feel familiar – the sounds in the bazaar and the smells of winter and spring in the early morning and the fried-fish sellers on the side of the road – are no longer there. Tonight, she will fight for her son and his future and for them to leave and go to Iran to be with Hamid.

The servant boy puts the bowl of potato ghorma on the dining table, adjusting the salad and rice to make room. Rahim is looking up at her over the steaming rice piled into a mound. His eyes are studying her face, he seems to be waiting for a sign of her state of mind, waiting for the boy to leave so that he can talk to her.

Rahim, she begins in a quiet voice, when the boy has left, we can't stay here.

Her spoon is in her hand, but she hasn't touched the food. Four years have passed since they married, and they still eat from the same plate. He piles the plate with food, pushes it halfway between the two of them; she nibbles along the edges, taking small mouthfuls as he digs into the mound of rice and ghorma, from the centre, making neat bundles of food on his spoon, a little of each dish. He chews every mouthful thoughtfully.

Now he is looking at her, chewing slowly, his spoon resting in between mouthfuls.

Iran will be safe, she finds the courage to continue. Hamid has settled there, it's been two years and he will have made a good life for himself, we could join him and he could help us. Koko says she heard from the Sadigis that he has a job, Henna says, then stops.

My new job is a change I wasn't expecting, Rahim says. I know the bastards have demoted me, and as much as I would like to leave to get away from this job, I want to stay just to be a thorn at their side. He pauses now, as the servant boy enters with a jug of water.

Henna can see from the boy's face that he has heard the conversation, perhaps he has heard too much from Rahim. Perhaps this was a stupid mistake to raise the subject at dinner, knowing he may hear, he may report them.

She laughs a mechanical laugh to cover the seriousness of the subject, the sound of her laugh hanging unmistakably from the curtains and dripping with the candle wax that melts slowly as the minutes pass.

The electricity will not be back tonight, the boy says, I heard it from the neighbours. He looks from Henna to Rahim and back as he stands with his hands in a knot in front of his body, his white cap over light-brown hair, two brown eyes set in his white skin. He is the age Hamid was when Hamid became obsessed with slingshots, when he made one of his own, when he accidentally killed a bulbul with it.

Henna hopes that the meetings he has been attending recently as part of the new classes for youths will not cause him to forget Rahim's kindness in taking his mother and his siblings into their home, and finding his brothers small jobs around the city, preventing them from joining the growing number of homeless on the streets and in the bazaars.

Henna has many such students; the brightest are invited once a week to join special workshops designed to grow their minds according to Doctor Shams, but she knows they are being brainwashed to report what they see, small spies who watch and report on their own parents. It's a common occurrence for the father of one of these young people go missing, to hear one of these young men or women give a speech about the advances their country can make under the new government. She shivers when she thinks that, if they stay here, Tariq will be one of these brainwashed, mind-controlled servants of evil.

Tashakor, thank you, Rahim says to the servant boy, please go and have dinner with your family before the fighting begins.

The boy turns to go, as Henna turns to read Rahim's face. Waiting for him to pick up the conversation where she left off.

I can help the country if I am here, he says, as he goes back to his food.

It's a final verdict on the decision to leave. She doesn't have a counter to it without sounding childish and small-minded. She knows that he will judge her, that he thinks putting their own welfare first makes them materialistic. They are educated and capable and can help rebuild once the war is over, so they should be the ones to stay, he has told her on previous occasions. Abandoning this life will make them cowards who ran; they will be nameless and faceless without their watan, their country. They will lose everything that they are. Henna thinks of Hamid.

Rahim gets up to bring the radio to the table, to tune it to the station where the voice crackles with coordinates of tonight's bombing targets. *Maybe our area number will be called tonight*, she thinks, *maybe this will show him.*

The bombers are flown by pilots who are Muslim, who didn't think they were here to kill other Muslims, Rahim says. The farmers to the west have started to flood their lands at night, to signal where the farmland is; the water glistens in the dark and the missiles are fired into pools of water rather than homes.

He pauses. She nods. What Rahim and Henna don't know is that later the best of the Red Army will arrive, and that will mark the bloodiest phase of the invasion – these men who are trained to fight from a young age will not spare homes or people.

Now, they continue the meal and talk about other things. Through it all, Henna manages a spoonful or two, and she begins to feel the full force of desperation make space within her. She feels that the room has become claustrophobic, the ceiling low over their heads, she wishes the electricity would come back.

Rahim

Even though he became engaged, even though he married,
Rahim never really believed that he would become a father,
nor that his beloved country would be invaded and changed
beyond recognition, nor that in the same year he would experience
his first professional failure in the form of a demotion from public
prosecutor to a nondescript role behind a desk.

Last night, the gunfire, like intermittent drum beats in the distance,
made Tariq cry. Rahim could see the exchange of fire between the
government troops and guerrilla fighters, like fireworks on the
horizon, yellow and orange across the sky. From the radio he heard
that the fighting was on the outskirts of a village to the east. The voice
on the radio intermingled with the sound of a man's voice coming
through the window, a man walking on a rooftop somewhere close
by, taking his turn tonight to call Allah o Akbar in the darkness,
a darkness that is brooding and heavy across the neighbourhood.

Rahim called the one remaining local doctor when Henna couldn't settle Tariq down and they noticed his little body was heating up. The doctor did not answer. They decided to give Tariq some more time. Rahim chose not to call the family, he didn't want their mothers' fussing, their home remedies. As he paced outside the door, he could hear Henna comforting Tariq in their bedroom, she held a small wet cloth at his forehead.

He could hear her moving about the room, the sound of the metallic aftawa lagan, jug, pouring water. He wondered if the lanterns needed more oil, if they were to dim there would not be enough light in there for Henna.

Now, hours later, Rahim is running out onto the road, there is not a car in sight, and he is feeling guilty for not calling Bebe. The driver who could be called at all hours left town with his family when the war began. No one is answering the phone at Doctor Jahan's.

Rahim should have brought the car from the garage, a good fifteen minutes' walk, and parked it outside last night; now it will take him fifteen minutes to run to the doctor's house. He is losing time, and there is no time for worry and questions; he needs his body to move, he needs his brain to be quiet. He is running towards the doctor's house, his feet inside his sandals, the faint morning sun on his back, dressed in yesterday's clothes. He sees a taxi on the road, and waves at the young man sitting behind the wheel. The car stops, he hops in and tells the driver to take him to Doctor Jahan's.

The doctor is Rahim's only hope, but will he be there or has he deserted the city like so many others? Moments later, Rahim runs to the doctor's door, knocking fiercely as the taxi waits. He knows the doctor will think it's a home invasion, he prays the doctor will open despite this. He looks down at his dirty toes inside dusty sandals, he feels his unwashed face, his unwashed hair, he feels heavy with grime and unfit to be seen in public. This is what he has been reduced to, to facing a friend in this state, how disrespectful.

His stream of thought is broken by gunfire in the distance and he wonders how long he has before the fighting is upon him, before he is in the thick of it, before he leaves Henna alone in the world with his sick son.

The doctor's door opens a sliver and then quickly wider.

Rahim jan, it's you, what's happened? Come inside.

His grey eyes look into Rahim's with relief. The doctor is dressed in mismatched perahan tonban, his shirt a light blue and his pantaloons white. The doctor must have said his goodbyes just now, dressing hastily to face the end planned for him, like all those others who have disappeared around them recently.

Come please, Doctor Jahan, Rahim says, please, Tariq is very sick, he had a high fever and at first he was crying but now he is unusually faint and quiet. Something is wrong, and we don't know what to do.

Amadam, the doctor says and turns back, closing the door.

Rahim is running to the car and the doctor is running behind him with his black instrument bag. Jahan slides into the back seat beside Rahim just as the car takes off.

The sound of fighting is closer now, Rahim doesn't know how the bullets are not finding the three of them, hopes they haven't found little Tariq and Henna. He repeats verses of the Quran to protect his son, to free his little body of illness, to encase Henna and Tariq in Khoda's protection.

He prays right there, the ayatal kursi for protection, has a strong urge to kneel with his head touching the grimy, dusty floor of the car in submission to Khoda and his will. In his mind's eye he surrenders, humbled before all things that he cannot control, ashamed for his own arrogance, for wanting so much from life, when perhaps Khoda has other plans for him.

The driver is steering recklessly in the empty streets. The doctor holds onto the headrest in front of him looking straight ahead. Rahim is holding on to the base of the cream faux leather seat, trying to steady himself from sliding back and forth, from bumping into Jahan, ashamed that he wasn't able to exchange even a word of normal greeting with the doctor and grateful that the doctor seems not to mind, seems to have also abandoned the polite small-talk and greeting protocol, the expectation of social niceties.

We are here, the driver says braking hard, almost catapulting Rahim through the front window.

Rahim realises he has no money with him to pay the driver, the doctor is already inside the house. He asks the taxi driver to wait. Rahim goes inside and brings money out. He comes back to pay the driver, but the car has already taken off.

When he goes back inside the house, Tariq is crying. The sounds of Tariq's voice tears Rahim's heart, but he finds it better than the ghostly quiet of Tariq's last few hours.

Doctor Jahan is holding an empty needle in his hand. Henna is holding Tariq in her arms, sitting with her back slouched on the couch in the lounge room. She looks exhausted.

Rahim looks at Tariq's wet brow and hair, his red face and tears.

Thank you, he says.

Jahan raises both hands as if to say, no need. He begins to put his medical bag back together.

Rahim can see that Jahan isn't looking like his normal self, his grey eyes have sunk into his face. Rahim remembers that Jahan recently lost his practice, that he has been imprisoned, that his wife and children have left for Iran.

Shokor, everything is fine, Rahim jan, the doctor says. Tariq will settle down; he had a fever and I have injected something to break the fever. Please give him this syrup in four hours and then again at eight.

A lone teardrop is rolling down Henna's cheek. Her body is straight, rigid as she stands and she holds Tariq as if she is afraid of one of them taking him from her. He is still crying, but now it's a whimper. Rahim wants to hold on to Henna and Tariq but modesty prevents him doing it in front of the doctor.

It's not customary for the doctor to leave without tea, as a guest in the house, but they both understand the pause in the gunfire may not last long and the car is some walk away. He wants Jahan safe at home and begins to move towards the door with the doctor following.

Khuda hafiz, Henna jan, the doctor says, turning around to Henna momentarily, I pray that our country finds peace again.

Ameen, she replies.

Henna

enna enters a large mud-brick room, with shelves built into the walls containing ornaments and books and a Quran wrapped in a decorative cloth. In the far corner, the family's bedding is rolled neatly and tied with thick ropes. The room is carpeted with overlapping kalims, rugs, and the walls are lined with toshak, which double as mattresses at night and reclining cushions during the day.

Bebe Shereen is a large woman, with a white cotton chadar on her head, dressed in matching green pantaloons and dress. She is sitting near the door, a grey shawl over her legs. She looks up from her embroidery as Henna pokes her head in.

Come in, welcome, Bebe Shereen says, patting a spot next to her on the cushion, not standing up to welcome Henna, given that Henna is younger. Henna walks slowly over and sits beside Bebe Shereen.

A small stove sits in a corner of the room, a black kettle the size of Henna's fist coming to the boil over it.

How are you, how is the family, says Bebe Shereen, using the formal you. Aren't you Khoja's daughter?

She looks over at the kettle, walks over to it and turns off the stove, lifts its bobbing lid.

Yes, Khala jan, Aunty, I am.

Are you here for a tawiz? Bebe Shereen asks as she prepares the tea. Want some tea?

Yes and no, thank you, Henna says as Bebe Shereen continues to pour a cup for each of them and places one in front of Henna, sitting beside her.

I have come because I heard you know how to . . . Henna struggles to get the words out. That you make tawiz . . . Henna pauses.

This is the first time Henna has gone behind Rahim's back on anything. She hates the thought that she has brought their relationship to this point. A dark secret will now be between them, a scab will form on the surface of her memories. How will she look at Rahim again?

I have tawiz for most things, the woman says. Her questioning eyes, black, lined all around with surma, kohl, look in Henna and through Henna. Henna stops trying to avoid her gaze and looks up, allowing Bebe Shereen to see all the guilt that is there to see.

The surma has bled into the creases of the woman's eyes, smudging into her many tiny wrinkles.

Yes, Henna says, I am here for a tawiz. Henna notices herself squeezing her hands in her lap, she feels her jaw is tight.

What tawiz do you want, Henna jan? Babies? Sons? Removing an evil eye?

I want my husband to agree to leave Afghanistan, she says, feeling herself a child. *I am a desperate woman*, she admits to herself.

I will write you a tawiz, you will place this under your pillow, Bebe Shereen says.

Rahim is awake for morning namaz, Henna thinks, as she opens her eyes to the sound of him moving in the hallway and in the next room. She lifts herself onto her elbows, feels them sinking into the bed, and stretches her neck to peek over the far side to check on Tariq.

She is relieved to see that Tariq is still sound asleep in his little bed. There has been a lull in the fighting during the night; he will be fully rested, waking soon to giggle when Henna tickles him, her favourite time of day. She has had a deep and dreamless sleep and is feeling rested for the first time in a long time.

A stream of grey light is cutting across Tariq's face, creating a mask, from the crack in the curtains. The same light, Henna notices now, is illuminating the bedroom. Henna thinks the day has blossomed too bright to be time for morning namaz. Maybe he is going to work early.

Henna lies back on her pillow, pulls the covers to her chin and stills her body. She closes her eyes, a smile spreads across her face, her mind is quiet, and she is willing herself to forget everything that has happened recently, for a moment of peace, to feel the relief of a quiet night spent like the old days. Soon Bebe will come to see them, but for now she can rest in the solitude and quiet of the morning light.

Just as she has settled, Rahim walks into the room, his steps quick, ignoring Henna as he goes straight to the storage room door and disappears behind it. He must be looking for something, his furrowed brow and tight jaw concern her. Moments later he returns, and then Henna can see that he is half dressed in trousers and undershirt.

What are you doing? Henna asks.

He looks at her, opens his mouth, pauses, as she sits up on the side of the bed, surprised at how her peaceful moment has transformed into confusion. In the next moment he is pushing a key into her hand with a scroll of papers.

Take these, he says. Keep them on you, there might be a search, cover up tight, he says, as he puts on a sock and then another.

They are here, outside, I need to go with them, he says. He isn't looking at her, but she can tell that he isn't sure of any of his words. I will be back later, he says, they will bring me back, he continues as he puts on his shoes. Don't tell anyone, don't talk to anyone about this, don't come to the department looking for me, go to work as expected, he says with finality.

This reminds her of a conversation they once had, about the advantages taken from a woman looking for her husband. They have discussed that she is never to go pleading to anyone about him if he is taken. That she must pretend life goes on, that nobody must know her distress and disagreement with the decision to take him, lest she is seen to question the actions of the government, be seen as a traitor to the regime.

The question on her lips is, who would tip off the KHAD, the dreaded secret police, which is rumoured to be under the full control of the KGB? What is Rahim being accused of? But she stays quiet, watching him move around the room.

She doesn't know what to do to help him. She wishes he was leaving to divorce her, she thinks of their arguments, her stupid illnesses and turns of mood, and betraying him when she got the tawiz. In her mind she has given him a difficult marriage, she fears she is a bad mother.

The inside of her mouth feels like the bark of a dry tree trunk. She remembers walking along the naju trees, running her hand down the surface of their bodies, being present with all her senses to their rough beauty.

They have come to get him. He must have said too much in the company of Abdel Hadi or other party members at gatherings, in the company of the servant boy. Or is it her fault for going to the woman for the tawiz?

She is following him around now, with the key and papers in her arms. Where are you going, where are you going, she is asking, knowing she doesn't want to know the answer. He continues to move around her, taking his identity card from the drawer.

He stops, takes her by the shoulders and says, I will be back.

She can see that his eyes are blank, his hair dishevelled.

She tries to follow as he leaves the bedroom, but he closes the door and tells her to stay in the bedroom.

Hide the things I gave you, he says. So she tries to obey but can't think of hiding places for herself or the things. From behind the door she can hear his footsteps down the corridor, voices on the other end, and the front door closing.

She runs into the hallway, the papers and key in her hands, she realises she forgot to hide them so goes back to the bedroom and pushes them under her pillow and she walks back to the door quickly.

She opens the front door a small sliver, and down the garden path she can see the back of Rahim and the men who accompany him, quietly walking away.

Rahim

He follows the uniform. This was inevitable, thousands have been taken and have disappeared, why would he not be one of them? Someone must have reported something, but who, and what did they say? He has only ever given a nod to a covert operation, an idea that he knew only in theory.

The idea was brought to him when he began this new job, this demotion. It was a proposal from one of his administration assistants. The young man, who made tea, filed the papers from his desk, kept the office in order. One day, he looked at Rahim intensely, his body still, his hands beside him and asked, May I speak to you a moment, Rahim jan?

Yes, Rahim had said, closing the notebook he was writing in, leaning back in his chair.

What we do here, the young man had begun, in this new department, it's a good deed. We are returning confiscated things back to their rightful owners, things the last regime took from them.

Yes, Rahim had replied.

There are some things we know people don't want back or that we will not find owners for. The young man paused. In his eyes Rahim could see that he is taking a risk, and he knew it.

We have known your family name for many generations, Rahim jan. I was thinking to share this thought with you. I can stop talking now if you prefer.

No, please continue, Rahim said.

Then the young man looked down at his feet, then looked up and made a gesture with his hand, like a gun. Rahim understood then that he was referring to the weapons, which form a portion of the confiscated items they are meant to return to former owners. The new owners could be the mujahideen.

I understand, Rahim had said then. How will it work?

Now, Rahim feels that the agreement, the transfer of the weapons to the mujahideen, the whole operation, which he was not part of physically, had suddenly become real for him. The fact that he didn't personally understand the process, or see what happened, had helped him to brush things under the rug with Henna and not tell her. Now he feels a pang of guilt for putting his family at risk.

The young man had assured him that Rahim would not touch or see any of it, he just needed to trust that it was being done, to turn a blind eye when the time for the paperwork came, that the young man and his group has covered all tracks at work. The ammunition and weapons have gone through several hands; impossible to trace back to him and his department. Rahim had felt good at the time he agreed, he was not being completely useless to his country, while he sat behind a desk in a job several layers beneath his capability, he felt good to have this power against his oppressors to support the fight.

Now, Rahim thinks that someone from the inner circle must have spoken, someone close to the family. But who? He thinks back to the people he spoke to this week, this month, how far back must he go? He tries to think of whom he may have upset in the process of doing his job, but since his demotion, since he isn't investigating cases anymore, his personal interactions with people have significantly reduced.

He quietly walks down the garden path, to the black car which looks like his own car but is not. The man in uniform points the way for Rahim, palm open, gesturing diagonally, polite and calm, towards the car on the street. It's dawn, the birds chirp incessantly, the air is icy, the clouds white and innocent. He has a thick coat on, which feels too hot for him right now. He casts one last look at his home before entering the vehicle, the uniform patiently waiting for him to do so before he gets in the front seat next to the driver.

Both men at the front of the car have thick moustaches, both have shaved heads, both are wearing the same uniform; they could be brothers. Rahim realises they are twins. He has been fascinated by twins all his life, he wants to know things about twins, such as how alike in behaviour are they? He hasn't met any twins before, he always wanted to encounter some . . .

As they pull away from Henna, his child, his family and home, he thinks of what he can do, who he can call. He told Henna when the war first came and the disappearances began that should he ever be taken like this, she was not to petition his release, not to go from official to official, but to allow their fathers to do this work.

Henna

A song plays in Henna's mind, Ahmad Zahir crooning about loneliness, his heart about to burst. It is one of the songs he sang on the stage when Henna and Rahim went to see him on their honeymoon in Kabul. That visit seems a lifetime ago, especially because the singer himself is no more. It was reported in the media that he died in a car accident near the Salang Tunnel. There are rumours that he was killed by someone in the Taraki government. This happened six months before the Roos arrived in December '79, when the Soviet Union rode into her homeland, under the pretext of upholding the Soviet-Afghan Friendship Treaty of 1978. In a way, Zahir's death, which was announced on his 33rd birthday, marked the beginning of the end of all that Henna had known to be her normal life. And now, Rahim is gone and she doesn't know where he is, or how he suffers.

The rice grains have curled and softened in the fading light of the window. Henna stares at the plate before her. The empty spot beside her. Bebe and Haji Mama have asked her to come eat dinner with them but she wants to be alone.

Her skin aches to touch Rahim, her thoughts are thoughts of him, she is nothing, non-existent. She realises how nothing matters, nothing matters without him, the world doesn't exist without him in it. Henna is surprised by this realisation.

She tests herself. If the war stopped, if all her silly childhood dreams of lazy afternoons and sweet treats materialised, if all the people she disliked at work disappeared, if all the wealth of the world were hers, would it be enough if he wasn't there to enjoy it with her? The thought leaves her empty. He has not died, but what about the day when he does? What is a lone bulbul without its mate?

Everywhere she looks, she can see an emptiness in the shape of Rahim, this song from their honeymoon in her head, the voice of tragedy ringing in her mind. She sent Tariq to stay with Koko and now she regrets it. She wishes he was here as a reminder of Rahim.

She misses the curve of Tariq's cheek as he nestles into her when she picks him up. She misses the warm cloud of his breath.

I will give anything for you to come back, Rahim jan, she says out loud.

Rahim

Rahim is brought to a man, heavy set, sitting behind a desk in a large office that was once a dining room, at the back of a building Rahim knows from long ago. It's the sprawling property of a friend of Haji Mama's and was well known for its springtime flower gardens. Rahim wonders where the family have gone, if they left this place to the KHAD in exchange for their passage out of Afghanistan or are they all . . . ?

Rahim can see that the furniture has been moved or rearranged haphazardly in the large room. In the corner, the tall, ornate mirror which once hung in the hallway, with its carved wooden frame, is now on the floor, beneath the legs of a wooden chair. This is the new makeshift prison and offices of the regime.

Welcome, Saranwal Sahib, the man says, calling him by his profession, a title he no longer officially holds, making Rahim cringe.

Salaam, Rahim says.

The man does not respond, choosing to exclude the customary lengthy greeting of asking about the wellbeing of family and friends. Rahim stands before him, waiting.

The man's tie and collar cuts into his thick, fleshy throat. His skin is dark, he has pockmarks on his cheeks and his hair is thin and oily. He has the look of someone who works all night, goes home to change and comes back to work. He rubs his hands together. They are alone, the two of them. The uniforms have gone and shut the door behind them. Rahim thinks of what he could do to this man, how he could dive across the desk and pull the necktie hard, watch as he struggles to breathe and agrees to let Rahim go. They look at each other in silence. How much does this man know about Rahim? Probably he knows everyone's names and ages and connections. Watan farosh, swine, this man has sold his country out.

Why have I been arrested? Rahim asks, noticing that his hands have formed fists even though he has rehearsed this moment before, many times. He practised how he would stand, how he would stay calm, what he would say. None of these things are going according to plan.

The thoughts he has are forceful and strong, and he can feel that in his body they create energy and a push for movement. He will jump this man, he will deliver a fist to his face, many fists, one in the name of the nation, one in the name of innocent lives lost, one in the name of Henna, one in the name of his son Tariq, one in the name of every Afghan ever born.

The man smiles, maybe he can read Rahim's thoughts. Rahim can see that the man is pleased to hear the sign of rage in Rahim's voice.

I studied for seven years in the Soviet Union, the man begins. I saw perfect order and unity in everything. I understood communism and the order and organisation it brings. Something we lack in our country, because we are backward. He pauses.

I worked with Daud Khan to overthrow the monarchy in 1973. But when Daud Khan became president, he threw me in prison for insubordination. While Daud was pro-Soviet friendship, I don't think he went far enough in implementing socialism properly. Which is where the new party needs to take things and why our comrades are here.

Something happens to Rahim when the man has finished speaking, his body takes control and he forgets about the fragility of his situation, the dangers of a young wife on her own, and he lurches at this man, aiming for his throat, ready to kill or to die.

When he comes to, he gets up from a damp concrete floor. His clothes are wet, sticking to the side of his body. His eyes slowly adjust to his surroundings. He tries to stand but feels a sharp pain in his head, mostly at the back and his forehead. Have they brought him to Pole Charkhi Prison? He can remember that there was not more than one man in the room, he marvels at how instantaneously other men appeared, even though the door wasn't open.

A lot of time must have passed because his throat is dry; he doesn't remember what happened after he felt all those hands on him. He thinks of Henna and Tariq. His family, his job, his home, his good friends. He sits up, only to lie back down where he is. His eyes open long enough to see the makeshift cell is a small room, the concrete floor is cold, there is nothing in the cell but the stench of stale human waste. A wooden door with a rusted handle is closed on him. He touches his forehead again, it's bleeding. His body aches. He sleeps.

He hears footsteps, two men, no four, or are there more of them? He is being picked up and carried somewhere.

He wants to fight but he is tired. He sees an image of himself being tortured. He remembers being asked about a name he does not now remember and at the time he did not recognise. He remembers asking them to call Haji Mama and Abdel Hadi.

He allows the dark of the night to smother his thoughts, he is ready to be sent to the end where Khoda will judge him on the scale of vice and good deeds. He knows most men who are captured end up in Pole Charkhi Prison.

His old life feels as though it was months ago. He remembers the pain of a boot to the side of his body.

He cannot keep his head up, he finds his body aches more than when he first woke. He can feel that he is in the back seat of a car, with a stranger driving an endless road, to an unknown destination.

You are being let free, says the voice of the driver. It seems that you have a friend in the party, but if it wasn't for Professor Hadi, you would rot there.

He chooses to fall asleep again, he doesn't have the energy to question.

When Rahim wakes, when he finds that he is in a bright room, he can see that the ceiling is white, that there is a cobweb he recognises. He is lying on a bed which is firm; from the corner of his eye, he can see the burgundy curtains of his home.

He closes his eyes as relief and disbelief wash over him.

Henna

He comes home in the early hours one morning; Henna is asleep, she has taken to sharing the bed with Tariq. The servant boy is sleeping on the floor of their bedroom because she has nightmares. The two and half days have passed in mourning.

She has gone to school, she has kept a brave face; when asked about Rahim, she has said he was invited away for work, not a shadow of dissent has passed across her brown eyes no matter how much scrutiny has been focused on her, no matter how much interrogation she has borne under the cover of solicitude from Doctor Shams and his cronies, the teachers at school and from the household staff. She has been strong like he asked her to be, she hasn't betrayed the pain of their separation and she hasn't heard a word about him.

This will be the first and last lie I tell him, she promised Khoda on her first night alone, feeling guilty about the tawiz, removing it from her pillow, hiding it away.

She thought she was joining those other women, women whose husbands and brothers and fathers have disappeared, never to be heard from, never to be reunited into the normalcy of family life, a gap left open, a gash, a wound, not even a grave to mourn over.

Now, she falls on Rahim like he is life itself, like he is her last breath, like he is the lake in which she wants to drown. She is almost afraid that he may be a mirage, but no matter how weak her knees are, how loud her sobs, his frame is solid, his body is holding her up.

She can see that this hurts him, her full weight squeezing him, kissing his face, his hair, his hands, abandoning the shame of her affection, abandoning the rules of conduct in front of household staff, her nostrils full of the scent of him, and his coat which smells damp and foreign. She can see that his body is bruised and broken, and he flinches from her attentions, but she doesn't care.

Rahim

Haji Mama is sitting on the single sofa, one arm limp by his side, the other on the armrest, holding his head. He looks deep in thought and concern at the idea Rahim has just expressed to him. It's his how-can-you-be-so-stupid face, which Rahim knows well, which means that Haji thinks the idea worthless, the concept beneath him, not even worthy of a reply.

Bebe is next to her husband, on the other single sofa. The light is poor, casting shadows on both of their figures. Rahim is trying to discern if one of them will say something, so he is looking from one parent to the other.

Well? he says eventually. If I send them both, then I would follow maybe in a year's time, if things haven't calmed down?

Rahim feels as if he has been taken over by a fever. The fever, or is it a spark, has taken over his brain. The spark of a new thought, maybe it is fear, maybe it is sacrifice, maybe it is guilt, he doesn't have

160

the distance from it to know what it is. Perhaps one day he will be able to tell. The idea itself has taken hold, the form and the substance of the spark, which made him believe that letting them go without him would be better. Now he can't access that spark in order to describe it to his parents properly. It has died somehow, which is why they are reacting in this way.

When did you come up with this scheme? Bebe asks.

This is a shock to her, this idea of her son leaving his family alone in exile, while he stays back to look after his parents and his country. Rahim understands their concern, this is a change in thinking they would not be prepared for after his imprisonment, since things have begun to take their ugly shape, to really fall apart on him; before now, the discussion has always centred around how to get him and Henna and Tariq out together, then to be followed by both sets of parents and siblings. This new change in the plan is an unthinkable shift for his parents.

We have talked about this, Bebe says. Your father and I, and Henna's parents, are safer here than you in your situation. They took you once, they let you go because Abdel Hadi stuck to his honour of shared salt and let you go; the next time you can forget about coming back home.

We need to put our hearts aside, Rahim says to Bebe, who had her face turned to Haji and now turns to look at him, incredulous. We need to think with our heads, and if I am rational about this, then staying would be the right thing to do.

What would Henna say? Bebe asks. Thinking of Henna's reaction makes something else click inside him. He is like a kite, taken by the wind of words, in any direction. He cannot trust himself anymore. *What would she say?* he repeats to himself. He doesn't have the answer to this.

She will understand, he says, unconvincingly.

At this Haji stands, his legs parted, his arms folded behind his back, positioning his body towards the door, towering over Rahim who sits on the sofa opposite his parents.

Rahim can sense that Haji is going to deliver a verdict, a permanent position which will not be disputed, going against him would mean breaking familial bonds.

No son of mine, he begins, looking Rahim squarely in the face, will abandon his young wife to the foreign world, no son of mine will sacrifice his future and her safety for my sake. I don't need you, your protection or your pity. This is the end of the conversation.

With this, Haji calmly walks out, calm even though his eyes had turned red and large, even though his voice shook with the kind of anger that Rahim has rarely seen. Rahim exhales, which Bebe misunderstands as a sigh of protest against Haji.

Bebe pushes her palm towards him, No, she says and gets up to go. Your father is right, and I stand by what he said. Tomorrow you will put these foolish thoughts behind you and you will sort out your paperwork.

Rahim sits for a moment alone, looking at the weak flame in the alakain, its sooty glass casing. It's late, Henna will worry about where he has gone. He is surprised and relieved for some reason, unable to access the anger that usually arises when Haji passes one of his stubborn verdicts.

He feels light, the burden of a big decision has been lifted from his shoulders.

Rahim is in Kabul on an important errand. A heavy curtain of worry has settled upon his brow and an alternative future is unfolding in the theatre of his mind. This future is darker than the one he saw this morning as he dressed himself, as he said goodbye to Henna and kissed his son.

Horns toot as cars fight for road space around the main intersection a few blocks away. His thin, curly hair is hanging around his head like a cloud, a small wind gently ruffles the tips. He looks up at the houses along the urban hills of Kabul, they look like wooden boxes stacked precariously on top of one another, their windows sparkling like diamonds in the noon sun. Dirt pathways mark the hills like tattoos, connecting anonymous doorway to anonymous doorway. This morning he saw this same scene and said goodbye to these hills, those doorways, the snow-capped peaks of the Hindu Kush in the distance. But now he feels trapped by it all.

The smell of stew and fresh bread is coming from somewhere nearby. Thick grey smoke escapes a smattering of chimneys and yawns across the sky, joining the undulating voices of the muezzin in the air, calling all humanity to worship. His broad square fingers press his temples. As his thoughts bounce around about his next move, he sees his friend Sadiq walking towards him.

Sadiq's grey wool suit sways with his movements, enveloping his tall thin frame. Rahim hasn't seen his university roommate for many years. He can see Sadiq coming closer, but he doesn't move. His small round eyes have many thoughts behind them. The two tall men embrace like two giant grasshoppers, exchanging greetings. There is a pause, Rahim has run out of words.

So, how are you, really? Sadiq probes in a low, intimate voice.

What can I tell you, Sadiq, everyone is well, but . . . Rahim begins in the silence created by Sadiq's gaze, then stops, shakes his head, looks down at his hands. His hands seem so useless to him. You know how life is, we have lost trust in each other, a supposedly close friend put me in prison, then vouched for me to be released. I don't know why he did what he did, does anyone know why they do the things they do anymore? . . . I wake in the middle of the night thinking I am trapped in that horrible cell; food has lost its taste. I am being watched all the time. They gave me a new job, tracking down people who have become ghosts . . . I want to serve my country but this isn't a job for a public prosecutor . . .

Rahim breathes out, looking away from Sadiq. What Rahim doesn't mention to Sadiq, for reasons more of modesty than trust, is that his department is helping pass unclaimed cars and weapons to the mujahideen.

If it wasn't for Henna and Tariq, I would have joined the mujahideen, he says.

Rahim feels relieved talking to this familiar face from his youth. It is a gamble. If Sadiq has switched sides like most people, then he will lead the KHAD directly to Rahim . . . and then prison will be his endless fate. But this is Sadiq, who cooked potatoes for dinner on cold nights in the corner of their dorm room at university. They have shared salt, he has to trust this man.

Sadiq takes a cigarette box from his coat pocket, lights two cigarettes and gives one to Rahim. Sadiq takes a puff and exhales, his lips in the shape of a zero. His eyes, two candles of intense light, stare into Rahim's dim bulbs.

Where will you go? And you will need a good reason to leave, Sadiq says. You are going to get caught with their stalling techniques, he says, knowing this is what Rahim is thinking. Or you are going to be disappeared.

We wanted to go to Iran but I have been accepted into a law scholarship in Delhi, Rahim replies. Thanks to Haji Mama's old friends, I am supposedly going to learn from the Indian legal system so that

I can come back and help improve our legal system. Everything is ready to go, but I have just been told the tickets are being held back for some reason and I think I am trapped in a stalling technique . . .

Sadiq straightens his body. He seems taller than a moment ago, he flicks his half-smoked cigarette to the ground and steps on it.

Go visit a man named Mr Singh at the Indian embassy, he says. And tell him Sadiq sent you.

Henna

enna is stoic in the discreet dismantling of her home. As she sits on the lounge-room floor, their valuables are spread around her like treasures. Some small piles of jewellery are to be donated, some to be stored, some to be sold. She cannot carry all of this into their new life, she must leave behind the gifts from her wedding, her silverware, china, velvet and silk fabrics waiting to be cut and made into gowns.

She picks up a plate, one from her most valuable dinner set, a fine, white, bone-china plate, gold and indigo threads running around the rim, a gift from Khoja that he bought on one of his trips to Europe a long time ago. She carefully wraps the piece in newspaper, and sees falsehoods, propaganda, slogans cover up its beauty.

For a moment Henna forgets the reason behind the momentum to leave and wishes she could put everything back in its place. She shakes her head at her own simplicity, her own materialistic desire to keep everything as is, the comforts of her past life.

She realises she has never really sacrificed anything in her life so far, that this will be the first time. She wonders if this means she is now living the prescribed hardships of life that wizened elders talk about. *Let us live in a tent, at least there will be freedom, there will be safety*, she reminds herself.

Tariq is drawing something on a notepad beside her as he makes up a story. Henna looks at his long lashes and his eyelids which are fine like tissue paper. Rahim is the one who had wanted to stay, but he is the one who initiated their move in the end. Was it the tawiz that did it, or was it Rahim being taken or their son growing up so quickly without a chance at being safe in school?

The first thing Rahim did, following his week of convalescence, was ask the servants to take all the beautiful rugs from the floors of their home and get them washed. The removal of the richly coloured rugs began the dismantling of their home. Henna saw this act from Rahim as the signal that he was preparing her for departure, moving the rugs out to acclimatise her to the idea that things were about to change.

Let's simplify our lives, he said to Henna when the rugs were gone, let's keep a few possessions and donate the rest to the rising numbers of homeless who beg on the streets, to the makeshift shelters which are forming around us.

When this was done, and some things were given away, and sold, and passed on to family, he came home and told her, This is no longer our home, we will go.

She didn't say that she had expected this was what he was doing when he asked for the rugs to be washed, she was just glad this was the decision he had reached.

Speaking with Khoja and Koko, Henna can see that they can't accept this is happening; Koko refuses to talk about it, Henna knows it is hurting her. Since their world changed, Koko says she has heard little from Hamid, Nargis and Roya. Now Henna is also going to leave her. How will Khoja and Koko cope without them? She tries to bring up the subject with Koko and Khoja but they keep saying to Henna, we'll talk once you have tickets in hand. They won't let you leave, nobody is allowed to leave, many people have tried and failed.

Despite the passionate talk from family, despite the whispers and plans made at underground meetings by people who hate the regime, the constant struggle of mujahideen for freedom, she knows things will not change soon. These thoughts sadden her, how long since she has sat beneath a tree to read, how long since she has gone on a mela, a picnic, to Takht-e Safar?

Her son will be safe and one day will be reunited with Koko, Bebe, Khoja, Hamid, the family. Will he care? She thinks of Delhi, is it the right city? Should they have gone to join Hamid in Iran? Things seem to be going well for him. *Why the questions?* she thinks, getting annoyed with herself. It had to be Delhi, that is where the scholarship was available, that is where his work could allow him to travel to.

Henna has initiated their English practice; she and Rahim have some understanding of it from school but they have recently begun to practise in earnest; it will be their only way to communicate once they reach India.

Now, she sits on the newly cleaned rug on the floor, she runs her hands back and forth against the rough and then soft threads of the rug with the elephant's foot design. Rich red and burgundy hues. Somebody's hands ran a pomegranate dye through this, a hand tied the knots on every strand. She wonders if those hands still do their work, if those hands are still safe.

The things for the trip will be packed away in a series of brown suitcases and hidden in the doolab in their bedroom. This room, which doubles as a shelter during air raids, is beginning to have no standing room for her family.

In a few weeks, only a superficial shell of her former home will remain. For now, to unsuspecting friends who visit, her life will seem as it always has. The burgundy curtains of the living room will blow in the wind as they always have. The servants – polite, well trained – will serve tea to guests in porcelain teacups and serve delicate elephant-ear pastries dusted with fine white sugar.

They will spend a lot of money on bribes, and Henna will come to admire Rahim's ability to bribe powerful friends in powerful places. She will watch Rahim continue to go to work, his senior bosses unaware of his plans. She will watch Rahim lie to people saying, We will be away for maybe a year, if we can stand the hot weather in Delhi.

Dear Henna,
First, Salaam, and second, may this letter find you well. I am well, my body has healed itself in my old muscular form and I have found a job in a nice office with some new Iranian friends that I have made.

There are many pretty women around, nobody told me that I had only to cross the border to find such beauty. If you and Koko were here, I am sure you would have found me a wife by now. Alas, wives are for men who are not awara, homeless, who are not bechara, directionless. For a while, until I make enough money and our beloved home can be peaceful, I will depend on the kindness of strangers, and that is not what a man who marries can offer a woman.

Enough of this sad talk, no more reminiscing about distant times now fading into the background of my ageing mind. Is it me or does the mind age more rapidly when one is away from home?

Tell me, how is my nephew? In your last letter you said he looks a little like me. I hope he is as handsome as I am, though with your and Rahim's features interrupting things, the likelihood is low! Of course, I joke, forgive me, beautiful Henna.

I miss our times together and I leave you in the hands of Khoda jan, knowing one day we will be together again. Don't worry about me, everything happens for a purpose. Please kiss Koko and Khoja's hands and give your little family all my love.

All will be well. Khoda hafiz,
Your brother,
Hamid

Today, Henna is feeling more lethargic than usual, this has been happening for a few weeks, building up in severity. She started packing this morning, and before noon she took a break to lie down. Now she wants to lie down again as she feels the Earth's strong magnetic force is pulling her down to itself.

If she were teaching today, she would have to give the class a textbook to copy from, having no energy to stand and talk, unable to deliver her lessons with her usual focus and intensity.

Now she hears Bebe's footsteps in the hallway. She can hear Tariq and Bebe exchange greetings. She can imagine Tariq has abandoned his toy box when he heard her come in and call his name. Bebe tells

Tariq she has come to take him to the stream, his favourite place to explore and play under Bebe's watchful eyes.

Henna pinches her cheeks and presses her lips tightly together to get colour in them, straightening her clothes, fingering her fringe to make herself presentable.

Henna opens the door to Bebe standing with her hand ready to knock, in mid-air. Bebe smiles, scanning Henna's face a moment, making Henna uncomfortable at how Bebe's deep-set eyes enquire about everything, all at once, without saying a word. From Bebe's face Henna can read that Bebe isn't fooled, that she isn't good at hiding her irritation, that she can see Henna's sallow expression.

They kiss three times on each cheek, Bebe running a hand down Henna's hair, smoothing down strands.

Why do you look like a ghost?

Henna knows Bebe is speaking from a place of love, but today she is tired and wants to sleep, and doesn't want to defend herself from the suspicion in those eyes, that something is wrong, that she is hiding something.

Henna doesn't answer, she lets the question die in the quiet of mid-morning, in between the chirping of bulbuls coming from the window. Even though it is rude to have this elder woman standing around, Henna is tempted to lie down on the bed and nap.

You need to go to the doctor, Bebe continues. It's been more than a week, why isn't Rahim doing anything about this?

Before receiving an answer, she continues, I will send over lunch, don't cook anything. I don't understand why Rahim insists on using the separate kitchen and house when we have everything over at the main house.

Before Henna can respond or protest, Tariq bursts into the room.

Bebe, let's go, he says while looking to Henna for a reaction.

Yes, go with Bebe, Henna says, smiling at them both.

He looks like you, so much, Bebe says, bending down to kiss Tariq again on his plump cheek.

A week passes this way, Bebe ordering food, Henna not feeling better. Rahim and Henna put the lethargy down to Henna's mental state. They are leaving for Khoda knows how long; the stories of death and fighting fill most conversations, there is fear in every goodbye.

When things don't seem to improve Rahim tries to find a doctor, but even Doctor Jahan is not in Herat anymore. They decide to invite a midwife, the one who delivered Tariq, to examine Henna, which won't be as accurate as seeing a doctor. The midwife tells Henna that she is pregnant, though she isn't able to determine exactly how far along Henna is in her pregnancy. She says the baby could arrive in six months, it could be three or less.

If the child is to be born in Herat, the trip must be postponed and the paperwork redone to include the newborn – an impossibility to bribe and plan again.

The unborn baby forms a chasm in their normally animated talk. Henna doesn't want this other child; she has her hands full. She hasn't felt the symptoms of her previous pregnancy, there was no tell-tale bump as she had with Tariq.

Henna is sitting on the front steps of the house as their luggage is loaded into the trunk of the taxi. Two months have passed since she found out about her pregnancy. Koko has cut Henna's hair short, shoulder length. Henna has pulled her fringe to one side with a bobby pin. A heavy chadar is around her shoulders, ready to be thrown over her head and body. Like other women in Herat who didn't wear the veil before, she has picked up this practice of wearing chadar since the war began; it is in defiance of a regime that seeks to remove their deen, religion, it is a way for her and other women to feel safer in public while the invaders roam the streets.

Rahim is holding the taxi door open, his hand shielding his eyes from the sun, waiting for Henna to get in the back seat.

Henna walks over slowly, she feels that her shoes are made from heavy bricks. She pushes away the thought of her child being born on the plane. She dismisses the thought of her child being born on the way to the airport.

Their family is gathered around, she cannot look at their faces. Tariq is being kissed and cuddled by Bebe and Koko. Haji and Khoja stand together near the taxi, engaged in conversation about the benefits of the young family leaving to safety as was Khoda's blessing.

Henna can hear the concern beneath their words. Even Haji's shoulders are rounded today.

She watches Koko sitting beside Tariq, her arm around Tariq's shoulders. She lifts his face, holding his small chin with her fingers. He is silent, sulking, and lets himself collapse into Koko's bosom as she embraces him. Koko pushes Tariq away to look into his face, she squeezes his cheek.

Bebe says, There will be rice in India. Tariq looks at her. His favourite food. Henna smiles, as she remembers a few weeks ago when he made them put the platter of rice in front of him, nobody was allowed to touch it, and as he stretched over it protectively, he lost his balance and fell face first right into the middle. His face and hands were covered with grains of rice mixed with tears of frustration.

If there isn't, Koko continues now, Bebe and I will mail you some. She smiles. In an envelope, will that be good?

Tariq nods. Henna pictures a white envelope with dry grains of white rice spilling from it.

In the back seat of the taxi, Henna sits quietly with Tariq next to her. Rahim is in the front seat. She turns to see the family standing together as the car pulls away and continues to watch as they recede into the background, becoming smaller and smaller. Tears fall down her face. Tariq looks at her, leans over to wipe her tears. She puts his small hand into her own. Here she is, Henna, the weak and sickly one, who became a wife, then a mother. She has found the courage to leave her family, to hold a second child in her belly; she has found the courage to create a family of her own and she must also find a way to survive all that awaits her in this new world.

Rahim

Sweat beads begin to form on Rahim's forehead as he looks down the narrow aisle of the aeroplane cabin. He turns to the row next to him and looks at Henna's still face as she holds a subdued Tariq in her arms. An overhead locker nearby is snapped shut by a flight attendant.

The hum of polite chatter in the cabin abruptly ends, halted by two soldiers with guns on their shoulders walking through the cabin. They stop a few seats ahead of Rahim. A whispered conversation ensues with a flight attendant who is looking down the aisle in Rahim's direction, and then at the piece of paper they give her.

Rahim takes a deep breath and begins to rehearse what he will say, how he will keep calm, keep his hand steady when he draws out the paperwork for the scholarship, but his mind keeps wandering towards one image, where he has the soldiers in a tight grip under his two arms and he bashes their heads together until they are bloody and limp.

175

He has rehearsed the words in his mind – about the scholarship, about the papers, how to show the invitation – he remembers a hadith, a prophetic story, about predestination, that you must tie your camel to a tree, do your absolute best and leave the rest up to Khoda. He tells himself this is what he has done, he has prepared all that he could, the rest is out of his hands, so he begins to pray, sitting stiffly, not making eye contact with anyone.

He can feel the heat of Henna's presence across the aisle from him, her head and body is wrapped in a chadar which she has taken to wearing everywhere she goes, she is wrapped like a mantu dumpling as she sits. He can sense her breathing, thinking of the curtain of her hair as it brushes his face on some mornings as they wake.

The intercom comes to life with the voice of a flight attendant; she is now at the front of the plane with the two soldiers.

We will call out some names, please come to the front, she says. The first name comes, the second and the third. None of the names belong to Rahim. After the named men have been escorted off the flight, Rahim takes a deep, deep breath. He can feel his body now and notices that his armpits are wet, his back is wet; he wants to fall to his knees and prostrate himself before Khoda jan right here on this plane.

Rahim exhales again, a long audible choof sound escapes his lips. The doors of the aeroplane close, the engine kicks into life, and the plane begins to move. The nose of the plane is finally kissing the blue of the sky, the promise of freedom, the darkness of exile and an uncertain future are coming towards him at many hundreds of miles an hour. The cabin is unusually quiet. Modesty prevents Rahim from taking Henna into his arms. His arm is stretched across the aisle to her seat, he has taken her hand into his and is gently squeezing it in celebration as she looks into his face.

part three

EXILE

Rahim

Rahim is pushing a trolley stacked high with suitcases; he is leaning to one side because the suitcases are blocking his view ahead. His head feels heavy, as the noise of the aeroplane still rings in his ears; his skin feels sticky and gelatinous against his clothes. His stomach feels constricted by his pants, which seem to be belted too tightly around his body. He pauses to open his shirt buttons, the hair on his chest peeks through, he notices this, feels ashamed and buttons back up. All he wants to do is pour buckets of cold, fresh water onto his head to cleanse himself from the stuffy air of the cabin, which has attached itself to him. He is irritated by the volume of their baggage, thinking Henna has packed too much. Then he realises this is the concentrated entirety of their existence, on one trolley; their life in Herat has been folded into tiny squares, wrapped in newspaper and squeezed into these three suitcases and their little compartments. His memories, like the objects they own, have been

179

boiled down, truncated, simplified and transformed into small, folded parcels, which he has stored in the back of his mind, within the creases of his beating heart, between the pauses of his breath. There they are hidden and waiting to be unravelled, unfolded, aired, used and relived, soon, once he feels safe enough.

Henna is walking beside him; she has removed her chadar, her belly stands out in front of her, her hand in Tariq's as they walk at the child's pace. This is like being born, pushed through the canals of the airport, ejected in step and speed with the ferocity of the crowd around him. He is folded with his family and unborn child into the foreign smells of Delhi at night, into the tooting of horns in the traffic, into the gaze of the dark eyes of strangers standing under streetlights and the vociferating taxi drivers wanting his business.

Not a soul here is familiar in this city full of people, which has existed in parallel to his city, with lives that have existed in parallel to his life. This is the city where his life will converge and unravel into the layers of a different history, one that was already underway. He looks around at the crowds, at the people with places to go, who traverse this noisy city, marking it with footsteps of blue ink, like the tattoos that women in the villages of Herat wear on their chins. Not a soul here knows his family name; his professional credentials hold no value here; he is completely useless outside of Herat. Why did he study law? Why didn't he choose to be a doctor or a builder or something more transferable? He will make sure Tariq does not choose a profession like law, a profession that is useless as soon as you leave one place and go to another.

As the crowd around them becomes denser, Rahim picks up Tariq, pushes on the luggage trolley with his other hand, waits for Henna to walk a few steps in front so as not to lose sight of her as they swim against the flow of warm bodies, all going in different directions. In his mind, Rahim is simultaneously calculating the present and the future as he adjusts the cabin bag that's hanging from his shoulder. One day, when they return to Herat, these bags will be taken from him by the boys who ran all his errands back home, the car will be waiting with the driver, Henna will be dressed in a beautiful gown, Tariq will be an educated and handsome young man. *What a strange dream to dream*, he tells himself. How could these things ever come to be after all that has happened so far and is happening in front of his eyes . . .

He stops abruptly, because a man who is walking quickly past them elbows Henna, causing her to jump to Rahim's side. A rage rises within him, and he turns to the man. He lets go of the trolley, drops the shoulder bag to the ground and, with Tariq still in his arms, he rushes forward and grabs hold of the man's collar from behind. He pulls hard and the man falls to the ground with a thump. He lets go of the collar in response to the man's struggling, his gurgling sounds and foreign words, his arms flailing, beating like wings. Tariq begins to cry, really screaming from fear and holding tight to Rahim.

The crowd has made space for this commotion, but otherwise continues moving around it like nothing is happening, like a stream of ants flowing around a drop of water, carving a safer passage. At this moment Rahim remembers Henna and the bags, he has left Henna to be pushed around again. Fool. The man stands up and staggers away as quickly as he can, muttering angry words at Rahim, who is now searching the faces around him for Henna.

Rahim finds Henna standing a few feet away. People walk around her, a couple of women nodding their heads in irritation, as she blocks their way. An alternative route has formed around this foreign object that is his wife, as the column of ants carve an alternate course to avoid the obstruction blocking their path. He is relieved to see her, he wants to smile but his face is frozen. She is looking straight at him as if she has been there since the beginning of time, watching him, watching herself, watching their life change, watching the bodies of strangers behaving like ants. His eyes meet hers. Rahim cannot read them, her mouth is closed, her blouse is a thousand creases, her armpits wet but her face is completely still. No tears, no emotion at all. In moments he is by her side, Tariq is crying quietly.

Let's keep walking, she says, her composure unchanged as if nothing has happened. The taxi drivers are over there, she continues, as she picks up the cabin bag from the floor and puts it on her shoulder, not allowing Rahim to take it.

Now that they are in the taxi, on the way to a hotel, he is grateful for the English lessons she had initiated. The driver understood him and he understood the driver.

He thinks of the incident. He thinks back to when she picked up the cabin bag and put it on her shoulder. For the first time in their shared life together he realises that she is willing and able to share his burden; that he is not alone in carrying their struggles.

Henna

enna is standing at the open window of a kitchen in a small apartment in Delhi. Near her is Engela, the woman who lives here with her husband and three quarrelsome children. It's the first time Henna has lived in an apartment; this is a temporary arrangement with old friends of Rahim's who left Herat years ago.

She breathes deeply, as if there is not enough air inside the room. The acrid smell of something unfamiliar makes its way into her nose. Her body feels warm from within, as if there is a sun inside her belly and not a child. She was shocked to find, just this morning, that her upper lip is capable of sweat.

The view outside this small window is full of obstructions. She wants to see the horizon but cannot. Instead, Henna's eyes trace washing lines, cramped balconies, vividly coloured movie billboards showing handsome men and decorated women with violent red lips. Through the small windows across the road she can see people moving around apartments. There, in the tightly packed apartment block, the clothes are draped along the balcony railings to dry; the balconies seem to be held together with the special tape Khoja used to bind glued carvings together until they were dry.

Delhi seems like a city of precarious structures, upon which lives have blossomed. On the road below the kitchen window, she can see two large white cows meander, one of them is wearing a garland of orange flowers around its neck. The cows merge and separate from the flow of traffic, weaving their own pattern among thin men on nimble bicycles and motorbikes with whole families on the back. There are luxurious black cars with black-tinted windows which glide ominously along, men accosting street vendors wearing tattered grey singlets that were once white.

The line between road and pavement is blurred; a multitude of sounds arise from the bustle. She remembers being shocked by the sound of tooting horns on her first night here, because they continued all night long. The city hums under the hot sky, sitting full and plump like a fat cat. Henna wonders at the lives of its inhabitants, who appear to be happy, who smile despite the crowded streetscape, the traffic drowning voices and conversations. *How do they survive,* she asks herself, *how will I survive?*

Clarity of mind, openness of thought, dreaming in the daytime with eyes open, this can only happen when the horizon in front of me is open, Henna says to herself, remembering the gardens and fields of her old home, which stretched across the earth when you looked out the windows.

She tries to picture the scene, from when she was about eleven years old, the commotion when, after a week away with Koko and her sisters, they came home to find the old front wall gone, the customary barrier which separates every family home from the rolling fields around them demolished.

Koko was furious, Khoja unapologetic, as he and Hamid had taken the wall down to create an uninterrupted view into the fields before them, the garden's boundaries merging with the fields to make an endless expanse of green, which in the dark would forever frighten Henna but in the daytime provided comfort.

She tries to imagine that Hamid is somewhere out there, across from her, standing by a window above a sink like this one, looking over at her, that he can see she is alive in a different way from the way she was alive back home. She breathes the same air as he does, is he aware of her presence, is he also thinking of the gardens of their home? After all, they are both under this same vast and multifaceted sky.

She has a half-peeled potato in one hand, the dirt smeared across her white fingers, the knife in the other. She realises that Engela has finished chopping the tomatoes and is looking at her. Engela picks up the last remaining potato and starts peeling it quickly, as if to say, Henna, you are too slow. Which is true, she is peeling this potato slowly.

She can see that her presence in Engela's kitchen, in this house, is making Engela hot with anger. She can see the anger starting at the edges of Engela's reed-thin body, gathering in the pit of her fleshless stomach, rising to the top of her large head of thick, henna-coloured hair.

Engela's eyes steam like pools of water from a hot spring. No harsh words are exchanged, no fights have taken place, but there is animosity. Henna recognises in herself a feeling she despises, the feeling of being a child next to Engela, a caricature of a village girl married to a man much older than her, a pathetic nobody in this hot crowded city with nothing to her name.

Henna steps aside and Engela takes over peeling the potato without a word. Engela begins to make the salad for their evening meal, chopping the vegetables into squares, recklessly, as if she wants to cut herself.

On their first encounter, seeing Henna with Tariq and her belly full of the next child, Engela said that even though children come from a woman's body, even though women make children from their own pain, in the end they will be their father's. She told Henna a story about her own marriage.

Her husband Karim told her on the day of their engagement, From this day you need to forget about playing with your girlfriends and running back to your family. I am your everything now, you are here to raise my children.

From that day, a prison formed around Engela, an invisible cage held together by the magic of his words. A magic she had a role in strengthening because she believed it.

Why did I believe in this and why didn't I fight against it? she asked Henna, as she pulled the fragrant naaz boy, basil leaves, from the stem, causing the whole kitchen to smell like a garden. I didn't fight because I couldn't, Engela said, as she prepared their first meal together as friends. Mine was a marriage of shame. I had to pursue him to marry me, rather than him asking for my hand like Rahim did for yours. I had fallen pregnant out of wedlock and brought shame upon myself.

After confiding in Henna that first day, Engela kept her distance. Perhaps it was Henna's reaction to the story, Henna now thinks. Engela had reminded Henna of the time of her own engagement to Rahim, when under the apple tree, Koko had tried to explain why a short engagement is better for the girl and how offended Henna had felt at this suggestion that she too might end up being in Engela's shoes.

I should have been more compassionate to Engela, but it was obvious to me that such a life would never be acceptable for me. I would rather have killed myself, she thought, *than force a man to marry me.*

But then, what does it matter now? The war came and here they both are, Henna and Engela, now equalised by shared statelessness. Their values reduced to be the same, even though they have lived such different lives.

Henna thinks of snow as she walks out of the kitchen quietly, allowing her mind to move on. The pristine white of it is not to be found in the humid, stale air of New Delhi. She misses the snow.

Hamid

Hamid wipes his forehead with a dirty rag, he slings the rag back over his shoulder as he assumes his usual stance, hands crossing his chest, staring out the window at the narrow, bustling street below. This is Tehran, and he stands inside the small kitchenette of a tea house where he works as a kitchen hand and errand boy.

His guardians, who welcomed him to Iran, who promised Koko and Khoja a safe passage and a loving home for their son, who were to take him into their hearts, have departed for America. Their letters to Khoja, filled with stories of their wealth and success in Iran were all lies, shrouds to cover their damaged pride, lest Khoja find that his close friends have fallen from honour when they fled their home, to become nobodies in a foreign land, which does not accept them. They lived in squalor, struggled to find work, they waited for visas and departed as soon as they were accepted by America, leaving Hamid behind. Hamid isn't bitter. He understands their predicament; their lies to Khoja trapping them into a generosity they could not afford to offer Hamid but offered anyway. Your secret life of poverty is safe with me, he wanted to say to Khoja's friend. We are both the same now. We have both lost everything.

Hamid has been on his own for some time now. They paid his rent for six months; he had a roof, some pocket money, which has begun to run out. As soon as his wounds healed enough for him to walk, he began to do odd jobs here and there until he found this place, the place where he now stands. This rough and rude tea house, which would horrify Koko and Khoja and Henna and Rahim if they were to see it. He doesn't write letters to them often. There is nothing to write that he wouldn't be ashamed of saying; he is already ashamed of his last letter, so he decides not to write again until his situation improves.

He relives the shooting every time his eyes close, every time he waits for sleep. He remembers flashes of detail, his knees scraping against the dirt, the sheer-yakh man's body bent in an ugly shape before him. The hot sting through his belly, the spreading warmth down his pantaloons. The same feeling as when he wet himself in a dream as a little boy. It was warm, it was comforting. He didn't get to say goodbye to his family, thinking of Henna only, her face representing them all.

He has allowed his beard and moustache to grow, longer than they have ever been. His employer, an old man cynical with age, is kind to him. He bought him two sets of clothing when he first arrived and accepted the job. He washes and changes the two sets of clothing every two days.

The man pays him a small wage every fortnight, in cash. Hamid pushes most of it into the folds of his mattress and the rest he puts into smoking sweet opium, to calm his thoughts. His muscular physique has given way to a reed of a body, his skin sticks to his bones in places and sags elsewhere, he is a skeleton with a leather cover.

Here is Hamid, the son of Khoja, working in exchange for a pitiful wage, some meals and a roof over his head.

Henna

Henna opens her eyes and lifts her hand to brush a strand of hair from her face. She sees a tube fused to the back of her hand. There is a burning sensation where the tube tugged and she remembers she is in the hospital.

She feels the tingle of a chill through her body. Her mind soars, leaving this white room through that white door. It effortlessly floats in the air of the corridors that wind through the building.

She opens door after door, along dimly lit corridors, and each time she finds herself in this room again. There are no other rooms for her but this room.

She is longing for a room with her newborn daughter in her arms, with Rahim and Tariq beside her. The daughter she wanted to call Sofia. Perhaps a room with Rahim, Koko, Hamid, Bebe, Khoja, Haji Mama, Nargis and Roya – stroking her daughter's forehead, fussing over her, pushing the edges of the swaddle away from the baby's chin, waiting for Sofia to smile in her sleep. They clasp their hands in glee when she does. They pass from hand to hand boxes of sticky syrupy jalabi, pretty in flower patterns and crumbling creamy slabs of sheerpera. Warm eyes and honeyed voices cooing and stroking the delicate face of the child she created with Rahim. Her mouth is filled with the sickly sweetness of rosewater, and pistachio.

But these figures disappear, slowly they merge into the walls of this room. The cardamom-scented teacups dissolve with their golden green leaves and soothing warmth.

She thinks of her baby Sofia, dying in her womb. The daughter with ten fingers and toes, but no beating heart, the one who ceases to exist.

She saw pity in the nurse's eyes. Her moment of lucidity when the colours and sounds around her were sharp. She felt the crisp white edges of the hospital bedsheet graze her arm as she folded her body into itself and she prayed for courage and patience from Khoda as her tears rolled.

She felt Rahim lay down beside her and gently wrap his arm around her, tenderly holding her to him, she feeling his chest tremble against her back as he quietly sobbed. His love, she knew then, lives alongside her pain. She thought of Tariq playing with the landlord's children, those kind people who have shared so much of their lives in recent times.

She called on all her strength but wished to submit to her helplessness in the face of what has happened. Maybe this is what the poets mean about abandoning the self in exchange for refuge in the daaman, the lap, of the beloved. Refuge is what she sought with Khoda, as she breathed and prayed.

It wasn't the middle of the night, it wasn't dawn, it wasn't thundering brown sheets of monsoonal rain. It was a bright sunny day and she was carrying an innocent death within her. A rose bud that didn't become a bloom, a soul who visited for a time, in a hurry to depart.

There are no bombs or guns. She realises that death can exist away from war. Death comes to the most innocent and the most tainted of souls in equal measure.

Now, the rude, bright sun comes in through the window when all should be darkness in honour of her grief, in honour of her loss, in honour of the baby she wishes to hold and to call Sofia. She remembers Khoja's face, and he reminds her to be patient, they will be reunited with Sofia in the next life, she will embrace her child then.

Rahim

He remembers helping Henna to load the bathtub with their dirty clothes, adding water and washing detergent. He remembers Henna stomping on the suds to wash the clothes with her feet. The soap suds flew everywhere and soaked her hair and clothes. He remembers Tariq joining her in the tub, stomping along with her, happy to play this new game.

It's probably not a good idea to lift and move this much, Rahim said to the top of her head as she looked down at her feet. She said she didn't mind; with the forty-degree heat outside, this was helping her cool down. She didn't get as far as hanging the clothes outside.

Rahim thinks of the round face of the gynaecologist with the red dot on her forehead.

It was a stillborn, the specialist said, your wife's life was in danger. She wiped the sweat from her vast brow, her shiny gold watch around her thick wrist, her thick hair slick with coconut oil, the scent of it making Rahim feel queasy.

He wonders now if her air of superiority was because Henna was a refugee, a poor stateless awara, or because the doctor was a sought-after specialist. What is there to be proud of as a doctor, so helpless in the face of death? Rahim used to think that doctors are miracle workers; now he sees the falsehood contained within their profession.

It is between night and dawn. He adjusts his body as he lies in bed, alone. Henna is also alone, in her hospital bed. She's probably awake, like him. He suspects that she is thinking similar thoughts.

In the quiet of night, Rahim feels the full force of his situation, he feels homeless and stateless. It feels temporary, but he knows that it's permanent. At this time of night, every thought has the quality of glass breaking, the sound of a porcelain cup or a crystal glass making contact with the earth and shattering. This shattering momentarily, fleetingly, seems to come from within his own chest. He feels relief at the sound. Then comes the realisation that something precious has been broken, is irreparably shattered. But it felt good for a moment. Even if he went back to Herat today, it wouldn't be the same. The rupture has already occurred. Tears stream down of their own accord, without effort or thought.

This is a test, no doubt, he thinks, resting his head on his elbow. He begins to count his blessings. Sofia, their daughter, has perhaps left this message for her parents, that Khoda tests those he loves, every test can become a path that brings us closer to him. Now is the time for patience, dua and namaz.

He lists these blessings to himself, offering gratitude to his creator, starting with Henna and her love, for Tariq and his health and inquisitive mind, for the translating jobs, which are supplementing the

UNHCR cash assistance they receive, for the peace and safety from wartime violence.

In between these thoughts he wonders how many nights Henna will stay in hospital. He loves her bravery and their shared understanding and faith that Khoda will reunite them in the next life with Sofia.

He decides they will not write to their family in Herat about this, they will continue to live their lives, grateful for every morning that greets them in a land of peace and safety. Their family will think that their child lives and will grow. He will allow them to think that his dream of a minibus full of children is coming true.

Now, he gets out of bed for the night namaz, a healing namaz which will calm his mind and heart, a namaz in the last third of this long night, a way to focus his mind away from the pain of this world, a namaz that allows his soul to take over his mind and guide it to peace.

Hamid

He slept three hours last night; this happens most nights. He is so exhausted he doesn't undress this evening. On these nights he feels that he dies and is resurrected around lunch time the next day, to suffer through the rest of the day as a form of punishment. He tries to find meaning in his existence – always between death and resurrection – but there isn't much meaning behind how he came to be the man he is now that he can decipher. Perhaps Khoda is testing him or gifting him with some new purpose.

These days, when he begins to consider ideas he used to contemplate, such as the nature of the universe, of life, of beauty, the nature of thought itself, he finds he cannot think logically.

These classes of thought, once within his reach, now elude him. His thoughts are tricksters, running off in different directions or refusing to yield, promising a magnitude of mental capacity that he is not capable of reaching, commanding a range of meaning he is incapable of articulating, even to himself. So, he retires his thoughts, allowing them to dissolve, unable to join mind and body like he once did. His old thoughts, his old body, his old being have all been devoured by this man who looks at him from the mirror that reflects hollow eye sockets and a gaze that no longer holds purpose. A face that holds the perpetual question – Where am I? – and a mind that no longer knows.

Take the green tea to the customer with the blue shirt in the lounge, his employer says, as he walks into the kitchenette. His thick voice shatters Henna's face, which Hamid was just now remembering, into small shards of imagination, which flit away out the window.

Hamid looks at his employer as he begins to gather the cups and saucers in the kitchenette – fine china, like his mother's maid used to bring to guests.

There is a woman in the tea house, with a man who must be her husband. She has a tightly pinned chadar around her face. Her eyebrows are drawn like the eyes of the women in Khoja's miniature paintings; high arches, with sharp ends like the stingers of scorpions as they describe in all the love songs. Those creatures in Khoja's paintings were ethereal, timeless and ageless princesses.

He can smell the cardamom pods as he breaks them with the tip of his two front teeth, trying not to get spit onto the cardamom, lest the Iranian client acquire his Afghan disease. He squeezes the seeds into the round steel teapot, filling it with water and tea leaves, placing a tea-cosy on top to keep it warm.

He sets two cups on a pretty platter to please customers in the way he is taught. One for the man, another for the woman.

Hamid thinks of marriage, and questions himself. Does he wish to be married? Yes, if he listened to his heart, but there is no chance of it if he admits his reality. He has nothing to offer a marriage. He is poor, he is awara, living a transient life. Maybe some of the men and women who visit his tea room together are not married, maybe they are illegitimate couples, from distant towns. He knows this is an unlikely scenario given the government's tough stance on adultery and its punishments.

Besides, even if they are getting away with it, he can't judge them, for he is making use of illegitimate meetings with a girl himself.

Jameela, he says her name, the way she says it in her Iranian accent. She, an orphan living with her angry uncle and his family; he, a poor man working for the roof over his head.

Jameela is willing to take the risk to see him, willing to call this a friendship. They write letters to each other which express more than they both say in person when they meet, which isn't often.

When they do meet, they talk in short sentences with long pauses. He hasn't dared touch her or look at her properly. He wonders what her hair is like beneath her veil. *She is so innocent*, he thinks.

Their moments together are short, their conversation doesn't have the time to take root before she is gone. Until next time, friend, she says and runs off. Her body-length black veil catches the breeze as she walks around the corner.

He knows that he is betraying her, she may expect marriage, but he is a half-hearted passenger in this romance that will never blossom. He knows this because he is a being that is floating through life. When he writes to her, his words get away from him; the recipient of the letter he pictures is not Jameela, it is a silhouette of someone who loves him, who knows everything about him, who isn't shy and quiet like Jameela.

He can't stop himself from writing these full-hearted and poetic letters, even though he wants to. He tries to be dry but friendly, but he cannot. The letters unlock his tongue and make a poet of him at a time when feelings are hard to grasp.

For now, he lets the thoughts go. He will have to tell her his truth soon, that he is only a guest for a short while in her homeland. From her letters he can tell that she will be heartbroken, but she will come to understand that his own heart has nothing left to heal or nurture hers.

For a moment he is caught by surprise. An old feeling has returned, like an ingrown hair; he can see the shadow of what he felt but he can't access it, no matter how deeply he digs. The old question loop begins, *Why didn't Khoja teach me something useful, something the world needs? Not more artists, this is where art leads you, cleaning teacups.*

But how would Khoja have known that the war would come and turn our world to dust? reasons the Henna who lives inside his head.

Henna

This vase, in its packaging of bubble wrap inside a plastic bag, hanging off Henna's arm, is not as tall as the ones she recalls from her parents' house, nor as pretty, but it is a vase and it reminds her of Khoja, so she bought it. All the vases she has ever seen, in any home or any shop, always remind her of his papier-mâché creations, which he decorated with his paintings, and which occupied the corners of their home, his studio. They gathered dust in the storage spaces where Koko hid valuable ornaments she no longer liked.

This vase is made of clay and is decorated with flowers and a woman. She wears a bright-pink sari, her hair is parted in the middle, a large jewel decorates the piercing in her nostril. She looked sideways at Henna from the display table where the vase sat waiting for Henna to take her. Her gaze gave Henna permission to buy it. To spend money she can't afford. Henna didn't haggle for this vase in her broken English, she paid the asking price. She knows it is wrong to squander money this way; the shopkeepers expect you to haggle. But she was experiencing a rare moment of delight, she was exhilarated at her freedom to roam this street, her first outing in the city of sound and colour without Rahim, without Tariq and without the pain of the memory of Sofia.

She wanted to test her freedom, to learn about her new neighbourhood, the place she moved to this week. She left Tariq and Rahim together in their apartment, sitting enthralled by the colour and movement of a newly acquired spinning top.

She came out to find something to decorate the apartment, and she bought the first thing that caught her eye, which resembled something from the past. Her past, this web of imagery, of beauty and pain, holds her captive. She considers it precious to have a past, but for a moment she becomes one of the strangers who are now criss-crossing her path. She pretends that she has no past, that she exists only in the now. This elates her momentarily, a burden lifted for a time, to allow her to become someone else entirely.

She walks through the crowded streets, noticing the noises and smells, the cows with decorated horns, seeming not to belong to anyone, sauntering along the main road. She is blending into this crowd in her New Delhi clothes, no longer the daughter of Khoja, no longer known by name and birthright, an anonymous woman who walks towards a newfound destiny.

She will walk into the crowded shops and will be expected to haggle. And she will haggle like a local as soon as she regains her sense of self. For now, she nods and she speaks the few English words she knows. How much is the price of this, and thank you. Earlier, these words made the shop owner look at her puzzled, his large eyes intrusively scanning over her white face. She pulled her scarf tighter around her head and shoulders, Koko's voice scolded her, *This is what becomes of women who roam the streets.* Koko's voice faded as she walked out with the vase wrapped in newspaper, its shiny lacquered rim peeking at her.

The shopkeepers here, they don't know me, that is why they look at me directly and disrespectfully, why they brazenly ask a price, she now explains to the Koko who resides in her ear. In Herat, they used to bow with polite reverence to her, even if they had never met her.

Please come in hamsheerah, sister, take anything you want, their eyes cast down as they spoke. This is your shop, everything is here for you, take your pick.

It was a struggle to pay for things, they were embarrassed to name a price, she was embarrassed to push the bank notes towards them, the awkwardness of money coming between friends. Why was it so embarrassing, this introduction of money into the equation? Why did it feel like we were reducing something honourable to something lowly?

She allows herself to think of Sofia, the daughter she nearly had, as she sees a woman pass with a stroller carrying a tiny girl with kohl around her eyes and a bright pink ribbon around her head. But she locks these thoughts away in the place in her mind where other devastating thoughts reside, thoughts of Hamid the last time she saw him, thoughts of her old life that she cannot help comparing to her new existence. Her memories have acquired an angry edge. She is angry at herself. How stupid she was when she was young and wishing the 120-day winds would wipe away her life.

She is angry at her family, especially Khoja and Koko, for making it seem as if life would unfold as it always had done. Hamid had tried to warn her, to wake her, but she had not understood. Germany and Haidar's death had made him wiser than her. Nargis and Roya had both lived and seen more than her, moved to marry and create separate lives in a different city, seemingly without effort or fear.

She had remained inexperienced, left behind to learn all about life in a short space of time.

She will take this vase home, she will put flowers in it, she will think of Khoja and the vases he used to make. She will remember how Khoja used to hang a stone from the branch of the apple trees so that she and her siblings could reach and pick their own fruit.

That is all she will allow herself to remember. She has learnt this much about self-preservation in recent times, that one must not dwell.

Rahim

Rahim pays for the potatoes and onions and comes home. Today, his shopping is rushed, he didn't linger to make small talk with the friendly shopkeeper in an exchange made of his English smattered with Hindi. The shop is small, the shopkeeper has a turban and a friendly round face with a neatly trimmed moustache and beard. He usually holds Rahim captive with his knowledge about India. Rahim wonders at this man's patriotism and his political knowledge. Hindustan hamara hai, Hindustan is ours, the man says, meaning he wants all the different races who call this place home, speaking dozens of languages, following the different religious paths, to occupy this vast and varied country, to love Hindustan equally.

The last time they spoke it was about the advertisements on television telling men not to allow their mothers and their family to mistreat their wives. That burning a bride because of disagreements over dowries is illegal.

My daughter is in university, the man says. I will kill anyone who lays a finger on her.

Today, Rahim didn't linger to talk. The shopkeeper didn't appear to notice or even register Rahim's reticence. Now, Rahim is home, alone, and he is relieved that he made it here.

He puts the groceries down on the small table in the kitchenette. He sits, puts his hands to his head and lets the sobs come. He cries the way he did when he was a boy. He gasps for air, as waves of grief roll through his body. It was purchasing the groceries that undid him. Once upon a time he didn't have to measure a kilogram of anything, he didn't have to bargain with shop owners. Cartons of fruit and rice and vegetables were brought to the kitchen or grown on his father's property or picked and eaten straight from the trees.

He weeps at the romance of the way things used to be, at the abundance that they have lost – from a paradise of plenty he is reduced to haggling for these tiny bags of vegetables, lying on the table before him. This is the man he has become; this is how he provides for his wife and child, in small bags purchased from small shops. Perhaps his baby daughter Sofia was lucky to miss out on this life.

Rahim has been invited to tea. He is sitting in a guesthouse lounge room with three men, all of them new arrivals from Afghanistan, friends from his time as a lawyer long ago. All three are dressed in perahan tunban, in different shades of brown, and all have long beards. Two of them wear pakol hats. Large eyes sparkle at Rahim; these men are still connected to Afghanistan and the mujahideen in a way that Rahim can no longer manage. Mustafa, the most active of the group, is in his early twenties; the other two, Hossain and Matin, are a bit

older. All of them look older than they are as they sit on the edge of
the sofa and talk.

Mustafa is talking about Ahmad Shah Massoud. How he met him
in the mountains in the Panjshir Valley, how he spent twenty-four
hours with his crew. How he undertook a mission for the guerrillas,
a mission like the one they are talking about now, when he was just
a boy.

Rahim feels a wave of warmth and admiration for these men. This
feeling floods his body every time they call him Kaka jan, dear uncle.
Rahim feels he doesn't deserve this respect, but it reminds him that
he once used to deserve it.

Rahim's thoughts fill with dreams for these young men, leaders of
tomorrow's nation; he cannot help himself and says many times, you
are the future, don't give up. How can I help you? he asks.

Uncle, you are not required to do anything, Matin says. You did
what you could, risking your life, letting those weapons go to the
mujahideen while you were working in Herat.

They discuss a new plan in detail. They ask his advice about
targeting a well-known government official. Mustafa describes what
has been agreed. He picks up his empty water glass from the coffee
table and wraps a napkin around it.

Like this, he says, we will cover it like this, put it in the knapsack
like so, he says, twisting the glass so the bottom end is pointing up
under the napkin. I will be on the back seat of the motorcycle and we
will ride by, then turn and throw it when he comes out of the building.

Yes, this will work, Matin says. The rider is good on the motorbike,
he is young, he is fast.

The conversation comes to an abrupt end. Each man sits back on
the sofa, in the way that people push their plates away when they have
finished eating.

Their eyes, their posture, their silence shows Rahim the contemplation, the dream, to do something against their common enemy. To free their home. To save their families. To restore order. At this moment, in between each breath, scented with the perfume of ambition, each man also feels guilt.

Rahim can see that each man knows they have a lot to lose if they get caught as the perpetrators of this assassination. Each man will say goodbye to someone they love.

Rahim decides to say nothing of this to Henna. On this island, with these men, Henna does not belong, she will not cope. He will spare her this knowledge of war, of his hand in this.

Beyond death and statelessness, the uncertainty of their future, war has created an expanse where insidious secrets are born and held between people who would otherwise be close. And it isn't just between husband and wife. He thinks of the lies they tell their family about Sofia still living, the truth left lingering only in the passages of his heart.

Rahim suspects that Hamid isn't as well off as he makes it sound in his letters either. He believes that Hamid is hiding his reality from those who love him too, so that he can save them the heartache of his reality. He multiplies this possibility by the population of all of Afghanistan, all those people hiding their truths to protect their loved ones, and before him looms the enormous and undeniable reality that war's wounds are not all physical, cannot all be counted in the number of dead and injured.

Despite this realisation, he understands that he will protect Henna from the truths she cannot stomach.

Rahim

Henna steps out in front of him, wearing an emerald dress that flows down to the floor. She made the dress herself, choosing the fabric from a store nearby which they visited a few weeks ago; the rainbow-hued silk in the window caught their eyes. She used a second-hand sewing machine he purchased for her in Old Delhi. He thinks she has done a good job of it. On her neck and ears she is wearing the emerald set Bebe gave Henna on their engagement day. The gold filigree is holding small emeralds in the centre, a memory of a magical lifetime long ago. Her hair is up in a bun and the scent of her peach perfume merges with his breath. He looks her up and down.

You are beautiful, he says. He realises it has been a while since he said something like this to her.

Henna blushes. Is my make-up okay?

Yes, he says.

He takes the sash she is holding; he winds it around her waist and fixes it in front of her body into a bow. She slips on her shoes with the small gemstones glued on the toes. Rahim watches, unable to move, flooded with emotion. Tariq is dressed in black trousers, a white shirt and black school shoes; his hair is combed to one side. He jumps up and down in excitement, pulling Rahim's hand towards the door.

Rahim looks at the reflection of his small family in the mirror as they pass it in the hallway on the way to the front door. He imagines what people will think, how they will react to this family from another land, a refugee family coming to an Indian wedding. They go downstairs to find the street in front of the flat has been transformed into another world. It's a brightly coloured canopy of delights, a colourful series of tents covering the sky. The road has been blocked and converted to a banquet hall. There are tables with pretty flowers on them, chairs of ten surrounding the tables, chandeliers hanging and china glistening and sparkling – everything is opulent, competing with the jewels that ornament the bodies all around.

This spectacular kaleidoscope of colour lifts his mood for the first time in many months as his landlord – with his broad smile, kind face and big bulging eyes – comes to greet him.

Welcome to my son's wedding, a grand occasion, he says. He shakes hands with Rahim, warmly, and says, Very nice, as he shakes hands with Henna, tilting his head to the right and left in approval. The ceremony will begin soon, he says, gently directing Rahim to their decorated table.

Rahim feels like he has come to a jashn, one of the street festivals of Herat. He remembers the last time he took Henna, when they were engaged – he becomes embarrassed as he remembers his jealousy and the way the night ended. Now he takes her by the hand, as she takes

Tariq's hand, her eyes smiling into his; the three of them sit down inside this coloured tent of wonders. The smell of warm Indian cuisine wafts in, people are walking around with flutes of masroob in hand. Ladies with dainty fingers hold white teacups full of hot chocolate. Tonight, he and Henna will pretend they are home. They will forget the past, like the wind as it pushes away the clouds to reveal the bright light of the sun after the storm. Tonight, they will enjoy their time on Earth and remember with gratitude that they are safe and together.

Henna

enna is standing on the balcony, her arms draped around Tariq's shoulders as she stands behind him. She can see grey smoke rising in the distance. The air smells stronger than usual, mixed with the aroma of hot ghee from the next-door kitchen where the landlord lives. People have been marching with flags in the street below. Prime Minister Indira Gandhi was assassinated yesterday by her Sikh bodyguard. The army has been called in to suppress the violent riots where Sikhs have been targeted. Sikh homes are being burnt; people have died. Henna bends down and squeezes Tariq's face against her own cheek to suppress her shivering, she retreats to the lounge, settles Tariq at her feet with one of his English books, and sits on the couch.

She takes up the unpicker to undo a seam she has incorrectly sewn on a simple shirt for Tariq, a hobby she decided to pick up for the first time a few months ago to keep her mind busy after she tried and abandoned drawing miniature art patterns she had learnt from Khoja. The memory of the work was too painful, the flashes of their old life too vivid, so she had put it aside.

She asked Rahim about getting a sewing machine, noting the expense of buying clothes. Before long he had found a second-hand one in Old Delhi. She has been cutting fabric, wasting it sometimes on her experiments; she has managed to make a few things so far which seem to fit well, including a dress for herself.

Her work doesn't get far before she gets up, goes to the door and locks the flyscreen and the front door. She checks the windows are all closed. Rahim isn't home, he has gone to the BBC office in town to do a translation job for a small fee. She didn't want him to go, but he insisted he would be safe.

Now, Gandhi's son, Rajiv, is on the television screen, he asks India to remain calm out of respect for her soul. Tariq begins to get fidgety and restless, and Henna thinks it's because he can sense her unease. She joins him for a while on the floor of the lounge room, turning off the TV. They hop up and weave between the cane chairs, which came with this furnished apartment, following one another in a kind of game. Then, in the kitchen, she gives him a glass of milk to drink. He takes the blue plastic cup. He begins to drink, his two eyes locked onto her face. She makes an effort to look calm, she gives him a smile, you are all we have, she says as she brushes aside his fine brown fringe.

War has followed them here, unrest has followed them; where will they go next? She will bring this up with Rahim, she will ask him to begin submitting the forms, to apply for refugee status somewhere else.

Last night visitors came to see Rahim, colleagues and friends from his past. Most fled with their wives and children and have recently arrived in Delhi. Some of them are part of the Afghan resistance and tell stories of torture in prison and injury in battle. Meeting these old friends, or friends of friends, hearing their stories, keeps Rahim connected and involved with what's happening in Afghanistan. He needs to detach, she thinks, he needs to think about the future.

Six months have passed between letters from Herat. Henna receives the tattered, tampered, ink-stained, thickly folded messages with cautious celebration, lest they hold bad news.

Khoja is writing satirical poems, short stories and jokes. He writes of the good news that Roya and Nargis are coming to Herat, they are bringing their children and husbands with them. He and Koko are preparing the house to welcome them back.

He is disguising his political opinions and news of the mujahideen's successes within his creative writing. The censorship office misses the meaning of his secret messages most of the time. He describes mundane details of daily life to comfort Henna and Rahim with a sense of closeness.

It is at the end of one of his carefully crafted letters that Khoja mentions her brother, saying he has heard from Hamid, who is doing well. Henna is pleased that Hamid is staying in contact with Khoja, pleased but also disappointed that her last two letters to him remain unanswered.

Hamid

Hamid has met this man three times, this man who likes to meet late in the night, sitting on the steps of Hamid's workplace. Every time they meet, this man makes Hamid promises. Hamid knows the promises can't all be true, but he feels good when they talk about the passage to Delhi. How safe it is, how free he will be when he gets there. Hamid hasn't told this man about Henna, how he has a sister there and how his sister would now have two children. How he is an uncle to Henna's son and daughter.

Hamid has stopped smoking, and with the remainder of his savings hidden under the mattress – what he didn't give to the man for transport – he has purchased two small plastic toys. Each toy is the length of his index finger. They are two tiny dolls; one for Tariq, a man wearing a turban, and the other, a girl wearing a red dress and pantaloons, for Henna's daughter, who must now be born and living under this same sky without knowledge of her uncle Hamid.

He rehearses his future conversations with Henna. He tries the same with Rahim but falls asleep before the conversation has fully unfolded in his mind. What will Rahim say, how will Hamid explain his life?

He wrote to Jameela two days ago, to tell her he is leaving. They had met that day but he had not been able to broach the subject. Partly because she is skittish when they meet and this is a heavy topic that would take time, but mostly because he felt afraid to see her broken heart shining in her eyes.

Hamid has gone to check under the brick where they leave letters for each other but it is empty. Each time he checks, he is surprised by how raw the pain is, this absence of her. *Maybe you loved her after all*, he tells himself.

In another life he would have married her, an honourable marriage that she deserves. *They would have sung Ahesta Boro for us*, he thinks, *a banquet would have served the guests, her cruel uncle and her fears would have faded into her past*. She would have become a mother and a grandmother; she would have lived a life protected by him. But he is not that man, will never be.

Henna and Rahim need not know about this phase of his life. He will renew himself to resemble the Hamid they knew, but he knows this renewal will only be on the outside. He has begun to do push-ups in the mornings, so that he doesn't shock them with this current appearance. He has just a handful of weeks left to change.

Henna

Afghanistan ke azad shod, when Afghanistan is free, Rahim says. They are in the lounge room of their new place, a home slightly bigger than their previous apartment. This is their third move since leaving Engela; another move because their last place was damp and lacked natural light. This apartment has two rooms, bigger windows, a balcony, nice neighbours and a leafy outlook. The wide quiet street doesn't have any traffic. Henna bought a badminton set and they sometimes play out there on a cool afternoon, with Tariq jumping to catch the shuttlecock from the sky, both laughing at his antics until their sides ache.

Henna had been searching for a home where the barriers between inside and outside are blurred, where nature is as entwined with her days as it was in Herat. This apartment was not only affordable but has a large tree with branches that hang over their little balcony and fill their lounge room windows with green.

Rahim is wearing his white pantaloons and singlet and is pacing back and forth in front of the small black-and-white television, which has the news on. He has his hands folded behind his back; his eyes look into an invisible distant future-scape, a version of the future that Henna wishes she could see.

She hasn't heard the whole of what he just said, and she feels guilty. She blinks at him, a furtive glance that she believes does not fool him. She looks at the back of her left hand, turning it to herself as if she is inspecting it; she looks at the knuckles with gathered skin that isn't soft anymore.

Sorry, Rahim jan, what did you say? She glances at Tariq out of habit. He is playing with his toys in the corner, repeating new words, some even in Hindi. Every day it's something new with him, he is changing in front of her eyes.

The heat in the room is tempered by ceiling fans. A small creaking noise escapes from the base of one of them. Henna wonders if it will behead them when the fan comes loose.

Rahim begins most of his sentences about the future with those words, Afghanistan ke azad shod. Everything he wants to plan starts with this. He casts a spell with these words. Eventually the spell is expected to do its work and make Afghanistan's freedom come to be. He expects his old life will be waiting unchanged when the country is free. Three million Afghans have crossed into Pakistan, another million or so are in Iran and only a small number to India. She thinks of Hamid, wishes he was here so they could talk.

Rahim has told her on previous occasions that when Afghanistan is free they will set up a new organisation together for orphans and widows. They will help the poor; they will visit places they didn't go when they had the chance. Like her, he misses the way fruit tasted –

pomegranates, figs, apples, grapes from the vine. She feels the same, nothing tastes the same as it used to.

Today, his talk of the end to the war stings more than usual, given the recent violence in Delhi. At first, talk of this dream was pleasing to Henna's ears, but now, away from Herat for this long, his words have become grating.

She wants him to stop dreaming of an end that may never come, to stop reminding her of what they have lost. She wants him to speak about the alternative life they must now lead, where all the money they own is not hidden in the toilet cistern. He needs to find a job which pays more than he is earning now, something beyond translating words to Dari from English. Something perhaps in the legal profession, maybe that will get him back to the man he was, a man of striving, a man of action.

She has seen their savings dwindle since the scholarship ended, despite the work Rahim has found translating for the Iranian news service and the cash assistance they are getting from the United Nations refugee agency. They probably only have oxygen for another year. Then again, she could be wrong. It could be longer or much shorter, given neither of them have had to count their money, plan for savings, create and maintain a budget before now. She wishes she could go back to teaching, to feel the energy of movement of the classroom, talking to the students, thinking how to help those most in need of her attention, imagining their futures, each one of her students a sapling that she hoped would become a giant tree.

A repetitive thought visits her, the future is now different in each of their minds. It doesn't contain the same hues they shared previously. He is seeing them back in Herat, she is seeing them anywhere but Herat. This thought frightens her. It is normal for husband and wife to disagree; she reminds herself to give herself air to breathe.

The news, Rahim continues, isn't looking good. Talks have broken down between the UN and USSR . . . They haven't managed to negotiate an end to the war, he says. We can create a new organisation to help educate girls, something like what they have here in India, he says. We can start in the villages.

We are out of onions, Henna says, to interrupt this painful dreaming.

Okay, I will get some this afternoon, Rahim says, stopping to face her, seeming unfazed by the change in subject.

He goes back to his pacing, stops again and says, That qabuli you made yesterday was delicious, what will you be cooking for dinner?

Something new, she says, unsure of what it will be.

She has been trying different recipes, trying to recreate the dishes of their homeland. Having never maintained a cooking schedule, she is piecing together what she can. The results have been varied but she will keep trying. She wants Tariq to know these foods and for Rahim not to miss them so much.

Hamid

Hamid has a pen in hand, a lined notebook resting on a piece of cardboard on the bare floor of his small box of a room. He lies on his stomach, on his mattress, thinking what to say, how to relay the good news of his imminent arrival.

Dear Henna,
May Khoda jan shine his blessings on you, may you and Rahim jan, and your two kittens be in good health.

It's amazing that our sisters and parents will be reunited in Herat but you and I will not be there. Did you hear that Nargis and Roya and their husbands and kids have all gone to Herat because of the fighting in their region? I learnt this from a letter from Khoja, he is really happy to have them back.

I am coming to you, I am coming to Delhi to see you. I don't know what day it will be but I will call you once I arrive at the airport. Until then, know that your brother is in good health, he has saved up money, and is on his way to you.

Hamid takes his pen off the paper and stops writing. He is thinking about the consequences of writing this letter. Is it for him that he writes, to make himself happy, or is it for the benefit of Henna? Who knows why he does anything these days. He cannot trust his intentions, he cannot trust his own lies, which come through in this letter. Where to begin? Will he ever write letters without thinking of Jameela?

He shakes his head as if waking from a dream. What's the point in making her worry? I will go to her with open arms. I will call her from the airport. With this thought he takes the paper, tears it into shreds and pushes it into his pillowcase. He lies back onto the thin mattress momentarily, wanting to stay there all day. But it is noon, and this is a short break before the tea house opens for the day.

He gets to his feet, the last few days of exercise propelling him forward with more energy than he thought he could muster. He remembers that tonight he will sleep with the shredded letter to Henna inside his pillow, that soon he will see her and say the things that he wants to say to her face.

Tomorrow he will prepare to fly; at the crack of dawn he will wake and take a flight to Delhi. His things are packed in a small duffle bag, he will meet the man and will be given his ticket at last. For now, he has dishes to do, then a night of restless sleep and meaningless dreams before his new life begins.

Henna

From the pull-chain cistern, water is pouring down and over the toilet bowl, a solid sheet pouring onto the toilet, then flooding the bathroom floor. The wall-mounted cistern is far too high for Henna to reach and look inside. She is frantically pulling the metal chain to stop the flood. The water pours over her shoulders and she is wet from head to foot. Tariq stands at the door of the bathroom, jumping up and down with excitement at the spectacle.

Mummy, Mummy, he yells, laughing, look at the water!

When pulling the chain doesn't stop the overflow, Henna climbs on the closed lid of the toilet. Standing on tiptoes, half her hand can reach the cistern cover. She tries to slide the heavy cover to the side with the tips of her fingers and it begins to give and move aside. She is careful not to drop it to the ground. Now there is a gap wide enough for most of her hand to fit inside.

She pushes her fingers into the gap, the water runs down her arm and down her sleeve, she feels the cold of it as it slides all the way down her body to her feet. Her fingers can feel the plastic package just inside, so close. She shifts her body a little to the left and grabs hold of the corner of the package and gently pulls the package out.

She gets down from standing on the toilet with the package in her hand. Tariq starts to walk towards her and she says, No, no, stand back, you will get wet.

He looks for a moment like he is about to cry but she smiles at him, her wet hair clinging to her cheeks. Water is pouring on her head and down her face, she breathes out sharply to stop the water getting into her mouth. The swish of her breath sprays water everywhere and makes Tariq laugh.

She pulls the cistern's metal chain one last time to stop the downpour. Miraculously, the water stops overflowing. She asks Tariq to look away. He takes both chubby hands to his face, turns his back to her and waits for her to finish. She takes off her clothes, wraps herself in a towel. She walks past him to the bedroom, keen to dress quickly so she can check the contents of the package.

It is filled with the last of the money Khoja and Haji Mama had given them, stored in the cistern so that when the immigration inspectors come to their home, they won't find it. Rahim has heard that if they find money, they think it is stolen. They wouldn't believe it belongs to them, sure that it must be black market cash. Refugees are poor, how can they bring savings with them?

Now, hours later, she is standing at the door of the apartment, looking through the small square window as Tariq sleeps. She will not open the door if there is a knock unless it's Rahim. The apartment is full of bank notes laid out single file to dry. It was a game Tariq enjoyed playing in place of learning the English homework, which their new tutor Pushpa has given him and Henna.

Hamid

Hamid is in an interview room in Delhi Airport. He is sweating, the room is hot with only a small fan in the corner. Hamid is thirsty. He has been waiting here for many hours. They took him as soon as he landed, an Afghan, neatly dressed, travelling alone, false papers. A few coins jingled in his trouser pocket as he followed the uniform to the interview room at the airport. The sound of jingling coins reminds him that this is all he has to his name, these pennies, only enough for a taxi to Henna. He has spent all the money he did have, all his savings, paying the man who guaranteed him safe passage. If the prospect of a bribe arises now, he will have to call Henna.

Now, as he sits in the interview room, his bright-blue polyester shirt is sticking to the skin on his wet back. He is sitting on a hard wooden chair, with his back hunched, his elbows on the table. His hair was shiny and clean when he looked in the bathroom mirror on the plane, checking himself when they were close to landing; now it is wet with sweat around his forehead.

He has worked hard these past few weeks to regain his old self. He hasn't acquired his previous body, or his previous mind, but he has stopped the opium, he has had a haircut. He needs a smoke. A smoke would calm him down, stop him from acting stupidly and from looking like he doesn't belong in this country.

He straightens up in the chair, sits with a hand on each thigh, spreads his thighs apart and pushes his chest out. He feels what he supposes a peacock feels when fanning out its spectacular tail. *I should sit like this, exuding confidence, when they interview me. They need to know that if they let me in, I will be useful to their country.* He quickly tires of this posture, folds his back again, begins to finger the corner of the laminate tabletop, where the laminate is beginning to peel off, his hands trembling. He can smell himself. He smells pungent and unpleasant. He used a nice-smelling soap to wash. Now its scent has all gone. He was ready to see Henna, to face Rahim, as a new man, recently glued back together by a plane ticket to Delhi.

An Afghan man visited him in this room a few hours ago, with the uniform. He was an interpreter. *What a strange thing to say*, Hamid thought, when the interpreter told Hamid in Dari, with his Kabul accent, Speak only the answers to the questions this officer asks you and nothing more. They didn't exchange any other words, no greetings, no Salaam, how is your family. It's hard to tell what time it was, what time it is now. The translator had a smile of recognition in his serious eyes when Hamid looked deeply into them. A man who wore normal clothes and belonged and lived in Delhi. Perhaps this man will help Hamid, because Hamid told him that he is Khoja's son. Hamid told him as he was leaving that he has come to live in Delhi with his sister

Henna and her husband Rahim, son of Governor Haji Mama, but please don't tell this to the uniform.

Hamid wishes he was by that stream, the stream of his childhood, the stream that ran across Herat's lush green body in the days of peace. In the summer's dry heat, he and Henna would retreat into the woods and find a natural clearing between the trees. A fresh, cool wind blew through the clearing even in the heat of summer, the air itself was different. This clearing had nature's cooler installed, a phantom wind blowing only there and nowhere else, a phantom wind that stopped if you went out of the clearing and into the rest of the forest – perhaps a djinn's breath, they joked, his spine tingling with a mix of fear and pleasure at the thought of this clearing being haunted by djinn. He and Henna together, laughing.

He remembers sitting beside the stream, the djinn's breath on his face, cooling his wet hair, rockmelon juice dripping from his mouth, his fingers sticky, the sweet flesh of the fruit on his tongue.

Dipping their hands in the clear cool waters, they would smack their lips and laugh for no reason. Flies would circle restlessly, jumping from nose to rockmelon flesh, trying to get at their feast, he shooed them away and Henna pretended she ate a fly and spat out a seed.

A fruit so juicy, clutched between his two hands.

Fruit eating is a messy business, he said to Henna.

Yes, she agreed. It needs to be consumed right by this spring, just like this, so you can wash as quickly as you have eaten.

Heaven, he had said then, this is what heaven is. Right here, right now. His belly full of rockmelon, they lay by the banks of the stream for the rest of the afternoon until the sun's heat was tamed by the wise old moon.

Then they walked slowly home, dizzy from their siesta, famished for the iftar dinner spread awaiting them at Koko's dastarkhon.

Koko had forgotten what she had asked them to do, she would think they had fasted a full day, while they had dodged her nagging requests and spent a few hours in paradise.

Now, he wishes he could taste that rockmelon, swim in the stream, laugh with Henna. He will never again taste rockmelon so sweet, while squatting along the banks of that stream, a thick strip of it at his mouth, taking a bite, the juices running, his eyes closed, breathing, biting, laughing and chewing all at once. He picks up the styrofoam cup and takes a sip of lukewarm water. He wishes he could fast a day and come to Koko's dastarkhon to eat once more.

The door of the windowless interview room opens and the man who first took Hamid from the airport walks in. The Afghan interpreter follows. He closes the door behind him. The Afghan sits opposite Hamid. The uniform reminds Hamid of all the men in uniform who came to reside in Herat – different uniforms, different agendas, but uniforms still. Hamid wishes men in uniforms did not exist.

The uniform pulls one of the skeletal chairs towards himself and sits opposite Hamid, next to the interpreter. The uniform is small in stature, dressed in a khaki collared shirt and tie, the thick waistband of his matching trousers alarmingly tight around his middle, his felt hat with the insignia of the Indian coat of arms.

I am sorry, sir, he says, his large eyes unblinking. We will have to send you back to Iran.

The Afghan opens his mouth to interpret, but Hamid has understood it all before the Afghan says a word.

Hamid suddenly feels relieved, joyous, happy, light. He breathes out, a huge weight lifted from his shoulders. He is happy that he doesn't have to face Delhi, a new city, another new life, begging for work – but most of all relieved not to face Henna and Rahim. He has already said goodbye to them.

The shame of who he has become, of what he has become, of how he looks – a failure – compared with what he was. None of this will be revealed to Henna, or to anybody who used to know him. He has their letters in his pockets, letters that were inspected when he was first taken into this room, letters from his family. It dawns on him that his anonymity, his distance from Herat, is much safer, is less work, requires less energy from him. He can go back and be the man he was in Tehran. He can live his days as he has been, remain quiet, write sparse letters, and distance himself from those who knew him once upon a time.

Then age will catch him and before long the man he used to inhabit, who has already died, that man will also be free. *Let them remember that Hamid, who is no longer me; let them think he lives a life of happiness, when in fact he died a long time ago.*

Rahim

Rahim carefully folds the letter from a friend, less a friend and more a contact, someone he met a long time ago, who works in the immigration department in Delhi. A long time ago, when Rahim was a prosecutor, this man crossed his path. This man was young then, in his early twenties.

He fled to India to start a new life. Now, they have crossed paths again, since he saw Rahim's articles in the Iranian paper, the articles Rahim has been hired to translate and then re-write for the Iranian news service from the English-language news sources. Work Rahim has begun to enjoy. Many people have come forward since Rahim's articles began to show up in the Iranian newspaper – old faces, old stories.

Now this man has become a confidant; from inside immigration, he has offered to help Rahim and his family to apply for refugee status in a new country. He has written to Rahim that Hamid tried to enter India with false documents, has been rejected and sent back to Iran.

The letter says that Hamid mentioned he is the son of Khoja but did not mention that he knew Rahim and Henna for fear of implicating them in this crime and agreed to go back quietly without a fight.

Now, Rahim has a decision to make. Should he keep this from Henna? Or will he tell her? And, if so, how will he tell Henna without breaking her heart? She is finally on the mend, she has started to sleep through the night, is starting to do things on her own again.

He tears the letter into shreds and throws it in the garbage bin. The loud clanging sound of the metallic lid startles him as he drops it accidentally to the floor.

Rahim jan, everything okay? says Henna from inside, with mirth in her voice, as she often teases him about bumping into things.

Yes, I am fine, he says, as he runs his hand down his face and takes a long audible inhale, pacing on the balcony. Choof, he breathes out loudly a moment later, sending his dua to Hamid.

Henna

Pushpa's small wrists jingle with thin glass bangles in purple and red. She wears a mustard knee-length shalwar kameez, tunic and pants, and a dupatta, scarf, wrapped around her shoulders. Her hair is parted in the centre and woven into two thick plaits that fall down her back. Blue ribbons weave through her plaits and tie at the ends with bows. Henna thinks these ribbons are like a river, flowing through the night of Pushpa's thick hair, carrying the memories and history of this girl that Henna has come to know as her and Tariq's English tutor.

Henna was delighted to make a new friend, a local girl who can teach her, who can help her son with his homework. She is glad the school had this introduction program, this access to extra help for pupils like Tariq, which Henna is paying a little extra to benefit from. Henna now stands watching them, as Tariq has his daily lessons before he goes to school. He sits beside Pushpa, cross-legged, in the already humid air of the balcony, on rugs upon the floor. He repeats every sound after her. He is learning sound by sound, part by part.

Henna thinks now of their adventure the other day when fresh-faced Pushpa came to pick them up for a visit to her village, early in the morning. Tariq was excited to leave the house, to visit his teacher's house. It was a kind invitation from the teacher, an idea which she agreed to on the spot.

She had assumed the teacher lived somewhere nearby, but the seemingly never-ending journey made Henna believe the girl was leading them not to her home village but somewhere else. Did the girl have a more sinister plan? Had Henna's simple mind caught her out, and was it about to deliver her and Tariq straight into the hands of some evil awaiting them?

Henna's mind ran wild with fear all through the drive in the taxi, so much so that she now doesn't remember what she saw outside the window of the runaway car. She imagined the unbearable guilt of something happening to her and Tariq. Rahim would never forgive her; he would never recover from the loss of his wife and son. She saw Rahim looking down into the deep graves where unknown hands lowered their bodies. A thousand nightmares visited her, of kidnappings, killings and rapes. How could she have trusted this girl?

Finally, they stopped at the edge of a city of huts and Henna prepared herself for struggle. She was quiet and tense but didn't want Pushpa to notice any change. So, she smiled as she paid the taxi driver, looking at him one last time, as if he were her only link to freedom and now he would drive away.

Driver wait? Henna asked Pushpa.

Pushpa said, No, I know another one, he can take you back.

And then the taxi was gone.

Pushpa led Henna and Tariq through narrow walkways, deeper and deeper into a maze of poverty. Women were sitting in circles making pancakes of dung, which they stuck to the walls of huts to dry.

There was a strong smell of loosh, a mixture of mud and rubbish. Henna fought the urge to hold her nose in the presence of the people who lived here, who stood to watch them pass in procession, into the winding pathways of the temporary-looking dwellings.

Tariq held Pushpa's hand as stray dogs passed. Henna tried to calculate her escape, looking at a woman here and there, directly in the eye, so that perhaps these women could remember seeing her when the police came, when the investigation began.

Soon enough, they arrived outside a hut. Pushpa's home was compact, with a low roof. Hamid would not have been able to stand up in it, his outstretched arms would have touched the sides of the hut. Pushpa's open palm gestured for them to enter. Henna bent her head and entered the hut. Beneath her feet she saw a tattered mat and, in the corner, folded thin, were blankets and sheets. She sat down on the bare mat and put Tariq beside her. Tariq, thinking this was a special new game, was smiling from ear to ear. Henna didn't want to upset him, so she retained her stiff smile as Pushpa signalled with her index finger, one moment, and disappeared.

Henna remembers sweating like she has never sweated before. She waited for the dacoits to enter, wearing red bandanas around their greasy hair and carrying curved daggers, pointing into her face. She waited for a chloroform-soaked rag to be pushed against her mouth.

Shortly, an old woman entered. It was dark in the hut, but as the woman placed a steaming cup of milky chai in front of Henna, she could make out a face that had lived many lives. Placing another in front of herself, the woman positioned herself, sitting cross-legged and silent, opposite Henna. Shortly after this, Pushpa joined in, with her own cup. The three of them made a circle of tea drinkers.

Seeing as this was the tea party she had been promised, Henna immediately relaxed. Koko's voice was still audible in a corner of Henna's mind, although it was quieter now, still whispering to her. *Stupid girl, what if the woman's husband comes home, what if the woman's husband has an evil eye.*

As Henna picked up the glass tumbler of hot tea, Tariq moved to sit next to Pushpa, squeezing in beside her. This made the old woman giggle, a toothless giggle which rippled through her thin cotton sari and wrinkled arms. Then Pushpa giggled, looking at Tariq's beaming face looking at her. Henna giggled too, looking at them, in reality laughing at herself. The three women drank sweet tea together in silence while their smiles filled the gap of a shared language.

In her dream Henna is sitting on her side, her legs folded beneath her. She is on a hill, beneath a tree with thin, dry arms reaching up in all directions. There are small white shokofa, apple blossoms, growing along each branch. On her head she wears a black veil, which is draped over her shoulders and her body and threatens to take flight like an ominous bird every time a gust of wind blows. She is alone, beneath a sky of black clouds and a burning sun, which has just begun to set behind a mountain in the distance. A vast burial ground surrounds her, tombstones are everywhere. Also, there are fresh mounds of dirt dotting the rolling black hills near and far, beneath which new deaths have recently been concealed. The sky is grey, but there is an openness about it, it is a wide sky, it is Khoja's open arms.

She is sitting in the semi-darkness of a crepuscular sun, she is sitting beside Sofia who is still and quiet and in her grave. It is a small grave, stretching in front of Henna, the length of her forearm.

Henna had helped to wash her daughter from head to foot, polishing the perfect skin with the soaking sponge, to cleanse the body of an already pure soul. She had covered Sofia in a white shroud and sent her back to Khoda, back into the earth in Delhi.

Now, it begins to rain. Fat drops of icy water which Henna can feel on the top of her head and shoulders. Drops like the ones that fell when the toilet flooded.

Henna watches the rain fall over the gravestones all around her, the drops breaking like clear glass and running down Sofia's head-stone to wash away dirt and dry decomposed leaves which must have accumulated over the years since Henna has been away, living a life in another country, far from Sofia.

Henna finds that she has a twig in her hand and, using this twig, she begins to dig a tiny hole in the mound of dirt beneath which Sofia sleeps. She wants to make sure that the water can flow, that Sofia can get water from the rain to break her thirst.

Rahim

Henna has started to watch an Indian soap opera recently. She has become wrapped up in the story, the drama, the characters. She tells Rahim about the latest twist in the plot, the latest intrigue, when he gets home from work. He likes to listen to her stories of what happened in the drama each day, what he has missed since they started watching it together a few weeks ago. Now, the drama plays, but the sound is mute. She is sitting beside Rahim on the sofa, her cup of black tea between her two hands. Steam rises from it as she holds the cup, her legs folded beneath her, her face turned to Rahim.

It's been a long time since they talked properly, since they planned their future. Rahim is cautious, he doesn't want to do anything that may destroy this precious exchange of thoughts and plans. He doesn't want to say anything that may discourage her from sharing her true thoughts with him. He doesn't want to talk over her and is glad she is in this bubble with him, even if its temporary, just for this hour. The bubble has the air of Afghanistan in it. She is doing the talking now. She is sharing beyond day-to-day instructions and movements.

He takes a deep breath, a quiet, slow inconspicuous one, so as not to signal inadvertently his joy or boredom. Not to spook her or distract her.

Three years have passed in New Delhi, she says. While our bodies occupy Delhi, our minds are still in Herat, she continues. We live in temporary arrangements, but how long can we keep this up? It is a limbo between Herat and Delhi.

Rahim says, Yes, we are eating borrowed food, we are experiencing borrowed emotions, we purchase temporary, perishable, cheap things that can be thrown away at a moment's notice.

At this point their views diverge about what to do. Rahim thinks, but doesn't say, they will be going back any day. In this unknown land he doesn't have any financial security, he doesn't have any interest in buying a home to settle down. He is waiting to go back.

He knows that he will never settle here, or anywhere that isn't his ancestral home. The bridge between his past, his beliefs, his culture, and the rest of the world is vast. Henna thinks they should make a move. She says the situation in Afghanistan isn't improving. A speedy end to the war seems unrealistic. The money they brought from Afghanistan is running out.

Okay, he says, we will look elsewhere.

Just like that, the decision to apply for refugee visas to Canada, the USA and Australia is made. He believes there is no use in arguing with her or holding on to their current existence. Once you are uprooted it doesn't take much to choose where you live next, there isn't much sense in thinking too much about it. Wherever he goes, it will not be home, and eventually he will have to return.

Tomorrow he will start the process by calling his friend in immigration to take up his offer of assistance, he promises Henna. She seems pleased.

Henna

Henna watches the city blur as the taxi races towards the airport. Splashes of colour appear, merge and disappear, morphing into the grey of the morning landscape as the city dissolves into farmland. The colours she sees are like the body of a beast within which she has lived her recent life. She reflects on the contradictory and unexpected turn of her days and nights since they left Herat. She reflects on the kaleidoscopic hues of Rahim's temperament. He has become quiet, less in control, more introspective and pensive.

She reflects on the changing nature of her own views, her relationship with Rahim, her role as a mother, now moving on to a new life. This new life will be revealed like a new moon, emerging slowly from behind woollen clouds, will form into a swollen disk of light. She has morphed into many women in her recent past, is constantly evolving. Like a moth to a flame, she has been drawn to a new sense of self.

She has lived many lifetimes in her short years here, many more than she lived throughout her life in Herat.

Now, she breathes over the overwhelming noise in her head. She thinks of Sofia. *Sofia, we are leaving Sofia here*, she says to herself. She is afraid these words will form out loud and Rahim and Tariq will hear them.

Perhaps Rahim is thinking of Sofia too as he sits in the back seat of the taxi beside her. Henna looks at him as he looks out his side window. He is whispering dua as he always does when they embark on something new.

Choof, he says, at the end of the sura he was reciting to himself. Choof, he breathes the sound over Tariq's head, who is sitting between them.

Henna rests her hands in her lap, she feels the fabric of her blue crepe dress. She thinks of the day the rickshaw wheel came away and flew down the hill, as she and Tariq and Rahim sat wide-jawed in the passenger seats behind the driver. The danger was palpable. Had they fled war only to be killed on a busy road in Delhi?

She will miss the red heat of Delhi and its warm monsoonal rains, the young women running out of their homes onto the street to stand beneath the rain, their faces held up to the sky. The brown rain pouring down their faces and their thick long hair, believing it will heal acne and improve their complexions.

She will miss the kindness of strangers and the warmth of her friendship with the landlord's wife, who did her best to soothe the pain of Sofia's departure. Who brought over freshly made chapatis. They shared many meals together, and Henna cooked for the landlord and his wife. The shared daal, qabuli and lamb kofta, the couple's appreciative smacking of lips, which pleased her as a new cook and a broken mother.

Now that she takes stock, she is relieved to leave this city. To leave behind its talkh, bitter memories. This colourful city, which is Sofia's home. Henna knows that she will come back some day, that she cannot leave Sofia alone here without many visits during her lifetime. The distance to return will be great, both emotionally and physically, but she must find the means to do it as soon as they have jobs. She will be living on another continent, even further from her home. She is willing to take this journey.

A small voice of regret sounds in the back of her mind, but she shuts it out. It's Koko's voice, asking if she is sure of this move. Hamid's voice is saying, *run further, to safety*.

She remembers looking at a map of the world and seeing an island at the bottom. Tariq will get an education there, Rahim will find work, Henna will become a mother and wife who lives in a nice home. They will save money and send some back to Herat. Things will start anew. In the suitcases she has packed new doilies, crisp, white, embroidered tablecloths and new bedspreads. She will take these out when they settle into their home.

The driver toots his horn as he overtakes another taxi. Rahim is quiet, Tariq is playing with a figurine. She wishes Rahim would speak, but he is deep in thought. She wonders if he blames her for the growing distance from Herat, for making him leave Sofia in this vast and populated city all alone. *Khoda hafiz Sofia, Khoda hafiz Hamid*, Henna whispers in her mind. Tariq looks up at Henna as if he has heard her goodbyes to the figures from her past. She pulls his head to her lips, delicately kissing the gloss of his hair.

Rahim

Rahim looks out the window of the plane as India passes below. Delhi is made of beautiful sparkling jewels scattered across the velvet of this dark and clear night.

Thank you for flying with Air India Airlines. We hope you enjoy your journey, says the voice on the intercom.

Gradually the darkness thickens around the bejewelled cityscape. Rahim thinks of the flat-roofed houses in Kabul as they flew over them, years ago. He remembers how, in the distance, sharp mountain peaks pierced the sky, his heart pounding in his chest, his mind full of fearful thoughts he dared not let loose.

Rahim doesn't allow himself to think of the distance he is putting between himself and those sharp mountain peaks that guard his homeland. He doesn't allow himself to cry out like a child, as his young son does when things seem out of control and too painful to bear.

He imagines that if he began to let himself go, his sobs would come in uncontrollable waves, the edges of them touching passengers in the seats all around and reaching down to the oceans below.

Henna is sitting with Tariq, in the same row as Rahim. Tariq's head is in Henna's lap, his feet are curled up, his eyes are closed and are seeing the dreams that children see, no doubt full of the small irritations that children feel at being misunderstood by adults. Henna's cracked lips smile knowingly at Rahim as he looks over at her. He expected her to be asleep but she is not, the cabin is dark but her overhead reading light is on, making her two large eyes and face clearly visible to him. Her eyes tell Rahim to be strong, as if she can see and feel his sobs even though he holds it all in. *She is braver than I will ever be*, he thinks, as he remembers Sofia, the daughter he didn't get a chance to meet. How stoic Henna was in the face of this loss, how his cup was so full of despair that, had she sought his comfort, he would have not been able to cope with carrying them both. He wanted to create a different life for her, for the children who would be born from their love.

Rahim wonders how long he will feel the absence of his family, the absence of the sights and smells of his beloved Herat, the call of the muezzin, the feeling of being useful and of service. How long will this absence be felt in every cell of his body?

He remembers the poem by Jalal ad-Din Balkhi about the reed flute singing of the agony of separation. He is like this reed flute, uprooted from his reed bed, detached from the place he belongs. He rests his forehead against the plane's chilled window as warm tears flow from his eyes.

Rahim is sitting on one of the cement benches in the courtyard of the refugee hostel, where they arrived two days ago. His legs feel heavy, as if he is still on the plane. His nose feels blocked. His breaths feel light, they are not the full, belly breaths he is used to taking. He tries again a couple of times, straightening his body as he sits, opening his nostrils like a horse. Another breath.

He can feel his stomach expand, but his exhales are not satisfying, they feel stunted, short, as if they are not reaching deep enough inside his body to refresh him.

Lā ḥawla wa-lā quwwata 'illā bi-llāh, there is no power and no strength except with Allah, he whispers to himself to give his chest space.

He has just returned from the campus shop, where he purchased an electric kettle. The kettle is on the ground near his feet. He looks at the top of the shiny box, waiting to be opened. It will make endless cups of strong black tea, which he and Henna will drink during their late-night whispered conversations as Tariq sleeps.

When they arrived in Sydney, Rahim expected the city to look different. Newer, cleaner, more modern. He mentioned to Henna how the glossy pictures of beaches and colourful birds and vast cities with high-rises appeared in the brochures of Australia he picked up somewhere. He expected everyone to be blond with blue eyes. In his mind the city was a mythical place with highways and buildings made of sparkling, pristine glass. As the taxi took them from the airport to Villawood, he saw a small cityscape in the distance, which transformed into old houses and narrow streets before opening to a busy highway, wide open lands and finally their destination.

He thinks of the lady in the shop who served him when he purchased the kettle. She was fat, fatter than any woman he had seen in his whole life, her thick, white hands a novelty to his eyes.

Now, his mind lingers on hands, on white slender hands belonging to a beloved in a poem, recited long ago. The beauty described by Khoja on a night of poetry recitals at their house. He smiles, thinking how poetry erupted, how it became a fight to the best line between Khoja and Henna. How the night burnt down to nothing, like the candles surrounding a room full of glistening moist eyes, how the beautiful words were freed into the open arms of dawn. Henna and Khoja were exhausted, everyone else – Hamid, his parents, Koko and the guests – was captivated. He was buoyed along, floating on the wings of beauty, the beauty of words. Then the birds chirped and signalled the time for morning namaz, breaking up the group.

The other day, Rahim felt glad to be rid of the Australian in uniform at the airport. This man spoke to him in condescending English. *I am a foreigner*, Rahim thought, *not a fool*.

Now, the meal bell rings. This is the invitation to eat in the cafeteria. The staff will spoon mushy potatoes, fried eggs, steamed rice or boiled vegetables onto his plate, as he drags his tray along the length of the metal bench. Rahim expects that there will be pork as well. He will be ready to wave it away. He assumes there are mixed utensils in the kitchen, spoons that stir both the pots of pork and the pots of vegetables.

He stands and begins a slow walk to their room. He will gather Henna and Tariq, they will head to the cafeteria for lunch. Yesterday, when they had their meal here in the evening, there was an unfamiliar smell to the food. He noticed that Henna was doting on him, that she tried to compensate for his not eating anything, as if this is all her fault. She sprinkled salt and a lot of black pepper on some vegetables and put the plate in front of him. He still couldn't eat, though he tried a couple of small mouthfuls to please her.

There are many families here, all from war-torn countries. *If it weren't for Henna and Tariq*, Rahim thinks, *I would get back on the plane and fly to Herat. But then where would I be without them?* he asks himself. The question and its associated guilt weigh him down. Yes, but, what if the war had not come, what if his path had not crossed with the invading Roos, what if he had lived in Herat in the generation his father did, what if the year of 1979 had not come? It's best to count your blessings, this is what Bebe said to him, the day before their departure when he bumped into her in the corridor, when she stopped to look at his face properly, when she read his mind, when he let her see the regret of the decision to leave in his eyes.

He counts his blessings now; the safety from war, freedom to practise his deen, religion, an education for Tariq, shelter, security, no knocks on the door during the night. The promise that Khoda expects from him, that he will respect and contribute to the land that gave him shelter. He needs to repay this debt to Sydney. He will make himself useful and find a job as soon as they come out of this centre.

Henna

An Ahmad Zahir music video plays on the television. It isn't footage of him, just a series of scenes taken from Hindi films and overlaid with his song. It can be heard in every room of the small townhouse in Sydney's west. The image isn't clear but the sound is good if Henna doesn't raise the volume too much. Henna closes her eyes as Ahmad Zahir's voice climbs and holds a note. *How does he do that, holding a note for so long, as if he doesn't need to breathe?* Henna thinks, as she brushes the dust from the top of the coffee table with the new feather duster she found in the two-dollar shop. Her hand stills as the note continues to hold, her eyes closed, her mind cast back to the last time she heard this song at his concert on their honeymoon.

She can see the night of her wedding now, when she and Khoja were in the centre of a circle of family. She remembers how the sash at her waist squeezed out her breath slightly as Khoja tied it, how he didn't look at her face while he tightened it around her, his hands shaking. With the knot he tied, he blessed her to go with Rahim, not knowing how far away this would take them from each other, her from Khoja, him from his hippy girl.

Henna found this music video in an Afghan shop. She did not expect that Afghans would have shops here. Rahim discovered the shop in Auburn within the first few weeks of moving to this house. She is glad to have left the hostel, that sterile place, although she met some nice ladies there. One woman's story has stayed with Henna, making Henna's complaints about life in exile seem insignificant. This woman, a short, small-boned woman with a colourful headscarf, was there with her four daughters. How can she have made it to Sydney by herself, Henna thought at the time. She admired the woman's strength, having lost her husband in the war.

Rahim took Henna to the Afghan shop as a surprise, delighted to show her the small store with tightly packed shelves of memories from home, stacked high with nokhot, roasted chickpeas, pistachios, roasted and sugar-coated almonds and much more. The music video section was the main attraction for Henna, and she bought two of the videos. Henna expected the man behind the counter to refuse her money as was the custom back home, she expected to fight to pay him, but he took it without much notice and she was relieved not to have the old tensions that went with paying for things in Herat.

Henna finishes dusting the coffee table and looks around the place, turning as she stands in the middle of the lounge room. The suitcases that contained her favourite homewares, which she had brought from Delhi, have been unpacked and their contents put in their places. She and Rahim have furnished the housing-commission home with couches, a dining table, a coffee table, a few colourful chairs, and beds from St Vincent de Paul. Henna has unpacked the doilies, stainless-steel cups, tablecloths, measuring spoons and spice holders that she brought from Delhi. They will live here, this will be their home, as permanent as it can be, even though they have no roots here, not like in Herat, where generations of her family on both sides were part of the land-scape, the history and the soil.

She looks now to the corner of the lounge room; this corner reminds her of Khoja. She bought a large amphora, which comes to her waist, and now sits beside the vase that she purchased in Delhi.

Now that the cleaning is done, she will wait by the phone and will practise her TAFE sewing lessons, the stitches her teacher taught them to do in class. Since she taught herself sewing in Delhi, she has now learnt the correct techniques; these lessons have developed her understanding and renewed her old appreciation for teaching and the importance of knowledge. This afternoon, she will attempt to fit a zipper and also do some invisible stitching. She reflects on the dress she had made for herself in Delhi and realises all the ways she now knows to do it better.

She and Rahim have created and dropped flyers in the letterboxes of houses in the neighbourhood. She designed the border on the flyer herself; it was the first time she had drawn anything since her youth when she learnt a few miniature patterns working with Khoja in Herat. Under Rahim's encouraging eye, she created an ornate border around the flyer, filled with patterns. She found that her hand was shaky, unsteady, there was no music to her brushstrokes, the fine hairs unyielding to her command, unlike the way they yielded for Khoja, the way he had taught her and she had begun to grasp, before it all . . . *What's the use of thinking such things*, she said to herself then, as she has learnt to do.

Starting a fresh piece of paper, she decided to create curves and patterns dancing on paper, and she would be happy to come away with a good-enough border of crisscrossed lines and dotted flowers, which is exactly what she ended up creating. Rahim offered to write the advertising text inside the border for her and she gladly accepted, watching with delight as his fingers held the pen and wrote the cursive letters with confidence. He took the flyers to the print shop and they made him a handful of photocopies. I am proud of you, his eyes said as he handed half the pile to her and took the other half himself to drop into letterboxes.

She learnt about flyers from an Indian couple, who she saw walking their street one afternoon, putting flyers in the letterboxes. The lady was wearing a sari as she walked, making Henna nostalgic. When she checked their flyer, it was an advertisement announcing a new Indian restaurant in the neighbourhood.

The next week she and Rahim were doing the same thing, inviting the neighbours to bring their clothing alterations to Henna. The sewing classes and the encouragement from her teacher have given her confidence that she has the skills to sew for money. She appreciates the ease of sewing, the solitude of it, so different from standing in front of the class when she was a teacher, requiring her to be visible, authoritative and in company of others all day.

Now, she takes her seat at the second-hand sewing machine in the converted garage, a workshop with a phone beside her and rolls of fabrics which she purchased second-hand. She is imagining how she will greet her Australian customers in English when they come. She must not be shy, she must look them in the eye, she must not let her pride get in the way of accepting payment. She will sew straight stitches in straight lines with her sewing machine. One day, she will have many customers and will open her own shop.

To keep herself busy today, until the customers arrive, she decides that she will make new pantaloons for Rahim, which he can wear to bed. She will make herself a straight, modern skirt and jacket, giving her the opportunity to practise zippers.

When the customers do come, she will show them her workmanship using these samples. With this, she gets to work, taking out white cotton fabric, spreading it on the table and working until it's time to pick up Tariq from school.

Rahim

Henna, this shirt needs ironing, Rahim says, as Henna comes into the room. He hands her the shirt, absentmindedly, as he looks for a tie. She takes it into the next room to iron it. He was waiting for her to say something, maybe a mirthful quip or encouraging word, but she leaves quickly, without making eye contact.

He realises she is probably in the middle of getting Tariq ready for school. He recoils from himself. He realises he has done it again, lived for a week inside his mind without letting her in. They talked about this a little while ago, the night after they moved into this house.

They had a talk, after they had calmed down from an argument. He can't remember what the fight was about, but he remembers how it erupted, how her angry words shook her and reverberated through her every feature. She had never been so disrespectful with her words.

Today is yet another day in his contract position. Today he will need to face the man with the folds of red skin on his neck.

Rahim will stamp and prepare paperwork and faxes for this sweaty man to sign all day. His mind, which he has known to be strong and brilliant under certain conditions, is underestimated at every turn since he arrived in Sydney and started to work in these short, contract jobs. He thinks it's because of his accent that they don't hire him for something more complex. He abhors his accent, the way it makes him seem slow, clumsy, foolish. He also suffers from being stiff and restricted due to his modest vocabulary, his lack of slang. He feels stuck, as if he's trying to move and look alive, active and vibrant while inside a pot of honey. There are witty expressions he cannot form because he doesn't know the right words to string together, he cannot contribute to the banter. He can't change this, he won't be fake about it. He pushes aside the now-familiar feeling in his chest, the sinking knowledge that, as public prosecutor and lawyer, he had this exact clerical work done for him by others.

I will work, I will put my head down, he thinks. *My son will be educated, he will represent our family name by making a difference in Australia. One day I will go back to build Afghanistan anew.*

Yesterday, like the end of every day, he stood in front of the sweaty man with the thick neck.

You are doing a great job, Raaheem, the man said as Rahim handed him a folder full of paperwork, meticulously written notes and stapled pages, which took a long time to print and compile.

Rahim has discovered that printing, faxing, putting papers in order, actions that require minimal thought, take him the longest. He drops the stapler several times, he loses pages, forgets them at the fax machine or the printer, he tries to keep the printing in order but they are always in the wrong order when he checks them after stapling them together.

Rahim is happy to work within complexity as long as complexity does not include process and patience and paperwork and administration.

Otherwise he makes a fool of himself. He is slow, he is meticulous, but this work is painful. What could he do instead? *Every choice we make comes with a level of pain, whatever level of pain is bearable for the longest time is the right choice,* he thinks.

A month has passed in the job. He has thought long and hard about his future prospects and discussed his feelings with Henna in their late-night conversations. Henna feels that he should do what makes him happy, and he has observed that at the end of every day an emptiness awaits him, he feels hollow as if he is wasting his life. The sacrifice just doesn't seem worth the work. As he puts on the shirt that Henna ironed for him, he goes over in his mind how he will tell his boss that he has decided he will not go back to this clerical job. Today he will resign and that will be the end of the tall, fat man asking him to print and fax things. Although his work is in a prison, somehow connected to the legal profession, it feels empty. He will join Henna in the sewing business at her suggestion. They will discuss it over dinner.

Henna

Henna is waiting to hear who was at the door, wondering if it's another customer with alterations. Rahim walks into the room shaking his head, his white singlet tucked into the pantaloons she made him. She notices his stomach has grown from when he first put them on; this pleases Henna, seeing that he is putting on weight in Sydney, a sign of improved health. He seems much happier since quitting his contract job and it has been good to work together on the business. She is pleased with the way he began promoting the alteration business after undertaking a series of short courses on marketing at the local TAFE.

It was a man, Rahim says, as he sits down beside her and picks up his cup of tea. He takes a sip and holds the cup out in front of Henna. She reaches for the thermos and fills his cup with fresh tea, her eyes still fixed on his face, she is unsure why he is stalling telling the story of who was at the gate.

Was it a customer? Should I go? she asks. Silence.

Well? she prompts.

No, Rahim says. She notices mirth is brewing in the corners of his mouth, she can see that he is trying to hold back laughter. Something about the look in his eyes makes her feel ashamed to ask about this mysterious visitor, perhaps she should let the subject rest, but she cannot.

Who was it, she says, her face breaking into a smile, her cheeks feeling a slight ache as she tries not to pre-empt anything with her own laughter.

It was a khastgar, a handsome suitor for you, Rahim says, bursting into laughter, his mouth so wide that she can see most of his teeth.

A what? she says, uncomfortable with the joke, unsure of why he would say such a thing. Rahim jan, is that really appropriate? she asks.

Rahim's face is not betraying anything more, his eyes full of laughter, his mouth smiling. He says, Don't worry, I sent him away. You are safe.

He picks up the remote to turn on the TV and appears to be content to move on.

Henna says, I'll take the remote and throw it through the window.

Okay, he says, putting the remote aside. Now he smiles, a shy smile full of light. It was an old man at the gate, older and uglier than me, Rahim says. He had a bouquet of flowers in his hand, expensive-looking flowers. It was as if he had just swum out of a river of cologne. He was dressed sharply and he asked me if Henna is home. I told him you are, and he asked if he may give the flowers to my daughter.

I told him I am your husband, and he blushed and walked away quickly, apologising. His name is John and he said he is sorry.

John is from my sewing class! What a strange thing to do, Henna says. Confusion makes her trace every word she has exchanged with

John. I made a cup of tea for myself and he was sitting there alone, so I offered him one too. Now, every day, he waits for me to make us tea. Strange, deluded man! Henna says and walks away.

Come, Rahim says, let's have tea, he says, patting the seat next to him. She can't help but smile and oblige.

Henna replaces the receiver on the telephone and slowly makes her way to Rahim in the kitchen. A soft smile rests on her lips, as if the person she was speaking to is standing before her. She is smiling because the conversation she just had was a wave of easy flowing chatter, as familiar and warm words were exchanged, as well as shared nostalgia about the past. She has been speaking with a woman she saw at a party last week, at the house of a new acquaintance.

On the night of the party, Rahim had sat with the men who took over the lounge room to talk politics, Tariq had been introduced to the games room with the other kids, and Henna had been ushered by the hostess to the large kitchen where the women were congregating.

At first, Henna didn't notice Zora standing behind their mutual friend's kitchen bench. Then Henna noticed Zora's hands, her red nails peeling grapes from a stem and collating them into a magnificent crystal bowl at the bottom of which pomegranate seeds glistened like rubies. She was making a multicoloured fruit salad for dessert, using the fruits of Henna's childhood.

Henna thinks now of Zora's face, how her red mouth opened, exclaiming, Wee Khoda jan, it is you. It took a few moments for self-conscious Henna to recognise this familiar face from the past, startled at the welcome when she was expecting everybody to be new to her. It took a while to reach Zora, as Henna had to go from woman to woman, working her greetings around the large kitchen, placing three kisses on every face.

They embraced then, once Henna finally made it to her. Zora's vibrant reddish brown hair had now been dyed burgundy red, her skin still as white as marble, her eyebrows still plucked in thin arches. Zora, the ambitious science teacher, the woman who had quit her teaching career abruptly to become a housewife.

Henna was enveloped by the strong scent of Zora's perfume, this widely smiling teacher who taught at the same school as Henna in Herat. Zora's memories of their home remain untainted, filled with joy and love. She is lucky, Henna thinks, to have left before the complete ruin of things.

Henna sometimes feels she had never fully appreciated their life, in that heavenly world that Zora describes when they reminisce. She and Zora had not been close, but Zora was always smiling, polite and friendly, the two had shared words here and there when they saw each other in the corridors of their school. Now, in their exile, a previously superficial friendship has gained deeper meaning and value.

I am happy to see your familiar face in this unfamiliar land, Zora jan, Henna found herself saying as their bodies parted from their embrace, the sequined trim around Zora's black top matching the sparkle of her dark eyes.

Now, Henna finds herself at the bottom of the stairs, facing the kitchen. I have invited Zora and her family for dinner, she says to Rahim, who is sitting at the kitchen table, scribbling a note in the margin of the phone book. Henna stands at the kitchen door, as Rahim looks up at her. He turns his head slightly to the side, as if to study her more intently, to listen more closely to her playful tone, the way he does when he recognises a new mood in her. She enjoys this attentive response from Rahim, when he takes an interest in her, in this absorbed way.

We can also invite a few other families, she says, taking a pen and paper from the odds-and-ends tray on the corner of the counter. She puts it in front of Rahim, knowing she is planting the seeds of a party, a party they have both spoken about hosting for a long time, since they came here, in memory of the parties in their old home, as a way of resuming a sliver of the life they used to have.

Although spoken about many times, the party idea has never come to life; it had been postponed to a point in the future that they thought would never be reached. Now, there are no remaining reasons to delay, such as the furniture being incomplete. Henna has extended an invitation, and now that Zora has accepted, the party is going to finally happen.

Rahim's glasses are perched on the tip of his nose, he is still looking at her, not joining in her excitement as she wants him to; she feels a rash of irritation rising at his usual caution before welcoming good news.

Go on, she says, please write the guest list and the shopping list.

He assumes his face of deep concentration as he takes pen and paper and begins to write down the names of their new handful of friends, including Zora, calling out each name as he writes it.

Then he pauses, looking up as if he has just remembered something painful.

What is it? she says. Don't you want to have this party?

Abdel Hadi is in Sydney, he says, looking up at Henna.

What? That watan farosh, traitor!

Yes, Rahim says, he should be on trial for war crimes, the bastard. The other night at the party, in the lounge room, there were a few men who have met him, they were singing his praises, about him being a patriotic, educated and eloquent intellectual from the time before the warlords ruled Afghanistan. They had no idea he was part of KHAD or that many died at his hands during the regime.

Did you say anything? Henna says, her knees weakening, her thoughts about the party dissolved. She pulls out a chair and sits down opposite Rahim, her body gripped by a familiar tension from that time when it wasn't safe to express fear or dissatisfaction with the government. Her shoulders and stomach remember what it was like to hold herself within a shell that did not belong to her. She feels every cell in her body move to self-preservation, as if there are spies everywhere again, and it isn't safe to verbalise the oppressive nature of the government's rules and innuendos and threats.

She remembers Abdel Hadi visiting her home in the old days, before he became a party supporter, as he talked with Khoja about art and literature. She liked to watch him as he took the glass cup and twirled it in his hand, the leaves performing an elegant dance in a sea of green tea. She remembered that his was the voice that initiated her betrothal.

Henna had heard, over the years, about his stellar rise within the regime to become one of their high-ranking officials. He had risen far enough to be the catalyst for Rahim's release from prison, a welcome but strange favour that he bestowed upon them, even though at the time he was a key force behind the movement and the people who had taken Rahim. Does this mean he will want the favour returned in some way?

She shivers as she thinks what it will be like to come face-to-face with Abdel Hadi at one of these parties. She will not know what to do or say to him, she will be expected to continue the pretence of normality, just like she was expected to continue that pretence during the regime.

Rahim interrupts her thoughts with an edge in his voice.

I didn't know how to tell you, he says, but I wanted you to know before the party, before you hear about him yourself. I told them Abdel Hadi is a killer, he was in the secret police, Rahim says. I couldn't help myself.

Henna looks into Rahim's eyes, she can see that they are moist and red. She knows that he vividly remembers his time in prison, that still sometimes in the middle of the night, when she finds him walking the length of the lounge room, back and forth, he is trying to distance himself from his memories of that time, the time when they both had to pretend life was normal when it wasn't.

She is moved towards courage by the look in his eyes, a protective feeling overcomes her, a feeling similar to the one she experiences for her child, of wanting to cradle Rahim and his vulnerability, to give him a measure of her power, a power unconsciously nurtured within her in recent times. A power that she recalls Hamid used to see in her. She takes Rahim's hand, she looks into Rahim's eyes and she hears herself say, we will speak up against him at every opportunity.

Rahim

ahim is reading the morning newspaper, flipping to the world news pages where he might find stories of home. Today, he is astonished to find a small article with a photograph of Khoja in it. In the photo, Khoja has grown a full beard, his hair is dishevelled, and his eyes look straight at the camera. He has a book of his miniature paintings on his lap and is surrounded by his artworks. He has aged considerably. The article recounts his story and the destruction of his public works. It talks about the death of the great man, his wife, his daughters and their families in an explosion in Herat.

Rahim closes the paper. The next moment, he feels like he cannot breathe, but it is a sob that breaks loudly and without constraints as he sits alone in the sunroom of their home. Henna's whole family has been wiped away. He dresses himself, his knees weak, he washes and puts on his clean namaz clothes. He holds the Quran in his hands and he sobs for forgiveness and for courage to face Henna and his life.

He begs Khoda for bravery, to be the man he will be expected to be in all of this. He fears that he does not have it in him to be Henna's courageous husband. He wishes that he hadn't been chosen to be the one to tell Henna this news. Images of Koko, Khoja and the family flood him, memories of a blessed existence long ago, now lost. Memories of a man who created art and meaning for others, memories of a family . . . A feeling of guilt overcomes him. How could he have kept the news of Hamid's attempt to enter India from her? How will he face this?

Hours later, once he thinks he has found the nerve, he enters Henna's new shop. From the way she looks at him, Rahim can see she has guessed that something is wrong. Rahim knows that his face is not a reliable mask, that at every turn his eyes betray him to the world. Especially to Henna, who can peer into them and see every atom that makes up his existence. There is a woman in the change room trying on a dress Henna has altered. Rahim sits in the back room to wait. He hears the woman pay and leave, the bell at the door tinkling as it closes behind her. He comes to the front of the shop, which they have called Sofia's Alterations. He sees Henna has flipped the 'Closed' sign on the shop window and locked the door.

Tell me it isn't true, Rahim jan, tell me something has not happened, Henna says, as she walks towards him, her voice full of sorrow, her eyes full of tears. This scene has happened many times, except that every other time Rahim was able to say, No, you are expecting the worst, no, nothing is wrong, it's the electricity bill that has me worried, not news from Herat. But today, she is right to cry.

Rahim and Henna are dependent on new friends to serve the customary black tea and sugar cubes to every visitor in their home as part of the funeral. Zora has taken Tariq to stay with her older children for the week and is in the kitchen dispatching tea trays, while her husband sits beside Rahim, in the position Hamid would have taken if he had been here.

The house has an austere quiet when the visitors leave at the end of each day, as Rahim walks through it, turning off the lights before bed. Henna's ornaments and the decorative pot plants and furniture have been moved to the spare room to make space for as many chairs as possible. Their friends have added folding chairs, which now line the walls of the house.

At this moment, the house is full of people as a melodious voice reads the Quran, playing continuously on a tape recorder. The voice is loud enough to be heard in every room. Nearly every chair is taken as people line the walls of the house, sitting in silence, listening. Once in a while, people raise hands to pray for the deceased. Those who have prayed leave to make room for newly arrived guests. More Afghans than Rahim would have thought existed in Australia have emerged from different corners of Sydney and started visiting as soon as the deaths were announced on local Afghan radio program.

Men and their wives come to pay their respects and give condolences. Most of them knew of Khoja and his work, some knew him personally, a few didn't know him at all. The women kiss Henna on both cheeks, their elegant, perfumed veils loosely covering glossy hair. Rahim is grateful for their comfort to Henna, but he looks away every time Henna melts into their arms and into her grief, he can't bear to see her in so much pain.

Rahim has tried to comfort Henna, but nothing seems to calm her. Every night he breaks a Valium tablet in half and gives one part to her, taking the other himself. Food is piling up in the fridge, untouched, and keeps arriving with new visitors. Rahim hasn't any appetite, but he eats mouthfuls of blessed halwa because it's the right thing to do, forcing small mouthfuls onto Henna as well.

He thinks of the funerals he attended in Herat, men and women coming to the mosque, staying for the Khatem, the reading of the whole Quran from end to end, a simple meal shared with halwa, alms for the poor, dua sent for the dead.

It is our duty to share in the grief of a fellow human being, Haji Mama used to tell him when he took a neatly dressed Rahim to the funerals of friends and strangers from a young age.

Humans are social creatures, his father had said, you must respect society's customs, you must contribute to it, so that you can live respectfully within society, rather than live an individualistic life on the outskirts.

He had lectured Rahim, every time. It was the same lecture, no matter how old Rahim was, this was their drive-to-the-funeral conversation, as Rahim coined it to himself.

The first time he went to a funeral with his father, Rahim remembers being about ten years old, sitting in the back seat, feeling like a grown up. Rahim remembers his father's voice, he remembers looking out the window as the snow-covered trees and streets of Herat passed them by, he remembers suppressing his delight at the invitation, marvelling privately at this initiation into the ways of grown men, of going places with his father as his elder brothers had done. It took subsequent funeral visits for Rahim to grasp what his father was saying, and many more years to believe that his words held truth.

Haji and Bebe's life was spent thinking about their death, in the way that young people think about marriage in the Western world, Rahim thinks. Reflecting on his own death has been a good way to stay humble, to never forget the purpose of life, which is to go back to your maker with a sound and pure heart.

Khoja and Koko had also shared these same values, talking often with his parents about how their children would be there to bury them when their time had come.

The irony is that they have failed, despite their preparations; no one could have predicted the way life shaped itself, the way war drew them apart from Henna and Rahim and ruptured their lives. Today, Henna is not present to mourn the death of her family in person, to grieve at their graves, to say a proper goodbye. They say there is a healing that occurs when you see the shell of a loved one, empty of the soul, the body no longer occupied by the presence that made the person who they were. Henna will not have this chance to heal.

Rahim is sitting stiffly in his chair, his back is aching from being in the same position all day. He has not left the house in what seems like weeks. It was only two days ago when the news came, yet now their previous life, which held Khoja and Koko in it, seems like a distant fantasy.

The latest Sura comes to an end, waking Rahim from the nightmare inside his thoughts. The men who are seated around him in the lounge room raise their hands in front of their faces. One says a dua.

Amen, the rest say.

They lower their hands and stand to leave. Rahim stands from his seat and walks the men, the last group for the day, down the hallway and to the front door. He positions his body with the open door behind him and, as they pass, they hold his hands in their own. He is grateful that these people have given their time to share in sorrow and contribute their dua to those who Henna and Rahim have lost.

Hands to chest, heads bowed, Inna lillahi wa inna ilayhi raji'un, they say as they bid Khoda hafiz, verily we belong to Allah and verily to Him do we return.

Hamid

Hamid is walking in a dream. Ahmad Zahir's voice sings of unrequited love over the bazaar. The shop doors are open, but nobody is here. Herat's bazaar is empty. Hamid's Herat is empty. Red dust covers Hamid's feet as he walks, barefoot. He isn't feeling tired today as he traverses this street, which is quiet and still but for the sound of the song coming from a decorated rickshaw, the kind he knows they have in Delhi – he has seen them in films. The rickshaw is standing by the side of the road, its speakers turned up high, its seat empty, the engine running. Maybe it's waiting to take him to Delhi? Who is this music for? For Hamid? Like a painted bride, this rickshaw waits at the side of the kerb. Hamid thinks it waits for him, but he is not yet ready to leave. He is delighted to be home, in Herat. He wants to find Henna, Khoja, Koko, Roya, Nargis, Rahim, he wants to see them first.

Hamid enters a familiar antique shop to find Sultan, the shop-keeper, perched on a stool. Hamid is glad to see a familiar face. Sultan greets Hamid with a friendly smile, and Hamid tells Sultan that he is visiting from India, he has come to take his family to Delhi with him, that the rickshaw is waiting. Sultan says he knows Khoja will be very happy to go with Hamid.

Sultan disappears behind a curtain of red glass beads, which jingle and separate, swaying in the wind that blows inside the shop. The song continues to play, now becoming louder, even inside. Hamid begins to inspect his surroundings.

A bowl of gemstones on a nearby countertop reminds him of an old grudge he has against Khoja. He always wondered why Khoja gave his gemstones and artworks and antiques away to people. It took many hours of work and heartache to acquire these things. Hamid thinks of Henna now, she was also a gem that Khoja gave away.

Epilogue

The white room is quiet except for the music coming from a small television hung high from the ceiling. On the television, a beautiful young woman skates on ice in a blue and silver outfit. She is skating for Russia.

She completes a somersault as the music builds. She lands gracefully on her two feet, her body in the shape of a swan. She is flawless and poised. The crowd applauds. The commentator, a woman's voice, describes the technical difficulty of the perfectly executed choreography. The camera pans across the judges, they look pleased, they make notes.

Henna watches the ice skater glide across the screen once more. Arms open as if in flight. The music seems to keep the skater and Henna's breath suspended mid-air with invisible thread.

The woman twirls into her third somersault and it looks perfect again, a bird in paradise, but she fails to land properly and falls to her knees. The crowd gasps, Henna gasps, the voiceover is concerned for the performer's limbs. The skater rises from the fall, limping but determined to continue. She takes flight again, another twist and jump.

Rahim has dozed off. His thin white hair trembles in the draught which is coming from the air-conditioning vent in the ceiling.

Henna is sitting next to Rahim's bed. She reaches beneath the white bedsheets to hold his warm hand. She goes back to the magazine lying in her lap, holding the tips of his long, elegant fingers gently in her hand.

Hamid has been writing more regularly to Henna about his life in Iran. She folds these letters into tiny parcels like tawiz. She kisses each one and collects them in a special case in her bedroom. Henna thinks now of Tariq, he will come to visit later. He has chosen to study law despite his father's guidance to do something different.

The dialysis machine churns Rahim's blood through its tube and back into his veins. Henna watches the blood of her beloved with both love for him and awe at Khoda's creation.

Life hums through Henna and Rahim's bodies, through their connected hands, as if they are the one person, and they are together as they have always been.

It begins to rain outside. Henna thinks of the snow in Herat.

Author's Note

At nine years old I wrote my first novel in a scented diary with a lock and key. I would sometimes enter the writing competitions for children run by the newspaper. One day there was a competition for short story writing and I submitted the whole diary, with the key, as my entry.

At the heart of what I wrote back then was the seed of the story you have just finished reading; the story about a family who became refugees, like my family did when I was four years old. I have rewritten this story many times during different stages of my life. Each attempt brought me closer to the novel I really wanted to write.

At its most traumatic, the Soviet invasion of Afghanistan caused death and destruction, while creating one of the world's largest refugee populations. At its most subtle, the war displaced identities, sense of self, and carved emotional scars which cannot be conveyed through statistics.

Behind every indigo burka we see on the news is a life full of complexity, a story that is unique about love, loss, resilience and courage. A woman whose dreams have been broken and rebuilt numerous times, only to crumble inside a new war. Behind every on-screen image of the remaining skeleton of a building in a crowded bazaar is a family with customs, generations of stories, a rich heritage going back centuries.

You are about to read the short story that was the genesis of Henna, Rahim and Hamid's own journey. While it no longer fits into the novel, as it was written so long ago, the novel would not be complete without it, and so I am compelled to share it with you here.

Paper is falling from the sky. I am in the garden, it's a sunny day. It comes back to me in slow motion. I'm three years old. My father is often amazed at the fact that I should remember this far back into my childhood. I tell him these are unforgettable memories.

The paper continues to fall, communist propaganda rains down on us. The helicopters are so noisy, so high up in the sky. I stand looking up, my arms are wide open. I want to catch all the pieces of falling paper. At least it's better than when they shower us with bullets.

Mother is at school across the street, she is a teacher. You can see the school when you go outside the huge walls of my grandparents' property. The walls, made of thick hay and mud, I remember the walls. The height of them makes me feel protected. I imagine these walls to be strong enough to stop the rockets.

I go inside the house to play behind the dark blue couch in the lounge room. That's where we hide when the sirens sound in the middle of the night. One night I hear my father pray for us to die together if we are hit. That night he holds mother and I close to him. I can feel him shivering as I secretly share his dua. I've never seen father frightened before.

Now I play with my big red doll when it happens. I hear a loud noise. I know it is a bomb. I run out into the garden. I find my hand in my aunt's hand, I am being pulled behind her. Small feet trying to catch up.

Everyone gathers outside, smoke rises from the direction of the school; I see it come over the wall. The noise deafens my ears, there is screaming and shouting on the other side, where Mother is.

We run out of the gates, into the street, though I am hesitant, as I don't want to see her pieces lying before me. She would have been coming home for lunch now.

All I see is smoke. My heart has stopped, my knees shake, I know she's gone. Everyone is crying. I watch the smoke. I don't say a word. My grandmother holds me, my head at her chest. I want Mother to walk out of the smoke. That's all I want.

I break free of my grandmother, I stand alone, but I do not cry. After that, I don't remember what happens. What I do recall is my mother, running out of the smoke. She runs towards me. I'm in her arms. I can smell her; she smells of Mother. She holds me tight. She cries as she whispers, we have to get away from here.

My mouth is dry.

Acknowledgements

Thanks to Khoda, Allah, the Most Gracious, the Most Merciful for my countless blessings. I am grateful for the blessing of being able to create this novel in a place of peace, safety and beauty. I pay my respects to the traditional owners of this land where I write, the Wangal people, and the Aboriginal elders of this country.

Thank you to Madar, the consummate creative, the storyteller whose stories have engaged me and fed my imagination. Thank you to Baba, my late father, in whose heart the gardens of knowledge and curiosity blossomed. Special mention to my husband Qais Wadan for believing in me, and my sister Doctor Bilquis Ghani for showing me strength. Much love to my brothers, Abdullah and Mahmood, my loving extended family, and my nieces Naenae, Eshy, Anouk, Yasmine, Zara, Mashal, Nooshie the little caterpillar, and the cutest twins Ava and Alia. May you all grow into proud, wise women like your mothers and grandmothers.

Thank you to my teacher, guide and friend Emily Maguire, who helped me understand myself as a writer, who gives generously to all, all of the time.

Thank you to the friends I call Home, my writing group; Jane Carrick, Rowena Harding Smith, Patrick Forest, and Andrew Turner, who write, laugh and share much, openly and with authenticity and acceptance.

Thank you to extraordinary editor and friend Alison Frazer for helping me sharpen my manuscript, and Kate Benecke for her meticulous work on the facts and histories.

Thanks to the Richell Prize team for shortlisting my manuscript, and WestWords and the Cultural Fund Copyright Agency for the Western Sydney Emerging Writers Fellowship, which connected me to amazing people, such as Michael Campbell, James Roy, Luke Carmen, and Alison Frazer, and exposed me to the amazing institution that is Varuna, the National Writers' House.

Thanks to the kind folks who read early drafts and contributed to my journey in different ways; Dominique Antarakis, Doctor Safdar Ahmed, Ferdinand Dickle, and Farhad Azad from AfghanMagazine.com and Kaka Jalil Ghai.

Last only because it makes sense chronologically in my journey, thank you to the Hachette team, especially to Vanessa Radnidge and Stacey Clair, also Alice Grundy and Rebecca Hamilton, for making my dream come true with so much grace and kindness in your words and actions.